The Eternal Empire: The Spark

Written by: Dylan T Horan
Illustrated by: Indy K

DylanTHoran.com

Dylan here, just wanted to give some shout outs and thanks.

First and foremost I thank you, for picking this book up, reading it, and with a bit of luck, enjoying it. I wanted to write something I was proud of, anyone who enjoys it and wants more brings me joy, and yes, there will be more to come.

I need to thank my wonderful illustrator Indy K whom put up with my inability to describe what I wanted well and still somehow brought this book to life in ways I never could have.

Also, I thank my wonderful editor, Del's Diabolical Editing. Trust me when I say that none of you want to see what this looked like before she got her hands on it. For putting up with all my mistakes, and making me laugh with your notes, a sincere thank you.

To my wonderous parents who have been by my side my whole life, none of this would have been possible without your support in life as a whole.

My dear friends, near and far, those whom have even left my circle since I started this. You have been invaluable to me and I cherish you.

And most importantly to my old teacher, Glenn Williams. Without you, I never would have found my passion for writing. You changed my life. Thank you, for all eternity.

Chapters

Prologue: The Final Stand

"Sir, the enemy has halted their advance." Lord Bradford stared at the monitors that displayed the battlefield as the officer spoke to him.

"Of course they have." He responded in his gruff low voice, "This is the impenetrable Fortress of Eilon. We could hold the Empire's entire army here until the end of time," he smirked. "We have enough resources to stay within this mountain for over a decade. They might choke us out eventually, but our defense will drain their time, resources, and most importantly their pride."

The Eternal Empire. Over half the world was under their rule. Now with the Kingdom of Estates all but under their control and their constant fighting to increase their borders. It was here, at Mount Eilon, that the last forces of the Kingdom of Estates would take their final stand. Most of their country had fallen ten years ago when the Empire first debuted the power of the Archangels. The seven most elite warriors the Empire had to offer, wielding mech suits so advanced they dwarfed the Angels the Empire used, and utterly crushed the Knight Mk.[1]2's of the Kingdom. Not only that, but they each had unique psychic powers the world had never seen before that completely changed the landscape of the war.

After the fall, the utter destruction, of their capital New Hope, the Archangels left to go fight in other areas of the world leaving only one behind: The Archangel of Death. He rarely made an appearance, not only on the battlefield but in the media as well. Every citizen knew the faces and personalities of the other six Archangels, but next to nothing

---

[1] MK – Military shorthand for mark, designating the current generation.

was known about him. Yet Lord Bradford did know one thing. Where Death went, nothing but utter death and destruction followed, and victory for the Empire was assured.

"The Empire won't wait that long." Earl Crownley, his second in command, walked to his side as they kept looking over the battle lines, "The Archangel of Death will come for us here."

"Good," Lord Bradford smiled. He pulled out his phone and quickly made a call, "are the Royal Knights ready for service?"

"Yes, Milord." The voice responded swiftly.

"Good. Tell them to be ready at all times. They are not to move until I give the order." Before a response could be given he hung up.

"Really think they'll be able to defeat the Archangel of Death?" Crownley asked him.

Lord Bradford took a deep breath and pulled out a cigar. He cut it with his combat knife and lit it, taking a few puffs before responding, "I think we're all going to die here. In this mountain, but if we can bring the Archangel of Death down, if by some miracle we can kill him? We'll give the rebel cells and the rest of this world a glimmer of hope. A glimmer they *desperately* need."

The room fell silent. They had all known this would most likely be their tomb, but it hit home when their own Lord, the last leader of the Kingdom, as the Royal family had fallen when New Hope did, told them it. "And if they fail? We'll die as god-damned heroes anyways, facing the end with our heads held high, our guns run dry, the ground stained with the blood of our enemies alongside our brothers and sisters! We are the Kingdom of Estates! We will never go down without a fight!" He encouraged them, "Long live the Estates!"

"*Long live the Estates!*" Everyone in the command center responded.

Bleep ... Bleep ... Bleep. Bleep. Bleep.

The green dots on the screen showing the position of every one of their Knight Mk.2's, one by one … they started to go dim.

Tch! "Sir!" A voice came over one of their radios, "We're dropping li-" An explosion and static cut the rest of it off.

"He's too fas-" Another one came in seconds before it was destroyed.

"How the hell do we fi-" Another. And another. And another.

"Sir," The officer controlling the screens spoke up again, "There's no enemy Angels that have moved! Could this be…"

"It's him." He blew out a puff of smoke, "The Archangel of Death."

Everyone in the room froze for a moment before another voice came in over the radio, "Sir, we've got a visual!"

"On screen!" He demanded. The largest of the screens blinked over to a live feed of the battlefield. There, in the dimly lit hours of dusk, standing out against the glow of the fires and the piercing lights of all the mechs…The Scythe. The frame of the Archangel of Death. It was more compact than even the smallest of the mech frames in the world. Able to shift and change its configuration with such speed it was unbelievable to see. It's pitch black matte paint and lack of any lights, not even the smallest LED's dotting its edges, made it nigh impossible to make out any details. In an instant it changed from fighter to jet form and disappeared from sight.

More insistent radio calls came in. His men were being slaughtered. Lord Bradford grabbed the command radio and broadcasted a signal to everyone. "The Archangel of Death thinks he can take us on alone." The rest of the Empire's troops held their battle line, unwavering, but not even firing. "Everyone hold your position! Do not move an inch! If you see *any* movement in the sky! *Shoot it with everything you've got!"*

The dusk sky lit up as bullets rained from the Knights of the Kingdom onto The Scythe. "How the hell does it move so fast!" More radio calls came in.

"It's like he can dodge bullets!"

"He's on m-"

"Come on hit him!"

"He can't get all-"

"For the Estates!"

"Shit!"

"Die you demon!"

The rain of bullets came to a stop as they all realized … they had lost sight of their target. "Anyone have eyes on him?" A voice came in.

"Nothing here!"

"Nope!"

"He's gone!"

"Did someone get him?"

"Hah! Like it would be that easy."

Beep.

The whole room's eyes snapped up to the monitor. A red dot had just appeared on their close-range radar … it was past their front lines … and speeding towards the mountain itself. The walls shook slightly as an explosion far above went off. "He's here! He's destroying our ground defen-" The call went silent as an explosion shook the walls again.

As Lord Bradford pulled out his cellphone his eyes opened in terror as the entire army of the Empire started to move again. He grabbed the command radio and screamed into it, *"Knights! Hold your ground! Keep the Empire from advancing!"*

He dropped the radio and quickly dialed on his phone again, "The target is now on our radar. Send out the Royal Knights. They are to destroy him completely and utterly. Leave nothing of his body! Let's put to test this regenerative power of the Archangels! Make the Archangel of Death regret ever being born!"

The Royal Knights. The most advanced Knights the Kingdom had ever made. And this was to be their grand debut. The Kingdom of Estates had fallen long ago, this last fortress was barely more than a well-supplied rebel cell group to the Empire, but their debut would be even greater to the world than the debut of the Archangel's … for they were going to kill one.

"Crownley," He spoke without even glancing back at him, "Take command of the main conflict. I'm going to observe the Royal Knights directly."

"Yes, Sir!" Crownley quickly took his seat and started issuing orders to the Knights fighting the Empire's main force as Bradford put on a headset directly patched into the Royal Knights' comms.

"RK 1 here. Com check."

"RK 2. Receiving."

"RK 3. I hear ya."

"RK 4. Loud and clear."

"RK 5. All good on my end."

"RK 6."

"Com check complete." RK 1 responded, "Engaging the enemy in twenty seconds. Attack plan Charlie, Romeo, Lima."

"Acknowledged." The rest responded as one.

"Enemy now on RK sensors." RK 4 said.

"He's a fast little bugger." RK 3 smirked.

"Indeed. Change to Bravo, Alpha, Charlie." RK 1 said.

"Yes, Sir. Contact in five ... four ... three ... two ... one."

The radio comms filled with the sounds of gunfire, shorthand orders that Lord Bradford didn't even understand. A slight smile crested his lips though as the battle continued. They were holding their own. His new Royal Knights were holding back the Archangel of Death. The Scythe was the scariest

Angel the world had ever seen, but it was also the Archangel's weakness. His psychic powers didn't seem to work within it.

In every battle he had been recorded in, he never once used his psychic powers while within The Scythe. He always had to leave it first. As long as they could keep him within The Scythe then victory was possible. Of course, this whole plan depended on this one assumption.

"6. Stay on him!" RK 1 ordered over the radio. "2, cover 5 as she gets unstuck! 3 and 4 on me!"

Explosions over the radio followed by a death cry cut off almost instantly, "Direct hit on enemy target! 4 lost." RK 1 reported. "2 and 5! NOW!" More gunfire, another scream, another explosion, "Target damaged. 2 gone. Lima, Bravo, Foxtrot! NOW!"

"Sir yes s-" The radio comms were suddenly overwhelmed with the sounds of incomprehensible screaming. A screaming filled with pain, sorrow, hurt, regret.

Lord Bradford's eyes opened wide. Everything had depended on this not happening. On his psychic powers not… "*Fire now! Fire everything now! Now! Now!*" He screamed over the comms at them. The sounds of their own screaming overlapped with the ringing of explosions and endless barrage of bullets made for a nigh unbearable cacophony that was soon followed by…

Silence.

"RK 1! Report!" Lord Bradford demanded over the comms, "Report! *Now*!"

Nothing.

There was nothing.

"*Dammit!*" He shouted as he threw the headset off. "Where's our close-range scanner? Why can't I see what's going on out there?" He yelled at the officers in the room.

"It was damaged in the fight. We're working to repair it as quickly as we can."

"*Get me eyes on the Archangel! Now!*" He screamed at them.

"We're working on that!" Another officer told him while furiously typing on his keyboard.

Suddenly a whole section of the dots on the radar went dark. Both green ones, and red. And then another massive section. And another. "What's going on out there?" He demanded.

Earl Crownley slowly put down his radio and stood up in awe. "It's … it's…"

"Visual established." One of his officers said right before the live feed came up on the main screen. There, in the middle of all this carnage … was the barely functioning Scythe. The air around it shimmered for a moment, and then every Angel and Knight near it exploded.

"My god…" Lord Bradford took a step back, "He really is death incarnate…" They watched as whole swathes of both armies fell in instants before the Archangel of Death.

"*Sir!* Enemy flagship just fired a missile of unknown composition!" An officer shouted at him.

A missile? At this point in time? The battle was already won. Was it another nuke? Some new configuration of the power of fusing atoms together? "Trajectory?" he asked.

"Sir it's…" The officer paused as its trajectory was displayed on the screens, "It's headed for the Scythe."

Everyone stood in silent shock as they watched the missile soar across the now night sky … and collide with the Scythe. For a fraction of a moment there was nothing. And then…

They were nothing.

Chapter 1: The Archangel of Death's Memorial

"We're here live, reporting from The Capital of the Eternal Empire! Today is the painful memorial for the amazing Archangel of Death, who sacrificed himself in the final battle over what was once the Kingdom of Estates. For the first time in years, all the Archangels, all the Princes and Princesses, even the God Emperor himself, have gathered together in one spot to remember the life of this hero and friend."

Stephanie let out a sigh of disgust as she sat down at the plain steel table. "We really going to watch this?" She asked as her friends, Jeremiah, Collin, and Teresa, sat down with her.

"Hey, sometimes it's worth seeing what sort of propaganda the Empire is spreading." Jeremiah commented.

"At worst," Collin followed up with, "This broadcast right here will anger all of us and steel us even more in our struggle against them." Stephanie grumbled as she sat back in her chair, but said nothing.

"The legendary Archangel of Righteousness! What do you remember the most about the Archangel of Death? What will you miss the most?" The reporter asked as she leaned down to hand the microphone over to him. The Archangel of Righteousness was the picture-perfect visage of a man. A fair, clean shaven, yet chiseled face, his blond hair perfectly spiked back. Sharp piercing blue eyes, muscles fit to break a tree in half, yet still lean. And dressed in the finest clothes the Empire had to offer.

A hint of sorrow crossed his face as he took the microphone from her, "He was our brother. Not in blood, but by choice. Not just our, but my, brother in arms. He may not have been as open as the rest of us, but I think that's what I'll miss the most. His distance, yet still knowing he was always there. The six of us others laughing and smiling and drinking while he sat in the shadows silent as ever..." He took a deep breath as a tear formed in his eye, "I feel like I should be able to just glance around and spot him avoiding the crowd as he always did. It's ... It's hard to know he'll never be there again."

"Can you believe this bullshit?" Teresa rose one of her hands up, "Trying to play with the masses hearts like he wasn't some mass murderer. A literal nightmare on the battlefield!" She had long auburn hair with honey eyes.

"It's the Empire's own broadcast." Jeremiah chuckled, "What did you expect?" He shook his head. He had spiked brown hair and soft green eyes.

"The Archangel of Hope." The reporter turned around to face the beautiful figure of the most beloved Archangel. Her fair, long white hair and golden eyes were mesmerizing to behold. "This must be exceptionally hard on you, as you were known to be closest to The Archangel of Death."

The Archangel of Hope closed her eyes and bowed her head slightly, "Indeed. He was always the outcast of us by his own choice. Can one blame him though? We are Righteousness, Hope, Valor, Justice, Wisdom, and Glory. All virtues everyone should aspire to, but he was Death. An outsider by nature, but if one took the time to get to know him? I'd say he might have been the sweetest of us all."

"Sweetest?" Collin spat out his drink as his blue eyes went wide. His medium length blond hair flying about him as he nearly choked, "They really are going heavy on the lies this time aren't they?"

"Of course they are." Stephanie spoke with a deadpan tone, "They just lost one of their best weapons. A weapon they paraded around as a person. The whole Empire will grieve for him, while the rest of the world knows of his sins." The other three stopped to stare at her in momentary silence. They all knew why she hated him so much.

The screen changed to a different reporter who was sitting next to a man dressed in exquisite royal garb. His pristine stature exuded a demand of respect, while also a softer side of kindness. "First Prince Clyster. You were the commander of the battle where the

Archangel of Death sacrificed himself. Not many details have been shared about it yet. Is there anything that's been declassified you can talk about? Such as the rumors of what's being dubbed the Chaos Bomb?"

The Prince gave a soft chuckle, "Oh my dear, now is not the time to discuss rumors such as that. Tomorrow evening, I shall be holding a press conference for the whole world to watch to go into extensive military details. Right now, is the time to remember the Archangel of Death. And what I will remember the most about him is his undying loyalty. His fearlessness and lack of hesitation when it came to doing what needed to be done. He kept the Eternal Empire his first priority, before his own life even. Any man, whether it be noble or commoner, Angel pilot or solider, scholar or farmer, reporter or cameraman." He gave her a slight wink and her whole face went pink, "Any citizen who puts so much faith and loyalty in this Eternal Empire: what my father, the God Emperor, has created, is worth more than a hundred, no a thousand royal guards!"

"And there's the self-praise." Stephanie scoffed, "Can't even hold a memorial without patting their own backs."

Collin turned down the volume on the TV so they could talk easier, "So, what's our next move?"

Stephanie shook her head, her soft brunette hair swaying over her pink eyes, "We need to lay low still. With the last of the Estates' armies now gone and its government completely abolished they're going to be on the lookout for any leftover rebel cells trying to fight a lost war."

"A lost war?" Collin shouted at her, "We're still at war!"

She rolled her eyes at him, "No. We were at war when we had an army. Now we are nothing more than terrorists in their land. I've already heard reports of other rebel cells trying to fight back, to go as hard as they could, only to be easily crushed. It's not like we can rely on the Eastern Dynasty or the Southlands to help. They're busy holding back the Empire against their own borders…" She took a deep breath and sighed, "Nor were we allies to begin with. If we want to keep up the good fight, then right now we need to hide. We *need* to live to fight another day. Wait until the crackdowns relax and the Empire dares to get even remotely comfortable in its control of our kingdom."

"We're really going to do nothing?" Jeremiah asked her in defeat.

She smirked at him, "Well, maybe not nothing, but we aren't doing anything big. Anything that might draw attention. At the very least, we will be doing nothing but lying low for another month or two. I'm still waiting for word from John's cell to see what he plans on doing. He hasn't made a move yet, and I'm hoping I can convince him to join us."

"You think you can get him to merge with us?" Teresa asked in shock.

She shrugged, "In all honesty? No. I fully expect him to launch a full-scale attack on the Empire. Upon which if he does, we will have to go underground for who knows how long. Maybe even move entirely."

"The men are restless," Collin told her, "What should we tell them?"

"I'll prepare a speech for them after tomorrow." She quickly responded. "I want to wait to hear what Prince Clyster has to say about the attack itself and their new Chaos Bomb before I say anything."

"You know it'll all be propaganda." Collin quickly remarked.

"Indeed." She scoffed, "But still. I know every single one of them will be watching it. So I will need to address it." She paused, "Tomorrow night I'll contact you all about setting up a meeting with the whole cell. Understood?"

"Understood." They all said as one.

"Good."

"We now go live to the God Emperor himself!"

"Now this I gotta hear." Jeremiah said as he turned the TV back up.

Stephanie pushed her chair back and stood up, "More power to you guys. I've heard just about enough of this nonsense for now. I'll watch a replay of it later tonight. I need some fresh air."

As she went to walk to the door Collin tried to stand up, but Teresa grabbed his arm, "Let her go," she whispered, "she needs it." Collin grumbled to himself, but sat back down and turned his eyes back to the TV.

Stephanie carefully made her way out of the abandoned basement in the mall they used as a neutral meeting place. It was somewhere her and her friends had found before they even formed the rebel cell, so they still used it. They lived in Empire controlled territory. They had for almost half of their lives. Ten years ago the Empire successfully took full control of Maynor Estate. After the utter destruction of the whole Reach Peninsula, every Estate in the southern reaches of the Kingdom quickly fell under their control.

They had blocked off or masterfully covered every entrance to the basement of the mall, but still, she always triple checked through the small slits in the concrete walls before using the door that was hidden completely behind hedges. Out in the open air again she took a deep breath and started to walk home. Their town was small enough they didn't need cars to get anywhere, as long as you didn't mind long walks. Most people still used them, even she owned one, but she preferred walking, jogging, or running. It kept her in shape. It gave her something to fill the time with.

If not for the increased police force imposed by the Empire, it was almost possible to forget this town had been conquered. Nothing had been destroyed, no major, or even minor battles had taken place near here, only small skirmishes miles away. The Empire merely waltzed in, deployed a platoon of Angels to watch over theirs and the neighboring two towns, and went on their way. The nearest large city, or what was left of it, Spoke, had a whole company of Angels alone as resistance had been heavy there. Exact numbers were hard to get, but in the Maynor Estate alone there were an estimated ten thousand Angels and an unknown number of soldiers.

Every township had at the minimum six Angels, with most having at least a full platoon of twenty-four. It all depended on population and levels of resistance. She was lucky. Most of the towns around here had gone peacefully, with any resistance going underground and planning before striking, often travelling to Spoke for any strikes, drawing attention away from their towns directly at least.

It was barely midday and would take her just over an hour to get home if she walked directly there. She sighed to herself as she walked the barren streets. Everyone was at home watching the broadcast. Even those who still hated the Empire. An occasion such as this, at best it was a sight to see, and at worst a slight against the Empire itself to miss it.

She slowed to a stop as she heard the hum of an Angel's thrusters coming from behind her before the pilot even spoke, "Halt, citizen!" It demanded as it came to land. She sighed heavily and looked towards the ground as she slowly turned around. "Why are you not inside watching the broadcast of the memorial of our glorious Archangel of Death?" It asked her in a demanding tone.

I could ask the same of you, she thought, but knew far better than that. She sighed heavily and worked up some tears to barely form in her eyes. Not enough to cry, just enough to make them watery, "I…" She spoke softly, "I … I just. I heard what the Archangels of Righteousness and Hope had to say, and it made me stop to think. The Empire might have conquered us and they are easy to try and paint as villains and oppressors, but you're all just people too. People like me. Even the Archangels. They have friends and family who care for them, who will miss them, who will cry when they finally die…" She paused for a moment, "I don't know, maybe it's treason to say this, but maybe you guys aren't the bad guys, and maybe the Kingdom of Estates weren't either. Maybe it's really just this war that is."

The Angel got down on one knee and placed an arm across it, "It's not treason to think such a thing, fine citizen. As someone who has fought on the front lines, I think I'd agree with you. Both sides have victims in war. Which is why the Eternal Empire strives to remove war from the land. Neighboring countries and kingdoms always end up going to war sooner or later. If we can unite under one flag, one banner, one leader, the God Emperor, then war shall be a thing of the past and peace and prosperity shall be showered unto all."

She let one tear fall down her cheek as she forced a smile and looked up at him, "Thank you, kind Sir. I think I'd just like to get some fresh air and think it all over. A walk in the woods to the east. I've always found it peaceful there."

The Angel stood up slowly and nodded at her, "I'm glad the Archangel's words could reach you. They have been given such titles for this very reason. Just make sure you are back within your home by curfew."

She nodded at him again, "Yes of course. That would be a silly thing to get arrested for."

"Indeed, it would." The Angel saluted her, "Long live the God Emperor!" and flew back off, patrolling the city from the skies.

Stephanie took a deep breath and relaxed. The Archangels were not people just like her. They were monsters, and the Archangel of Death had been the worst of them all. Bringing nothing but utter destruction, ruination, and death wherever he went. What she had said though, some of it was true. That pilot in that Angel? He was a person just like she was. Him, his friends, and his family. They were just on the wrong side.

Chapter 2: Past, Present, Future

Stephanie continued making her way out of the town and into the woods nearby. She'd been walking in these woods since she was but a young girl. To her, they felt like a safe haven. Somewhere where nature -- where life itself -- was unchanged. Just growing and existing as it should be, without the interference of humans, or war, or anything.

There was somewhere specific she liked to go to sit in peace. Somewhere her brother had shown her right before he left to go die trying to defend Spoke. A large boulder was in the trees that had flattened out at the top and grass had started to grow on. It overlooked the small river which ran through the area. It was his special place, and he had passed it onto her.

She finally reached it and sat down, letting the sounds of nature fill her mind. Serene. Calm. Peaceful. Wonderful. This is what the world was supposed to be like, this is what the Empire took away from so many. It was only a matter of time, especially now that the whole kingdom was under Empire control, until they started harvesting every single resource they could. The trees here for lumber, the water for power, the fish and wildlife for food. Soon this would be nothing but a barren wasteland.

She pulled out her phone and searched through her gallery. The Archangel of Death. No one knew what his face looked like. No one, but her. Only a small number of promotional pictures were available. His eyes were always covered by his hair, his face by his right hand. He never appeared at any events, in any videos, just a few small pictures when the Archangels were first announced.

He was there, in Spoke when it fell. When her brother died. The main battle took place to the west of the city, and therefore the Empire never felt the need to clean it up. When she was twelve, mere weeks after the Empire took full control of the area, she snuck into the abandoned battle zone alone and found her brother's Knight Mk.1, what was left of his corpse still rotting inside. She harvested its black box and snuck back home.

With an underground Knight diagnostic and repair system, she was able to access its contents immediately, but what she found was … astonishing. A video recording of when her brother died. The Archangel of Death, his long black hair always covering his eyes, his right hand over his mouth as he so calmly walked throughout the fallen Knights and Angels. His skin, pale as a corpse. Her brother, the brave fool he was, barely had enough power left in his Knight to raise the gunner's arm at him, but as he tried to pull the trigger it collapsed back to the ground.

The Archangel of Death's head snapped towards him and his hair brushed back away from his eyes. What she saw in them was terrifying. Black irises with snow white pupils. The veins bright red from tears, the eyes themselves even seeming to shake within their sockets. His hand shakily, slowly pulled away from his face to show tear-stained cheeks. As it finally stretched towards her brother, a scream, no a cry, filled with such pain she had to mute the video every time she watched it, and then static.

But she had seen the Archangel of Death. The boy who was no older than she was. The one who singlehandedly brought the whole of the southern area, and most of the Kingdom of Estates, to its knees. And what she saw in his eyes and face terrified her. It was calm and cold, but an undeniable pain and sorrow hidden deep within.

A pain and sorrow she now felt … because of him.

A few hours passed as she sat there in silence. She did her best to clear her mind, but that was a nigh impossible task.

She was the leader of the rebel cell in the area. Around fifty men and women were under her direct command. They had sixteen Knight Mk.1's and seven Knight Mk.2's and one old prototype two person Knight that was never put into full production. That was always a constant worry in her mind, but now this as well. Her brother's murderer, someone she vowed to kill one day, had been officially pronounced dead by the Eternal Empire itself.

She needed this time off from the rebellion personally just as much as they needed to take a break for their own safety. She slowly got up and started to walk home. She still had plenty of time to spare before curfew, just over two hours longer than she needed to get home, but it was better to be safe than sorry. Even if you came home before curfew, the closer to the deadline the more suspicious you were.

She had barely been walking five minutes before she stopped dead in her tracks. She heard a sound that wasn't natural, one that didn't belong here. She quickly lowered her body and quieted her breathing as she listened more closely.

Whimpering? It *was* whimpering … and crying. Followed by whispers she couldn't make out. Someone else was here and they were emotionally broken. She carefully, quietly, made her way towards the sound, doing her best to stay behind cover. There, not too far in front of her was a very frail man sitting down on a fallen long, shaking and rocking back and forth as he whimpered and cried. Her eyes opened wide. He was naked, and his body was so thin she could count the vertebrae and ribs as they pressed against his skin. The whispers, she tried her best to focus on them but still they were too quiet, too quick, too … panicked?

The man's medium length black hair looked as if he hadn't cleaned it in months; his skin pale as could be, yet somehow just as dirty. She slowly rose to her full height and spoke as softly as she could while still being heard, "Can I help you?"

Immediately the figure jumped and tried to scurry away, stumbling and falling onto the ground instead. He immediately shot back up for a second before bowing over, face almost pressed to the ground, while still facing away from her, "I- … I- … I- … I'm sorry!" He stuttered. His voice so soft she could barely hear him, and his words staggered between gasps for air, "I- … I- … I didn- … did-did-didn't know this was- … was- … this was yours…" It sounded as if it took every fiber of his being to speak, "*Please don't hurt me*!" He screamed and started crying profusely, "I'l- … I'll leave at once just pl-please, please, please please-please-pleasepleaseplease! I'm sorry! Sorry, sorry, sorry sorry-sorry-sorry…" his words continued to descend into a jumbled mess.

Stephanie stopped, completely taken aback. What the hell was wrong with this guy? He was so panicked, so fearful, so terrified. Why? What had happened to him? She very cautiously took a step forward into the clearing, "It's okay. This forest doesn't belong to me. Or anyone for that matter." It seemed as if he couldn't hear her as he continued with his begging and crying. She took a few more, slow steps forward to get a better look at him.

Suddenly she froze. The skin, the stature, the hair… No, it couldn't be…!

She shook the thought out of her head.

He was dead.

"Hey!" She raised her voice slightly to get his attention.

It worked. He instantly froze for a fraction of a moment, before falling back down begging, "I'm sorry! I'm sorry! Please don't hurt me! Please don't hurt me. Please! *Please!* I'll do whatever you want-whatever you ask! Just please, please, *please don't hurt me!*"

She took a deep breath and squatted on the ground, now no more than five feet away from him. "I'm not going to hurt you."

"Y-y-y-y-you- … you … a-a-a-aren't?" He asked her puzzled. His head slowly rose from the ground for a moment before he threw it back down, screaming "*B-b-b-but I deserve it!* I deserve it-I deserve it-I deserve it! I'm sorry I intruded on you! Please don't- … please! I'll do whatever-I promise-I swear!"

She took a deep breath. "Alright, I'll make you a deal. If you slowly turn and face me. I won't hurt you."

He kept whimpering as he spoke, "You- … you … promise?"

"I promise."

He nodded to himself while whispering, still unintelligible to her, for a few seconds before he slowly started to sit up. His whole body shook with every passing moment, cries and whimpers filled with fear escaping his mouth as he moved. He slowly, his hands shaking nearly beyond control, pulled his hair down in front of his eyes and tried his best to hold his right hand over his face as he turned around. His eyes fixated on the ground in front of her, obscuring his face as best as he could.

She froze. It couldn't be. *It couldn't be! He was dead! She was just watching his memorial!* She bit her cheek hard and steeled her mind. She had to know. "What's your name?" She asked him, maintaining a calm voice.

"N-n-name?" He asked her ever so softly, clearly confused.

She leaned forward slightly, cocking her head to the side. Her eyes faintly narrowed, both in confusion and curiosity. He was confused about his name? "What do people call you?"

"I- … I-…," He curled downwards and started crying again, "I don't know!" His whole body started to rock back and forth, "I don't know who I am! I don't know my name, my place! …I don't know anything except…" His eyes went wide and he completely froze, "Pain," He whispered, "Pain, pain, pain, *pain*!" With each word his tone grew louder until it ended in a scream that swiftly turned into back into whimpering and crying.

"Hey, hey, hey…" She spoke calmly, trying to get his attention back onto her without scaring him even more. Her hand reached out for a moment towards his shoulder, but she quickly stopped herself. He was like dealing with a stray cat, one wrong move and they are gone or lashing out. If he was who she feared he was, him lashing out would be the end of the line. "Focus on me, alright? Focus on me. Just look at me."

He slowly, barely, managed to gain a handle over his sobbing and looked up at her, hand still covering his face, hair covering his eyes. The hair. She was close enough to see through it. Her eyes flashed, catching his.

Black irises.

White pupils.

A wave of anger, of pure hatred rushed through her body. Her teeth instinctively gritted, her fists clenched, her eyes turned to slits. Before she even realized what her body had done he threw himself back to the ground crying profusely, "I'm sorry! I'm sorry-I'm sorry-I'm so sorry! I-I-I-I- … I didn't mean to-t-to anger you. I-I-I-I'm sorry please- … pl-pl-please … I-I'll accept whatever punish-punishme-ment you see fit!"

Just as soon as the anger had washed over her, it faded away. Was this *really* the Archangel of Death? And if so, why was he acting like this? Was this some weird sort of ploy … or did he truly not know who he was? No, it couldn't be. He was dead. He was at the apex of the Chaos Bomb's explosion. It utterly annihilated everything in a ten-mile radius around it. There was nothing left of Fortress Eilon. The whole mountain itself was just … gone. No downed Angels or Knights to search through. Nothing. Just a massive void where everything used to once be. The Archangels had insane regenerative abilities, but not even a god could come back from that…

"What's the last thing you can remember?" She asked him, very softly.

"Pain." He instantly responded, "I-i-i-i-immense pain and- … f-f-f-fear! Terror! It g-g-g-gripped my heart, my s-soul, my every thought!" His eyes shot up to hers and she was locked within them. It was almost as if she could feel the terror within them, it was nigh overwhelming, "And p-p-ain. *Pain!* It seared away my sk-sk-skin, it-it t-t-tore away my f-fl-flesh and bone! *It pierced my soul!*" His voice grew increasingly wild as his body shook, as if he was reliving the memory.

"Then what?" She asked him softly.

He shook his head violently, "I- … I … I don't … I don't … I d-d-don't…" The sobbing took over his voice once again.

She stared at him in shock. Her shock doubled when she realized what she was considering. This was her brother's murderer. The Archangel of Death. She should kill him, here and now, just as she promised … but if he survived the Chaos Bomb…

Her mind was running a million miles a second. The Empire announced his death. They genuinely think he's dead, they wouldn't have publicized it otherwise. He seemed not to remember anything except for pain and suffering and an honestly strange compulsion to submit. Why would this be? Did the Chaos Bomb really cause this much damage? She couldn't even imagine any atom of his body would have survived it but, she had a picture of him … and he looked almost exactly the same as that picture. *Steph you're insane … you're fucking insane…* She told herself while she took a deep breath. She couldn't believe what she was about to do.

"It's okay, don't think on it too much." She tried to smile at him, "I've learned it's best not to dwell on the past, especially the painful parts. You look like you haven't eaten in weeks. When's the last time you had some food?"

He tried his best to stop his shaking, but still spasmed every few seconds as he slowly looked back up at her, "E-eaten?" He stared at her confused, "Fo-food…?"

Her jaw did drop this time. He didn't even remember what food was? There was no way… "What about anything to drink … water…?" She tried instead. He merely cocked his head to the side and stared blankly. "My god, you really have no idea what I'm talking about do you?" She whispered softly. He simply continued to stare.

His eyes seemed to almost pierce through her skull, her mind, her soul, but there was a curiosity behind all the terror, the pain, the misery they held.

She shook her head and cursed silently to herself as she very slowly pulled out her canteen of water. "Water." She told him while she slowly, carefully, took the lid off. She brought it to her lips and took a small sip, over exaggerating swallowing. She then carefully held it out to him, "It's good for you."

"Wa … ter…?" He softly asked as he stared at the canteen in her hand.

"Yes." She nodded her head at him, "Take a drink. Please."

His shaking left hand slowly reached out towards the canteen and grabbed onto it. She lightly let it go and watched as he slowly, shakingly, brought the spout to his lips and took the smallest sip of it, swallowing just as exaggeratedly as she had. As he finished swallowing his eyes opened wide, his right hand slowly fell away from his face, and a wonderful sensation of joy washed over him. It was quickly replaced by his whole body shaking violently as he struggled to stay sitting up, "I- … I- … I-I am … n-n-not…" Tears streamed down his cheeks.

He dropped the bottle and she quickly reached forwards to grab it, but to her surprise he didn't move. "I-I-I-I do not…" his whole body started to violently spasm, "d-d-deserve … s-s-s-such … k-k-kindness…" His body started to collapse towards her, and she quickly caught him in her arms. She stared at him, at herself in shock. It was too late now. He had seen her too thoroughly, and there was no way she knew how to kill him. But if he really had forgotten everything…?

She paused for a moment taking once final consideration at the move she was about to make. No one else would make it. No one else would understand it. No one else would agree with it, but she was far from anyone else. She took a deep breath, and smiled softly. "Shhh," she softly told him as she held his body. She ran her hand along his hair, "Shhh, it's okay now. It's okay now." As she continued to cradle him, she could feel his whole body start to relax in her grasp, "It's okay. I've got you. I'm going to take care of you…"

"T- … t- … take c-care of…?" He asked, his voice broken as he cried in her arms.

"Yeah," she smirked. "Watch over you. Protect you. Feed you. Keep you safe." She tried her best to explain. How did he not know what any of this meant?

"No … no one … n-n-no one cares for me…" He whispered, "I d-don't d-d-deserve it…"

"Why not?" She asked him, still petting his hair softly. His whole body tensed up. "Shh … it's okay. You can tell me … it's okay…"

"I … I- …" She could hear the panic start to enter into his voice again, "E-e-everywhere I g-go … I only bring p-p-pain … d-destruction … *Death!*" His body started to shake violently again, and she held him tighter, "My hands are drenched in *Blood! W-w-why?!*" He started to scream through his sobbing, staggered breaths, "*Why are my hands d-drenched in b-blood?!*" He screamed out in terror.

She tried her best to keep consoling him, but her mind was elsewhere. He didn't remember who he was, what he was, or any details of what he's done … yet the weight of his actions seemed to torment him. Nothing was adding up to her. Nothing at all. She needed to get to the bottom of this. At worst, he was playing her and she was going to die, at best…? The possibilities were endless.

She forced a smile and kept sliding her hand through his hair, shushing him like a small child. "Shh, it's okay. I'll take care of you. I promise. Okay. I've got you now. It's okay … shh…"

She kept repeating herself for minutes on end before he seemed to finally get a hold of himself again. He turned to look up at her and she smiled at him, "Now. Let's get you to my home, okay?"

"H-h-home…?" He questioned, puzzled.

She sighed internally. *Of course you don't know what a home is. What's next, breathing? Ugh!* "Just trust me okay? You *do* trust me, don't you? Because I'll take care of you?" She waited for his response, holding her breath.

He slowly nodded his head.

"Can you do exactly as I say?"

He nodded his head more vigorously, saying nothing.

"Good. Now I'm going to need you to get up and do exactly what I tell you to. Deal?"

"As you command." He agreed softly while sitting back up away from her and getting to his feet. It was the first time he spoke without hesitation. And it was to obey orders…

She made a quick mental note of that and stood up smiling as well. An Archangel in the palm of her hand. If she could get him wrapped around her finger… First things first. She had to sneak him home. Naked as he was there was only one way to do that. The long old, abandoned sewer system.

Chapter 3: A Name

The journey back to Stephanie's home had been *far* more difficult than it had any right being. The old sewer system led directly to the decorative well in her backyard, allowing them to avoid any and all contact with people, but this man, whom she was all but positive was the Archangel of Death, jumped at every little thing. A drip of water from overhead had him curling up in tears. The squeak from a rat had him completely immobilized in fear for a whole minute. She was almost starting to doubt he really was the Archangel of Death. How could one who was so helpless be him?

If not for the recording she had of her own brother's death, hell, even without it, there was too much that was off putting about this man. He wasn't normal, that was for sure. Assuming he really was the Archangel of Death, did the Chaos Bomb really destroy his mind this much? Did it turn him into a helpless, pathetic, mercy begging, child-like person; alongside erasing his memory? Or were they unrelated? The video she had of him, tears had stained his eyes and cheeks. Who was the Archangel of Death, and why was he the only one without a virtuous title? A question she had never considered until now.

She climbed up the ladder and took a deep breath of the fresh night air. Her large yard was surrounded by hedges and filled with gardens. Her parents had been the richest people here while they were alive. Now everything they once had owned belonged to her. She looked back down the well to see her new companion still standing at the bottom. His right hand still covered his face, his left over it as if he tried to keep them from shaking.

"Come on." She called down to him.

He shook his head repeatedly, "I-I-I…" His whisper of his voice barely carried to her.

She sighed heavily, "You can do it." She softly called back.

He kept shaking his head, "I- … I'm- … t-t-too weak." He barely managed to speak. His shakes slowly got more violent. "I-I-I- … I c-can't stop-stop shaking!"

She closed her eyes for a moment before reopening them and looking down at him with the softest gaze she could craft, "Please," she whispered, "for me?"

His whole body froze for a few long moments, "F- … for you?" It was the most composed he had sounded since they started their walk to her home.

She nodded her head at him. He wasn't looking at her, instead still staring at the ground in the sewers, but she knew he could sense it. "Yes," she repeated, "it would make me very happy if you climbed up here."

"Happy…" She could barely make out the words as he spoke to himself, but they were just loud enough, "m-m-make her happy. Pl-pl-pleased? No. No! No, no-no-no! No one is ever p-p-p-p-pleased with me. B-b-but she said! L-lies? No. She wouldn't. But happy? M-me? M-m-m-make someone hap-py-py? No, no, no-no-no-no impossible. But what if? What if, what if-what-if?"

She rolled her eyes to herself. He wasn't going to be convincing himself anytime soon at this rate, and while her backyard was mostly safe, there was no accounting for any aerial flybys of the Angels. If they saw her reaching down into what was supposed to just be a decorative well, who knew what they would do. She couldn't believe what she was about to try. She stretched her arm out, down the well and made and a scratching motion with her hand, "If you come up here, I'll scratch your head." She called out to him in a teasing, singsong tone.

His eyes snapped up to look at her smiling down at him, teasing with her hand reached out towards him. His mouth fell slightly agape as for the first time since she had met him, the fear and terror in his eyes was washed over with a mesmerized joy. He nodded to himself after a moment and quickly grabbed onto the rungs of the ladder and started to pull himself up.

Stephanie stared at him in disbelief. It actually worked! She felt like she was holding her hand out to a lost puppy trying to get it to walk over to her. He was utterly pathetic. His arms and legs were shaking, and she couldn't tell if it was his normal shakes, or if he was barely able to pull his body up the ladder with how weak he looked. Probably both. As he neared the top, she slowly pulled her hand away. He froze for a moment and whimpered.

"All the way up," she told him, "Come sit on the ledge and I'll give you your reward."

Without another word he finished climbing the ladder and sat down on the side of the well. He bowed his head and closed his eyes. She smiled at him and placed her hand on his head. The moment she touched him he flinched for a moment, as if expecting pain, but stayed still. She rolled her eyes. If it was going to be this easy to control the Archangel of Death, then the hardest part of her plan was out of the way, or at least the part she feared would fail. That still left a lot of other problems though. Problems she would have to figure out sooner or later.

She slowly started to scratch his head softly and smirked as he leaned into her hand. "Good boy." The moment she said that his whole body practically melted as he fell towards her. "Hey!" She squeaked as she quickly knelt to catch him.

His eyes popped wide open as he landed in her arms and his breathing became panicked, "I-I-I-I'm." He could barely even get one word out, "*S-sorry!*" He cried, sobbing in her grasp. "I-I-I-I di-di-didn't…" He couldn't even manage to finish the sentence.

Stephanie couldn't help but chuckle. All it had took was two words and he melted in her hands. They had spent far too long out in the open though. She quickly picked him up in her arms and stood. "You're kinda cute." The words left her mouth before she even realized what she was saying. She stopped and blinked. *What? No. How? How could I?* Her body was completely frozen. *About him? Him?!* She quickly regained her composure, "Pathetic though."

He lay limp in her arms but pushed the side of his head against her chest, "I know…" he said softly. "I've ... I've … always been p-pathetic." His words came out calmly for once, but barely above a whisper. "Weak, soft, helpless, hopeless … I … I'm sorry." The tears finally started to come back.

She took a deep breath and started to walk towards her house, "Come on, let's get you cleaned up." She paused for a moment, "And myself, for that matter."

"Did … did…" He fought against his staggered breaths to speak, "Did I m-m-make you happy?" He finally managed to ask as she closed the door behind them.

She stopped and looked down at him. She blew on his face to get the hair out of his eyes and locked contact with them. There was endless pain, suffering, fear, horror, sorrow under his unique eyes, but … there was something else that stood out even more. A longing. She smiled and nodded at him, "Yes." He closed his eyes and melted in her arms. "You did well."

A slight smile crossed his lips, but he said nothing. He was lost within his own thoughts. He mumbled so quietly that even as she carried him up the stairs she couldn't make out what he was saying to himself, but he seemed almost … happy.

She walked into the master bathroom and carefully set him down on the tiled floor, "Wait here, okay?" She asked him.

He nodded at her; his hair falling back over his eyes and raised his right hand to cover his face again.

She walked over to the large tub and turned on the water. The sound of the pipes squeaking and the water rushing caused him to squeal in fear and curl up in a ball. She chuckled to herself as she let the water get warm before plugging the tub. "It's alright." She assured him, "It won't hurt you."

He tried to nod his head as he whimpered in the corner, still fearful of the sound of the rushing water. Stephanie stopped and stared at him. He most likely didn't even know how to bathe himself. She'd have… She closed her eyes and silently grimaced. The ends justified the means. The ends justified the means! She was putting up with this for a damn good reason. Pretending to care for him was only so she could use him, use his power, to strike against the Empire.

Did he even know he had power though? That was another question she faced. What if she was doing all of this work to groom him to her will for nothing? If he didn't know about the power, could he use it? If not, how would she reawaken it within him? Did he still have it? Was he still immortal even? Or had he expended the last of it all surviving the Chaos Bomb?

So many questions. And no answers. She couldn't even think of a way to figure out the answers. Not without shattering the trust she was trying to gain. She could easily test if he was still immortal. A .45 ACP round to his skull would tell her that, but then he might never trust her again, or worse, he might kill her. Time. Faith. Hope. She just needed to have some of each. This was her only real chance at striking out against the Eternal Empire. She wasn't about to give up on it just because … just because…

She took a deep breath and turned off the water as the tub was just over halfway full. She turned back to look at him, still curled up in a ball, spasming every now and then, and muttering to himself. She placed a hand on her head and rubbed her temple for a second before whispering under her breath "Fuck it." There was no easy way to go about cleaning him, she needed to bathe as well, and the tub was big enough.

She shook her head one last time, mentally fighting herself over what she was about to do, but finally began to undress. She wasn't sure if it was to her surprise, or if she expected him to have no reaction. On one hand any normal male would have been bleeding out of the nose by now, on the other hand, he himself had been naked this whole time and showed no signs of it even registering.

She finished throwing the last of her clothes to the side and looked back over at him. "Come on, get up now."

"Hm?" He seemed to snap out of deep thought as he turned to look at her, his hand staying by his side. She could see no recognition in his eyes that she was bare naked. For a moment she was hurt, but the thought of him … *him* … looking at her in lust was far worse than him not caring. She merely gestured for him to stand up and he slowly obliged. "W- … w- … what are we … we doing?" He managed to ask her.

"Cleaning up." She told him plainly as she carefully got into the tub. She gestured to the other side of it, "Get in, it's nice and warm." She smiled, "Trust me."

"Tr- … trus- … trust?" He asked as he walked towards the edge of the tub.

"Yes." She repeated, "Trust."

He nodded at her very carefully and slowly stepped into the tub. As soon as his foot touched the water he stopped for a moment. Fear flooded his veins.

"It's okay." She reassured him, "Trust."

He finished climbing into the tub and gasped. Within moments he slid down, submerging himself all the way up to his neck while letting out a soft moan. "It's … it's…" Tears started to stream down his cheeks as he looked up to the ceiling. His hair fell away from his eyes, his hands floating by his side, revealing a face of pure … joy.

It was just a nice warm bath, but she had never seen anyone so happy, so enamored. Tears flowed freely down his cheeks, and for the first time his body was motionless. There was no shaking in his hands, no twitching in his legs, no spasms coursing through his whole body. She stopped and stared at him in awe. How could something so simple mean so much?

"Hey," she said quietly, just loud enough to get his attention.

His eyes widened for a moment and in a rush his hand quickly shot out to cover his face as he looked over at her, "Y-yes?"

"I'm gonna have to give you a name you know."

"A … a name? I-I … I d-d-d-d-don't have one."

"I know." She smiled at him gently, "Means we'll have to come up with one."

He shook his head, "No … no, no, no … no-no-no!" The horrified tone started to creep back into his voice.

She quickly leaned forward getting over him and placed her hand on his head, "Yes … yes, yes, yes … yes-yes-yes!" She chuckled, "How about … A-D?"

His eyes went wide as her skin sat down on his, as her hand landed on his head. They locked eyes and she held his fearful gaze with a warm comfort. "A … D…?" He finally managed to speak up, "A … a … a name?"

"Mhm!" She smiled at him and sat back down on her side of the tub, "Your name."

"My n-n-name??" He gasped in shock, "I … I … I have a n-name?" His eyes went wide with excitement, "A … A-D!"

Stephanie started to laugh, "Yes. A-D. That's you."

He placed one of his hands on his chest and as he let his head fall back and rest on the tub again, "M-m-me. I'm … I'm A-D." His mind was lost in wonder once again.

She let him lay there in silence for awhile. She stared at him herself, lost in wonder as well. Words echoed in her mind *"He might have been the sweetest of us all."* That whole broadcast was nothing but a propaganda machine, but here she sat. With the Archangel of Death, or at least what used to be The Archangel of Death directly across from her … and sweet was a word she might've used for him. Pathetic, hopeless, helpless, idiotic, weak, were also words she'd use to describe him. But he seemed so … sweet. Full of child-like wonder right now.

"Hey, A-D?" She tried to get his attention.

He made no movements for a moment before he shook his head snapping back to reality and looked up at her, "O-oh! That's … that's … t-t-that's me!" He shouted out with a smile crossing his whole face.

She chuckled at him, "Yes, it is. Now," she grabbed one of the loofas on the side of the tub, "I'm going to teach you how to properly bathe. Okay?"

He nodded at her vigorously, "O-o-of c-course!" He responded instantly, "Anything for you," his eyes went wide. "Uh…"

"Stephanie." She told him, assuming what he wanted to know.

He nodded his head again, "A-a-anything for you, St-St-Stephanie!" He said it with such excitement.

She couldn't believe it. There was no way he was already wrapped around her finger this much. It was far too easy, but she didn't have time to dwell on that right now. She needed to keep on the visage. She couldn't let him think for nary a moment something was wrong, that there was any ulterior motive.

She placed some soap on the loofa and held it out to him, "Hold this." He quickly reached out and grabbed it, pulling it close to his chest. She grabbed another one for herself and put soap on it as well, "Now mimic what I do." She slowly started to massage the soap into the loofa.

A-D slowly started to squeeze the one he held and tried his best to perfectly mimic her movements. His hands shook with each squeeze; they barely held any strength within them. There was next to nothing to his body but skin and bones. No matter where she looked on it. It'd been a month since the fall of the Kingdom of Estates, a month since he was supposed to be dead. Had he gone this long without food? When did his body finally fully recover?

It also brought to question in her mind more ideas behind the regenerative powers of the Archangels. Did he not even need to eat? Or drink? Would their bodies just refuse to stop functioning anyways? She had no concrete proof … except for what sat across from her. It was going to take months to get him into decent condition at least, but it was more than going to be worth it. It had to be.

As the bubbles started to expand from the loofas and fall into the bath she stopped. "Good," she nodded at him, "now, keep following my lead." She held up one of her legs and started to scrub it with the loofa for a few moments before stopping and then gesturing at him to do the same.

He nodded his head and slowly started to reach towards her leg.

She quickly pulled it back in a gasp, "No!" She shouted.

His eyes went wide in fear and his arms shot back to his chest as he whimpered, "I-I-I-I-I-I'm s-s-s-so-s-s-sorry!" He said in panicked breaths.

She stared at him in disbelief for a few moments before a giggle left her lips, "Your own leg, silly." She shook her head.

"OH!" He almost jumped where he sat. "I-I-I-"

"You're fine." She said with a sigh, "Just caught me a bit off guard is all. You know, it's very improper to touch a lady like that."

"Sorry!" He squealed while shaking his head, "Sorry, sorry, sorry-sorry!"

"You didn't know." She said for him, "I'm starting to get the hang of this." She said more to herself, "Now, your own leg this time. Hm?"

He slowly nodded at her trying to hold back tears as he started to scrub his own leg. "Much better. Now," She rose her next leg, "We slowly go over the whole body…" He followed her every move, much slower and softer than she did, but within minutes they were clean.

For the rest of the bath he seemed more distant, quieter … she could tell he was afraid to make her shout again. She'd had more than her fill of coddling him tonight though and let him sit there in silence as she directed him out of the tub and showed him how to dry himself off.

It was getting late and she had a long day ahead of her tomorrow. Not only did she need to listen to First Prince Clyster's military press conference and prepare a speech, but now she also needed to buy A-D some clothes, since she had nothing for him to wear, get him a phone so they could keep in contact while she was out of the house, and buy more food for the two of them. She also had hoped to put in a few hours on her prototype Knight, Lady Love, but that seemed like a slim chance now.

She'd spent years working on the old thing, bringing it fully online. Early test runs with the model type proved to be too complicated for quick implementation. It was deemed too much for one pilot to use, and the amount of coordination for two pilots to work in sync was nigh impossible to find without years of training. She was the best damn pilot she knew, the best one any of the rebel cells who had heard of her knew. And this Knight would be a fierce tool on the battlefield if she learned to conquer it.

She didn't want to spend time cooking a proper dinner, so quickly put some chicken tenders in the air fryer while bringing out some robes to cover A-D. At least she had plenty of spare bedrooms for him to sleep in, but she couldn't decide where she wanted him in the manor. On one hand the room right across from the master bedroom would keep him nearby for simplicities sake, on the other hand? It was pointless to think about. What she liked or didn't like didn't matter. There was only one goal.

She showed him how to eat, just like she had with the water earlier in the day, but other than that they ate in complete silence. He was too ashamed and afraid to say anything, and she was perfectly fine with that right now.

After they were done eating, she put the dishes in the dishwasher and looked over at him as he sat, partially curled into himself in the chair. "Come on," she forced a smile, "let's get you to bed. I'm exhausted." He nodded his head at her and followed her up the stairs in silence. She opened to door to her old room, "This is your room now. You need to get some rest," she pointed to the bed. "Go ahead and lay down on that, close your eyes, and just relax the night away." She let her arm drop back to her side and sighed, "I'll be in the room on the next floor," She gestured to the stairs heading up to the third and top floor of her house.

"I'll come get you in the morning for breakfast." She yawned, "Make us a proper meal. Hm?"

"O-o-okay…" He said very softly.

"Hey." She said it with just enough authority to get him to glance at her. She held out her hand towards his head and waited.

It took him a few moments before he even realized what she wanted, but he instead shook his head. "No … no-no…" She could barely make out what he said, "M-m-ma-made you m-m-mad." He kept shaking his head, "Shou-should-be … be … be pun-punished."

Stephanie said nothing, but she placed her other hand on her hip, tilted her head to the side and glared at him. His eyes went wide as he gasped and quickly leaned his head into her hand. "Mhm." She said in a condescending tone, "That's what I thought." She started to scratch it, "Make it up to me by getting some rest okay?"

"Okay!" He squeaked.

She pulled her hand away from him and gestured for him to enter his room. As he walked into it, she told him, "Goodnight, A-D."

He turned around to look at her, "Good … goodnight, Ste-Ste-Stephanie."

As he finished wishing her a goodnight, she closed the door and let out a heavy sigh while rolling her eyes. She quickly went up to her room and collapsed on the bed. This was far more exhausting than she would have ever imagined. Not physically, but mentally. It was like she needed to watch her every word, every move, around him. One minor wrong thing and he turned into a pathetic crying ball of shame.

"The hell are you doing Steph?" She whispered to herself as sleep came over her.

Chapter 4: Alone Again

Sleep came surprisingly easily to Stephanie. Even with the Archangel of Death in her house, she felt he was far from a threat to her, for now at least. As she got dressed the following morning, she wanted to instantly run and check if he was still there, but she needed to keep her cool. If he was gone, she was probably dead no matter what she did. If he was still in his room, she was fine. For now at least.

She hopped onto her computer for a few moments to make sure all her security systems were still working fine, and more importantly, something she *hadn't* checked in a while, that all her emergency alerts for evacuating were still ready to get sent out. She might have been done for if things went south, but her people didn't need to die with her. She had ten different evac signals she could send out at any moment from her phone if need be. It was just a combination of three different meeting zones, each with three differing levels of how quickly they needed to move, plus one absolute emergency one that would signal an even higher level of need to rush and automatically link everyone to the nearest meeting zone.

Her parents may not have lived to see the fall of the Kingdom of Estates, but they had been more than prepared for it. To fight against the Empire once their home inevitably fell. Now all their tools and resources were at her disposal, and she used them to their full extent … or as much as she could. They had set up almost everything she used for her rebel cell. Most importantly they had left her, and her specifically, a note that arrived years after their death. Only for the upmost of emergencies they had a hidden underground bunker for her to use. The final, ultimate level of evac order also sent directions to computers at the meeting zones for her comrades to make it to that bunker.

Satisfied everything was still in place she made her way down one floor where A-D was staying. She crouched as she made her footsteps silent while she approached the door and cautiously put an ear against the wall. At first there was nothing, he seemed either fast asleep or gone, but then she heard it. The softest, quietest whimper.

She sighed lightly and stood up straight before lightly knocking on the door, "A-D?" She heard him squeak in fear, but he gave no response. "I'm going to come in. Alright?" She waited a moment to see if he'd respond, but he didn't. She carefully opened the door and took a step into her old room. The blankets were ripped off the bed and in the far corner of the room A-D had wrapped himself up in them and was rocking back and forth slightly crying to himself.

She took a few steps towards him and knelt down on the ground, "What's wrong?" She asked him softly.

"I-I-I-I'm sorry! S-s-sorry!" He cried out under the blankets, "Pl-pl-pl-please don't-don't hurt m-me-me!"

"I'm not going to hurt you. Whatever it is this time, I won't hurt you. I promise."

"Bu-bu-but I," he stumbled over every single syllable, "I cou-couldn't rest. I-I c-couldn't do what you asked!" There was an overwhelming fear in his voice. She was finally beginning to understand something. Failure meant punishment in blood to him. Failure over … anything. That would explain the terror he held at all times, his desperation to try and please her, his utter joy when she told him he had made her happy. But was this from the Chaos Bomb, or something ingrained into his mind?

"If you tell me why," she spoke calmly, "I won't be mad at all. Not even in the slightest."

"The-the…" His whole body started to shiver, "Voices!" He cried out, "I c-c-can hear them w-w-wh-when I close my eyes! They-they…" His ability to speak became lost in his tears.

She reached out and placed a hand on the blankets he was wrapped under, "What do they say?"

He shook his head violently. "No … no-no-no-no-no…" He pleaded with her.

"Come on, A-D." She started to peel away the outer layers, "You can tell me. Maybe it'll help."

He made no moves to stop her from peeling off the blankets one by one, "N-n-never … good enough." He barely whispered through the knots in his throat, "Not … g-g-good enough … always a … a failure. D-d-d-disappointment." He paused for a second, "I-I-I can't do anything right! I c-c-can hear the screams! *The cries of terror! Because of me!* Because-be … b-because of me…" He fell back into sobbing uncontrollably as she got down to the last blanket. His knuckles pure white as they clutched it around his chest.

"It's okay. I'd have trouble sleeping too if that was the case."

He shook his head, "No. N-n-no I f-failed you. I'm s-sorry! I'm not good enough! I c-c-can't do anything right! I shouldn't exist… Why am I alive st-st-st-still??? Why can't I just *die*?!"

Her eyes opened wide for a moment, he sounded so sincere. He wanted to die, but was that even possible? She'd do it without hesitation if she could. Her plan be damned. She wanted him dead just as much as he seemed to want himself dead right now, but all of this played into her hand. If these feelings, these voices, these faint ideas of memories were from before the Chaos Bomb…

She placed her hand on his head, "I'm sorry, A-D. If I had known resting caused you such pain, I wouldn't have said it would make me happy." She paused for a moment, "I'm sorry. There's nothing for you to apologize for."

"I-I…" He froze as though he could barely comprehend what she'd told him.

"And, if you makes you feel a little better," she added, "I'm very happy that you shared this with me. Thank you."

"Y-you aren't m-m-m-mad?" He cautiously asked.

"Not at all." She told him with a smile.

"You … y-you're hap-happy?" He barely managed to say, tears still streaming down his cheeks.

"Very much so." She responded without hesitation.

"I-I-I…" He started to breathe more frantically. She could easily see he didn't know how to handle what she had just told him.

She chuckled and stood up, pulling her hand away from his head and held it out to him, "Come on, let's get some breakfast made, hm?"

He finally turned around to face her and was stunned by the calm smile on her face and the offer to help him up. He very slowly, hands still shaking grabbed her hand and she pulled him up to his feet. "W-w-why?" He managed to ask her, "I-I-I don't … d-d-don't d-deserve this…"

"Maybe you just needed someone willing to give you a real chance is all." She told him as she led him out of the room, "Someone with a bit of patience and kindness. Seems like you don't know what either of those things are."

"I k-k-know I'm not worthy of t-t-them." He spoke softly as he followed her, hand still in hers.

"That was a past life. Here? Now? You can start a new one. Away from whatever horrors you witnessed in the past."

"Can … can…" He struggled more than usual to speak his words, almost as if there was a new fear holding him back, "Can I st-st-stay here with you f-f-for it?"

She looked back and smirked at him, "Wouldn't have it any other way." He froze in his tracks, her hand slipping out of his as she took a few more steps before stopping to turn around. His mouth was agape in awe, joy, excitement. More tears ran down his face, but these were of happiness. "Oh, come on now." She teased, "I know many people who'd consider that a terrible fate."

"They're wrong!" He instantly shouted back, "You are the k-kindest, sw-sw-sweetest, n-nicest person ever!" He quickly caught up to her and bowed his head low, "Thank you! Thank you, thank you-thank-you-thankyou!"

Her smile faded for a moment. He seemed so pure. No! She couldn't let herself think like that. He was the Archangel of Death. He was a monster. He was nothing more than just a means to an end. But right now, right here in front of her all she saw was a helpless and broken person. She quickly brought back her smile and pet his hair for a moment, "You're welcome. Now, I'm going to make us some waffles and bacon, then I'm going to help teach you how to clean up afterwards. Okay?"

He nodded his head at her, "Okay!"

She didn't quickly whip up breakfast for them, but she wasted no time. She knew at best her cooking was decent and that A-D was only so enamored by it because he had forgotten what food was like. Compared to what he was probably served while in the Eternal Empire this was garbage, but still, it felt nice to see someone enjoy every bite of her cooking so much. When it came to cleaning up, she did 95% of it; only asking him to carefully bring the dishes to the sink while she loaded them into the dishwasher, trying to explain why she did it. He had the want to learn, the desperate want to help her, but she was hesitant, for obvious reasons.

As she turned on the dishwasher she nodded to herself and turned to A-D, "A-D?" She addressed him, "I have something very important I need you to do for me."

"W-w-what is it?" He still stumbled over his words, even though she could see the excitement in his eyes.

"I must go shopping. Need to get you some real clothes, and more food for the both of us, but what's important is that you stay here, and you stay out of sight. It's already going to be a nightmare for me to come up with a reason why I'm buying men's clothes, the last thing I need is for someone to find out I have a man staying in my home with me. So please, leave all the drapes closed, don't answer the door, and try to remain semi-quiet."

He nodded at her, "Of-of course! I … I pr-pr-prefer the d-darkness anyways. And … and t-t-t-try to stay q-quiet."

She smiled at him as she walked into the living room. She grabbed the tv remote and showed him how to use it, "Feel free to watch anything you wish, quietly that is, or if you'd rather there's a small library down the hall. Read any book you wish. I'll either be back in time for lunch, or I'll bring some home with me. Okay?"

"Ye-yes!" He smiled, "I will … remain hidden. H-h-here." He paused for a moment, "Is … is this like how … how t-t-t-touching your leg was … uh … w-w-was improper?"

She chuckled at him, "Quite. Possibly even worse. Hence why it's best no one else knows about you for the moment."

He nodded vigorously, "Un-un-und-understood!"

"Very, *very* important," she emphasized, "If the doorbell ever rings," She paused for a moment, he probably didn't know what that was, "You'll know it when you hear it, or if anyone is at any of the doors knocking. Do *not* answer. Don't even go near the door. Just stay quiet and wait for them to leave, okay?"

He kept nodding at her, "Yes!"

She let out a small sigh of relief, "Thank you. Otherwise, relax. Make yourself at home." She finally made her way out of the house and to her car parked in the driveway. She'd promised she would be home by lunch, she didn't have much time to waste. Before anything she needed to drive to the other side of town and see if John had sent a messenger yet to the dead drop with a phone. She had sent a messenger to him over a week ago, unless they had been captured, which wasn't very likely, they had more than made it to him. So why hadn't he called yet?

A-D stood staring at the door after Stephanie closed it for minutes on end after she left. He was … he was … alone. Again. He gritted his teeth as his hands shook. It was only for a little bit … only for a little bit … just for a little bit. He kept trying to remind himself. She wasn't leaving him behind forever. She wasn't going to leave him alone again. Not for good. She wouldn't. She was too kind.

But it's what he deserved. It's what everyone else had always done in his life. His life he couldn't even remember, he just knew no one liked him. He didn't notice the tears dripping down his cheeks as he could barely stay standing staring at the door. She was leaving him just like everyone else. Just like he deserved. He was never good enough for anyone.

He dropped down to his knees and started to whisper to himself, "No, no, no-no-no-no-no … she'll-she'll-she'll…" His breathing started to pick up pace as he gasped for air, "I just-I ju-I … I just need to wait. She'll be-be b-b-b-back!" He slowly started to curl up in a ball on the ground, "Please … please, please don't leave me. Not again, not again, not again-not again!" The tears over took anything else as he softly sobbed on the wooden floor.

Chapter 5: Friends…?

There was nothing at the dead drop when Stephanie arrived. She didn't like this. John and her often didn't see eye to eye, but he rarely completely ignored her. There was nothing she could do about it right now though. She made her way to the thrift store on the far side of town, which made it far less likely she'd run into anyone who would recognize her in any capacity. She had no idea how she was going to explain herself if someone in her rebel cell saw her buying men's clothes.

A few sets of clothing was all she needed to get him. Basic and cheap. Later down the line she could buy him more, but right now she just needed to get him out of the robe he was in and into some real clothes. Enough for a few days at least. Then it was to the grocery store to buy twice the amount of food she was used to buying. At least he didn't seem picky about what he ate. She could only hope it would stay that way.

She had also decided to pick up food on the way home, she didn't want to spend the time cooking and cleaning up afterwards. She still needed to watch First Prince Clyster's speech about the new war technologies the Eternal Empire was finally publicly announcing, work on writing and scheduling a speech with the entirety of her cell, and with some luck she'd get some time to work on her prototype Knight.

After taking it out last time she immediately noticed some changes she needed to make to it before she would feel truly comfortable piloting it. How her parents had gotten their hands on this before they passed away baffled her, but so did much of what they left behind. Either way it had become her little passion project. If she could master this Knight, it would take an Archangel to stand against her.

She had managed to move almost all the controls to the main seat, but she doubted she could move absolutely everything to it. If she could train A-D to sit in the secondary seat they might be unstoppable. Of course, that was assuming she could actually train him on the details, rely on him for split second decisions in combat, and hoping he could work with her as one mind. She also still had no idea if his psychic powers still worked, or how she could control how he used them, but if she could somehow get him to use them to protect her, of even better to help her fight offensively…

Too many ifs. Far too many. She had to take everything one step at a time, especially with A-D. He was a ticking time bomb.

A-D finally got his crying under control and slowly picked himself up off the floor. "I-I-I just … need to wait." He quietly spoke to himself, finally believing what he said, "She s-s-said she'll be back, I just … I j-j-just have to wait." He slowly started to walk over to the living room, his hands held up by his chest as his whole body shook, "No-no-no-no one ever comes back though, but no one ever shows … k-k-kindness before." He argued with himself still, "S-s-she said it would be only for a bit. I'll … I'll wait until n-night. If…" He started to choke on his words as the thought tore into his heart, "If she's n-no-not b-back by then…" he started to hyperventilate, "she's … she's … just like everyone else."

He fell onto the couch facing the tv and tried his best to sit up straight, to maintain his composure, which at best was pathetic. Out of the corner of his eye, he caught his reflection in the endless abyss of the tv screen and instantly dropped his head down forcing his hair to cover his eyes and brought his right hand up to his mouth. He didn't know why he hated how he looked, or even hated himself so much, but he knew he should, he deserved it.

That terrified him. What had he done in his past; what was he forgetting, that caused so much hatred against him? Why did he feel – no, know – that he deserved nothing good? On one hand, he wanted to know what he was forgetting, on the other … Stephanie offered him a new life…

Through his teary eyes he spotted a thick book on the coffee table. She had told him reading was a good idea. He carefully reached out and grabbed the book. Opening it up his eyes went wide as the first page of the photo album graced his eyes. The whole thing was filled with pictures of Stephanie and other people he didn't know all hanging out, smiling, laughing, hugging, having fun. A-D ran his finger along every picture as tears started to silently pour out from his eyes.

\ \

"I'm back!" Stephanie called as she closed the door to the garage behind her. The last thing she needed was A-D freaking out over someone entering the house, best to just announce herself so he knew it was just her. "I grabbed some sushi for lunch and a ton of groceries to last us for awhile … hopefully," she made her way into the kitchen and set down all the bags. "For dinner I'll make some chicken and rice with some steamed veggies on the side. Sound good?" She quickly got to work putting away the cold groceries as she asked aimlessly into the house.

She heard nothing in response to her question, or arrival for that matter. Not even the slightest hint of movement. "A-D?" She called out for him as she finished putting the cold items away. Again, nothing. She closed the fridge and walked over into the living room and stopped in her tracks.

A-D sat perfectly still on the couch, with his knees up and a book resting against them. His eyes were red from tears, and she could see the stains on his cheeks of many that had already fallen. She quickly regained her composure and slowly approached him, "What're you reading there?" She softly asked. As she got closer she could finally make out the wide book resting on his knees and she gasped lightly, "Oh I had forgotten I left that out!" She walked over behind him, "Jeremiah wanted to look at some of the pictures we had taken over the years of us and our friends."

She leaned over the back of the couch and placed her finger on one of the pictures, "See that there is Jeremiah, and over here is Teresa, and that's Collin! We all go *way* back. This picture was from when we all graduated high school together." She chuckled to herself, "Oh I remember that day well. As soon as the ceremony was over we all quickly got out of those god-awful gowns and back into our normal clothes before nearly getting kicked out of one of our favorite restaurants for having too much fun."

"W…" A-D spoke in barely a whisper, "What's … a … f-friend?"

"A friend?" She asked him shocked. Now that he asked it, she had never had to consider what a friend was before, even less so how to describe one, "It's…" she took a deep breath, "it's someone you like spending time with. Someone who you care about deeply. Someone you trust, and feel that you can confide things in. And while sometimes they'll make you want to punch their face in, at the end of the day you'd do damn near anything for them."

"A … friend…" He spoke more to himself than to her, "I … I like b-b-being alone…"

"Well people always need their alone time too," she told him, "no matter how close you are to someone."

He shook his head, "No … no I don't … I d-d-don't like people."

"Why not?" She asked him.

"They … they d-don't l-like me." His body shivered for a moment as he spoke.

"Well, do you like spending time with me?"

His whole body stiffened up for a moment, "Yes!" He shouted out.

She chuckled at him, "Do you think you can trust me?"

He nodded his head vehemently at her.

"And you've shown you'll do things just because I ask you to."

His eyes opened wide and he looked back up at her, "Are … are…" his voice started shaking heavily, "are we f-f-friends?!" He finally squealed out.

She smirked at him and pulled out her phone, "There's one thing we gotta do before we can call each other friends."

"Wh-wh-what is it?" He asked her excitedly. She opened the camera on her phone and leaned all the way over the couch to get her head next to his while holding the phone all the way out. Before she could say anything A-D quickly made sure his hair was covering his eyes and covered his face with his right hand while curling up even more.

She sighed lightly, "Come on A-D. We need a picture together."

He shook his head at her, "I-I-I d-d-don't like…"

"Come on." She nagged at him, "I'll even let you still cover your face. Just put your other hand up like this and at least pretend to look at the camera for me." She held up two fingers on her free hand and forced a smile, "Just like this A-D."

"And … and … we'll be f-friends?"

"100%."

He sat in silence for a few moments before softly nodding his head, "Okay…" He glanced towards her phone and raised his left hand holding up the same two fingers as it shook in the air.

As soon as she took the picture, she pushed herself back up off the couch, "Ta-da!" She exclaimed and quickly walked around to sit next to him and show him it, "Look here! Our first picture together." He quickly relaxed as she was done with the camera and looked at the picture on her phone. She held it up next to the book, "Look at that. Now this is a picture worthy of going in here one day. Or even better a photo album you put together one day. Could call this 'My First Friend.'"

His eyes lit up and tears flowed from them freely, "F-f-f-f-friend?"

She nodded at him, "Friends." She smiled and ruffled his hair, "Now come on before the sushi gets warm. After we're done eating, we'll get you into your new clothes and then … then I'll show you something special. Something only my friends ever get to see. Deal?"

He nodded at her, "D-d-deal!"

Chapter 6: Mechphobia

"Now follow me." Stephanie told A-D as she finished putting the dirty dishes in the dishwasher. "What I'm about to show you, not many people know about it. So, I need you to keep it a secret, okay? Can't tell anyone." She stopped to look at him.

"I … I-I can d-do that." He responded as quickly as he could.

"Good." She smiled at him and led him to the small closet under the stairs. "It's a bit crowded but don't worry. Come on in." She told him as she walked into it. The closet was completely empty, and barely big enough for two people to stand in semi-comfortably. He carefully followed her and she placed her hand on the farthest wall. She paused for a moment and sighed, "Don't worry. Some things are about to move about quickly. I promise. It's safe. Just stay by my side, okay?"

He nodded, a hint of fear entering his eyes, "O-o-okay!"

She smiled again and pushed in the hidden panel on the far wall. Almost instantly the door closed behind them and enclosing them in pitch darkness. A-D jumped and gasped in shock, but managed to calm down slightly as hidden recessed lighting kicked in. "*And* down we go." Stephanie chuckled at him. Right as she finished speaking the hidden elevator they were in shot downwards. A-D squeaked again and grabbed onto her arm in a panic as they flew downwards. "I said don't worry." she reassured him.

Seconds after it started the elevator slowed down and came to a stop, the door opening on its own a few moments after they stopped moving. "A long time ago my family built most of these tunnels and used them for smuggling various goods through the country. The war changed everything though. Does the name The Eternal Empire mean anything to you?" She asked as she led him out of the elevator into the large open chamber below her house.

He paused for a moment deep in thought before shaking his head, "I … -I t-think I s-s-should know what that is?" He asked her. "But it…" he shook his head.

"Well long story short then. The Eternal Empire invaded the country where we live, The Kingdom of Estates." She turned to face him, "I know my parents were very busy during the early years of the war, but one day they just up and left in a hurry. Leaving my brother and I behind. Never heard from them since. Either way, they left all of this infrastructure for us to use as we saw fit. Maybe not intentionally, as it took me years just to figure out how to get down here, but here we are."

Her parents had disappeared just months before the Estate they lived in fell to the Empire. She had no idea what they had been up to during the war, but it was suspicious to say the least. She wanted to believe they had been helping their Kingdom in the war, but she couldn't rule out that idea that they might have been … traitors. Either way, they were long gone now, and almost certainly dead at this point with the whole of their Kingdom now under the Eternal Empire's control.

She stopped and took a deep breath, "Look, A-D," she addressed him in a far more serious tone, "I don't live a peaceful life. I'm a rebel. I don't respect the Empire's rule and dream of seeing them pushed back out one day. I fight them any way I can. Do you have a problem with that?"

He looked at her confused. "I … no!" He shouted at her while shaking his head once, "I-I-I-I … I w-wanna help yo-you. I don't … I don't know who-who any of them are, b-b-but you helped me. S-s-so-so I w-wanna h-help you!"

She smiled at him, "I was hoping you'd say that." She reached her hand out and flipped the large circuit breaker turning on all the lights in the room. It was a massive concrete chamber. A few televisions hung down from above and a plethora of wires stretched down to a large desk with a dozen monitors hanging all around it. On the far wall a huge steel door blocked off the only other exit to the place, but the centerpiece of the whole room was the mech standing in the middle of it.

It was larger than the base Knight Mk.1's and Mk.2's as the cockpit in the head was extended to let a second pilot sit below the main one while in its fighter form, or behind while in its flying stance. It was painted cream with pink accents and lines going around it, a personal job done by Stephanie to match her flight suit. A massive gun was held in its right hand, a thick shield in its left, a sword across its back, and twin missile silos hidden within its shoulders.

A-D froze as he locked his eyes on the mech. His whole body started to shake as he stared at it, and he shook his head vigorously. "No … no … no-no-no … no-nononono," he whimpered softly through tears.

"Hey," Stephanie turned around to face him, "it's okay." She reassured him. "What's wrong?"

"P-p-p-pain." He finally managed to speak up, "Pain…" He repeated while trying to point at her mech, but his arm was shaking so terribly he could barely lift it up.

She sighed and softly grabbed his outstretched hand, "No pain. Not unless I crash it that is." She chuckled to herself while trying to figure out what was happening. There was no way her mech, Lady Love as they called it, caused him pain. Was it just the idea of a mech frame in general?

"Don't make me get in!!!" A-D shouted out in terror, "Please … please-please-please-please *no!*" He dropped down

to the ground crying and shaking uncontrollably, "No-no-no-no-nonono please-please *no!*"

She knelt in front of him and forced a soft smile on her face, "What's wrong? I won't make you get in it, even though I was going to offer you the passenger seat, but I would like to know why a mech causes you so much … pain."

"No, no, no, no-no-nono…" he whispered to himself, "No-no seat only pain. *Crushing pain! Everything … crushed!*" He shouted out as his body spasmed down to the ground. She quickly caught him to keep his head from hitting the concrete floor and lightly started to pet his hair.

"There's no pain in there." She told him again, "No crushing, nothing like that. I mean, I'll be the first to admit the passenger seat is uncomfortable at best, but no pain."

It was as if he couldn't hear her. She held his head back and his eyes seemed to be glossed over. Looking nowhere, but as if he was seeing something. A past memory as they shook about in a panic. "F-f-flesh! *Blood! Bone!*" He cried out in horror, "Gone, gone, gone-gone-gonegone! Pain-pain-pain body turned to dust turned to steel. No … no, no-nono … no body left but the pain remains. *It screams in pain!*" His words turned into incomprehensible rambling and crying as his body shook in her arms.

"Shhh … shhh…" She softly comforted him, "It's okay now. It's okay. Not here. There's no pain here." Her mind was racing as she tried to maintain her calm composure. If what he was saying was to be believed… Then his body was crushed to dust; turned to steel. Becoming one with the mech frame? Did the Scythe not have a cockpit? Did it rely on his immortality as an Archangel? That would explain how it was so small, how it moved so fast and shifted so quickly. That would explain his fear.

"Hey, hey…" She brushed his hair to the side and looked down into his eyes, "Look at me A-D. Come back to me. Whatever it is you're seeing right now? It's not real. Right now, you are in my arms. You are safe. There's no more pain, no more suffering. I promise. I'm not going to hurt you."

Life snapped back into his eyes, and he froze for a moment, staring up into hers. "I…" He finally managed a whisper, "I'm … I-I'm sorry." He sat himself up and leaned forward, letting his hair fall back over his eyes, "Y-y-you're … not like the rest." His voice shifted back and forth from staggered to incredibly quick, "Y-y-you … you … you di-didn't leave me. Y-y-you came back. You haven't hu-hu-hurt me."

Stephanie sat back and watched him carefully as he spoke. She wasn't sure if it was a terrible gut feeling, or a good one, but she was starting to think that whatever tormented the Archangel of Death had nothing to do with the Chaos Bomb. "I-I-I-I-I'm s-s-s-s-sorry." He twitched as the words left his mouth.

She took a deep breath and sighed, "You just aren't used to it." She said for him, again. "That's okay. I'm not mad. I'm worried." Her heart stopped as those final two words left her mouth before she realized what she was saying. It took everything she had to keep her calm composure towards him as the rage bellowed up within her. How could she even consider being worried about him?! He was a monster? …Wasn't he?

A-D remained silent, sitting where he was twitching every so often. She quickly purged those thoughts from her mind. She needed to be alone when she thought about what it was she was doing, but right now, she needed to keep going forward with the plan. Getting his trust. She slowly stood up and offered him a hand, "If it's too much for you, I can lead you back upstairs, but I have to get some work done on her, so I'll be coming back down here."

"*No!*" He shouted as his head snapped up to face her, "I'll…" He immediately quieted down again, "I'll … I'll s-stay w-with you." He nodded to himself and took her hand.

She pulled him up off the ground and gave him a smile.

"I … I … I-I'm safe… W-w-with you-ou. N-not alone…" He shook his head, "Not-not-not alone."

"Don't worry, A-D, you'll get used to it sooner or later."

He nodded at her, whimpering as he did so. It was obvious, he was trying to convince himself.

"You know having an extra pair of hands down here will be very helpful."

"Help?" His voice lit up.

She chuckled to herself, "Yes, you can help me." She started to walk towards her mech.

He quickly scurried after her, "J-ju-just tell me what to do!" Excitement flooded every word.

"Now that's what I like to hear." She flashed a quick glance back at him. He was so easy to play, if only her very essence didn't scream at her for every moment she spent with him. *It's for the cause… It's for the cause…* Were the words she repeated over and over in her head. Thankfully working on Lady Love helped clear her mind. Aside from watching the military announcement tonight and figuring out how the hell she was going to address the rest of her cell, this was all she planned on doing for the next few days.

Chapter 7: Second Generation

A-D was barely helpful to Stephanie, but she managed to teach him the names of different tools so he could pass them to her while she worked on Lady Love. It didn't seem like she saved much time, but it all added up in the long run. She still had tons of work to do on it before she was ready to take it out again, but if he kept up his helpful attitude, she might be able to shave off a whole day.

She had stopped for now; it was already a bit past dinner time and First Prince Clyster's military press conference was starting soon. She took A-D back upstairs and made them dinner before it started. She found herself forgetting, and having to remind herself, that he was a monster: The Archangel of Death. He seemed so innocent, so broken, so pure. If he was anyone else… If he was truly a nobody…

She purged that line of thought before she could finish it and turned on the TV. The pre-conference had already been going on for hours, but that was just reporters speculating, spreading gossip, and the never-ending propaganda machine of the Eternal Empire. There was a countdown to the real deal in the bottom corner. Five minutes until the First Prince would take the stand. She looked over at A-D who ate his food eagerly, "Hey A-D?"

His head shot up to face her and he smiled. He … *smiled.*

"Yes?" He didn't stutter, he didn't hesitate, he looked over at her with genuine … joy?

She sighed to herself, she felt … bad … for what she was about to say. And she hated it. "I know you don't want to remember your past, but I want to know who you were. There's going to be some very popular people on the television soon. If the sight of them sparks anything in you… Will you let me know?"

He froze for a moment in fear before nodding his head, "A-an-anything for you!" He said excitedly.

She smiled back at him, "Thank you."

"Mhm!" He responded before digging back into his food. He was completely enamored by the chicken and rice. It was basic. She could immediately tell she didn't add enough seasoning to cover for the chicken not marinading. It was bland, boring, but it got the job done. And yet he was enjoying every bite like she had just spent a fortune on a meal at a 5-star restaurant. She smiled to herself; he would lose his mind when she finally cooked him an actual delicious meal. Maybe in a few days. Tonight was going to be a late night, after this press conference she needed to prepare what she was going to tell her cell, she was already stressing about it and could tell she would be exhausted tomorrow.

They were mostly done with their meals by the time the words she was waiting for aired over the television, "And now, Head of our military research and development, first born of the God-Emperor, our beloved … First Prince Clyster!"

The screen flashed over to a glorious stage. Banners of the Eternal Empire spanned the edges, Fireworks of gold shot off as the First Prince walked up to the podium. He waved his hand and bowed his head in respect getting the crowd under control, "Citizens of the Eternal Empire!" He addressed them all and they cheered in response, "It is, as always, my greatest pleasure to be surrounded by you all." The camera cut in-to a close up of Clyster as he spoke,

Steph glanced over at A-D as he watched the screen with her. First Prince Clyster was the leader of the Empire's forces in the Kingdom of Estates ever since they took over. First Prince Clyster was responsible for the downfall of Mount Eilon. First Prince Clyster *killed* the Archangel of Death.

And yet … A-D showed nothing.

"I've got some incredibly exciting things to share with you all today!" He beamed as he spoke, but soon a frown crossed his face, "But let's start with what you all are waiting to hear about. What might be our, no, my, greatest failure – the Chaos Bomb." The whole crowd silenced instantly, "It started as an idea to do good, to save lives. Something new that wouldn't leave behind the abhorrent radiation of a nuclear bomb while still being as potent and effective at clearing out heavily entrenched zones. Something that would keep our men and women safe." He paused as he glanced down, "But we were wrong. We could not have been more wrong. The detonation at Mount Eilon ... was over five times larger than our calculations suggested. We were playing with powers beyond our understanding, and it cost us something we can never replace."

There was complete silence as the First Prince paused his speech. Everyone knew what he meant, Even Stephanie. The Archangel of Death.

"All production of any Chaos Bombs has been halted immediately, Before we continue with this line of weaponry more research must be done. We still believe this can change the landscape of warfare, and more importantly, peacekeeping, but as of right now it is too unpredictable and dangerous even for our brightest of minds," he paused for a moment, "The Archangel of Death believed in us. He believed in the Eternal Empire. He believed in our scientists, and he believed in me. He himself offered to guide the missile into its target, and in turn..." He let the sentence remain unfinished. "A minute of silence if we will." He asked of everyone.

Stephanie once again looked over at A-D. Nothing. The Archangel of Death was known as the First Prince's dog of war. Clyster had just mentioned A-D by his true name. And still, it seemed as if nothing registered to him. She knew his memory wasn't completely wiped, as the damage of his past seemed to linger with him, but either everything related to the First Prince was wiped, or there was no major emotional attachment … damage…? Tied to him.

After the minute ended Clyster rose his head up once more, "Thank you all," he nodded at them, "while this is a hard time for the Eternal Empire, I am here to share our new military upgrades. I'm here to inspire you all! To bring us joy! Are you all ready to see what our research and development team has been up to?"

Resounding shouts of excitement filled the air.

A smile crossed his lips, "Now this is the Empire that I love and adore." He again paused for a moment letting the crowd die down a bit, "Now, over the years we have proudly announced many upgrades to our Angels. We've always kept them at the cutting edge, always giving them an advantage over our enemies, but it's been awhile since we last announced one, hasn't it?" Murmurs of agreement could be heard, "Well let me be proud to finally announce the new, not upgrades, but full retrofit for the Angels!"

Cheers erupted in the crowd, "Oh don't get excited just yet!" The First Prince chuckled, "I haven't even shared what that means!" He let the crowd quiet down again, "Past upgrades have been targeted ones. A new weapon, upgraded sensors, more efficient engines. Let me tell you. All of those? They dwarf in comparison to what our brightest minds have put together this time. This new retrofit effects ... well everything! Weapons, engines, sensors, armor, shielding, maneuverability, transformation time, pilot comfort, response time ... anything and everything you can think of. Which is why we are calling the upgraded models ... *the Second generation of Angels!*"

Cheers of excitement completely engulfed the audio coming from the TV. The First Prince had to practically yell into his microphone to be heard over them, "*Our normal upgrades take only a few hours, maybe a day at most to install. But this second generation requires a dedicated team of four, three whole days to install. As I speak right now this upgrade is currently being installed on our frontlines, and we have scheduled for every single Angel to become a second generation within one year!*"

Stephanie grumbled to herself, "Shit." This was far from good. The exact opposite of good even. A Knight Mk.1

couldn't stand up against a modern Angel alone, and a Knight Mk.2 was a test of better pilots. She had no idea how much was propaganda versus reality, but rarely did the Eternal Empire exaggerate their militaristic strength; if anything they were known for undercutting it.

Clyster used his hands to try and calm the crowds down, "Now, now, now … I understand you are all very excited about this, but what if I told you this wasn't the best thing I had to share today?" Almost immediately the crowd silenced. He smirked, "That's right. You all know me by now. I save the best for last, but this time. I've got a friend to help share – no show – the greatest thing our scientists and engineers have ever devised." The First Prince shot his hand out to his side and almost immediately an Angel started to land next to him.

It was both instantly recognizable and never seen before at the same time. The sleek, sharp design, the gold with blue accented paint job, made this Angel instantly recognizable as the Sword of Righteousness, but it was completely different from the Sword everyone was used to. It was much cleaner looking, much more refined. Much more *deadly* looking. As it landed the head popped open and the Archangel of Righteousness jumped out onto the floor. The whole crowd erupted in shouts of joy and awe as the First Prince stepped to the side.

The moment the Archangel of Righteousness jumped out of his frame A-D reacted, but not the way Stephanie expected. Before the Archangel's feet had even hit the ground A-D had grabbed the nearest blanket and covered himself in it, balling up in the corner, crying out, "I-I-I-I-I'm sorry! Y-y-y-y-you didn't-didn't s-s-see me! I-I-I-I didn't m-m-mean … I-I-I d-d-d-didn't know! Please-please-pleaseplease-don't-don't-don'tdon't! *I'm sorry!*"

Stephanie's eyes opened wide and she quickly reached out to him, "Hey, hey, hey … It's okay. It's okay." She struggled to speak over A-D's panicked ramblings, "He can't see you I promise. Okay?" She waited for a moment, but clearly wasn't getting through to him. She glanced at the TV,

Righteousness was currently waving at everyone and greeting them. She had a little bit of time before he would address them all. The Empire always took it's time celebrating its "heroes," but not enough to fully work this out with A-D.

She grumbled to herself silently for a moment before speaking up again, "A-D," she said softly, slowly, "I promise it's safe. If you come out of that blanket, I'll let you lay your head on me. We can talk about this later. Right now, I just want you to come here. Please?" She tried her best to sound pleading, desperate even … and it worked.

A-D's crying quieted as his stopped his shaking, "Y-y-y-y-you-"

"Yes." She responded before he could finish his question. She was running out of time. The Archangel was approaching the microphone. "Please? Come rest your head on me. You can keep your eyes closed if it makes you feel saf-" She wasn't even able to finish her last word before A-D shot out of the blanket and latched onto her, curling up and burying his head into her chest. She let out a sigh of … was that relief? She hoped that was how it came across at least and wrapped her arms around him, "It's okay, t's okay. Just stay here with me."

He nodded his head, keeping his eyes tightly shut and refusing to face the TV.

Righteousness held his hand up high and smiled at everyone, "*My fellow citizens of this glorious empire*!" He shouted at them and more cheers erupted, "I'm going to be completely honest with you guys. This new frame, *new*! Not upgraded, not retrofitted, completely new frame! This is unlike anything I could have ever dreamed of. Let me tell you, it makes the old Sword feel ancient and rusted beyond repair. I never thought that they would upgrade the Sword, I thought it was perfect for me, but these glorious men and women have proven me completely and utterly wrong! After spending the last week flying around in this new Sword I don't think I could ever go back to the old one!" Both him and the First Prince starting laughing.

The First Prince leaned back towards the mic, "Well let me tell you, Archangel of Righteousness, our scientists were going crazy over the new Archangel frames. Your abilities let them push engineering to its absolute limits." he turned to face the crowd. "Yes! You heard me right! It is not just the Sword, but every Archangel is currently, right now, in possession of a new frame!"

"I'd ask how in the world you did it," the Archangel spoke up, "but something tells me that explanation would be even beyond my understanding!"

The two of them shared a laugh with the crowd before the First Prince spoke up, "Truth be told I think some of the details might even be beyond me, and I'm the head of research and development!" Again, everyone laughed for a moment, "But let me see what I can do for all of you." The First Prince faced the audience, "The brightest, wildest, most creative, and innovative minds the Eternal Empire has to offer have done nothing but study you Archangels for years. Seeing what your frames excel at, what they struggle with, and most importantly, seeing what role you all like to fill in battle. With years of research, they started to develop even more refined frames made specially just for each and every one of you. In fact, these frames are so perfectly designed to each one of you, no one else could even attempt to operate them."

Righteousness nodded at him, "I can see it. It feels as if this frame knows what I want to do before I even do. Not only in how it functions though, but the comfort level. Everything is spaced absolutely perfectly for me!"

"Indeed, it is!" The First Prince responded proudly, "We spared no expense for our most prized and priceless warriors. Not only is everything spaced to the exact micrometer for each Archangel, but we made sure the comfort level was adjusted perfectly for you as well. Take you personally for example. We learned that you like your chair at a precise 111.111 degrees with a softness level of 6.89 out of 10."

The Archangels eyes lit up, "So that's why it's the most comfortable chair I've ever sat in?"

The First Prince blushed, "I think it goes without saying, but every Archangel deserves the absolute best the Eternal Empire has to offer. Without the likes of you keeping all of us safe... Well, I try not to think about it."

"And thankfully you don't have to." Righteousness responded, "Because we are all here, fighting day in and day out to keep this empire safe."

"Then making your seat the most comfortable you've ever sat in is the least we can do for you." The First Prince responded.

Stephanie started to tune out the press conference as it was now slowly devolving into a self-praise fest more than anything, as they always did. She instead focused on A-D, who was still holding himself tightly against her and shaking. She carefully grabbed the remote and muted the broadcast, turning on subtitles and making sure to keep an eye on them just in case there was something of worth left for them to share, although she was quite certain there wouldn't be.

She set down the remote and started to pet his hair, "What is it, A-D? What … what scares you?"

"H-h-h-h-he did!" A-D said frightfully, trying to point towards the TV. "*He hates me!*" A-D suddenly shouted out.

"Him?" Stephanie clarified, "The Archangel of Righteousness?"

A-D started to cry, "I … I-I-I d-d-do-do-don't know his name! But he hates me! *They all do!*" He once again started to shout through the knot in his throat, "*They never wanted to be seen with me! They hated me! Hated me!* Hated me-hated me-hated-me-hated…" His screams slowly devolved into repeated whispering.

Stephanie rested her head on his, while still lightly petting his back. Whatever fear, horror, pains he had… They seemed not to come from the Chaos Bomb, this all but confirmed it, but from his past life. He knew not who the Archangels were, but the sight of one on her TV sent him into a complete panic. She once again could hear the words of Hope in the back of her head, *"We are Righteousness, Hope, Valor, Justice, Wisdom, and Glory. All virtues everyone should aspire to, but he was Death."* The best lies were those rooted within truth, and Death being an outlier title amongst the rest of the Archangels was an undeniable truth. But was he an outsider by nature as Hope suggested, or was it by force? Because he wasn't like them?

Stephanie wasn't sure if this idea excited her or terrified her. On one hand, if he was an outsider not by choice, even if he regained his memories he might stay on their side… On the other hand … she was considering pity against the largest mass murderer in all of history. One thing was certain right now though, and that, was he was broken, and if she played the part of a caretaker, he was hers to command.

She continued to lightly pet his back and sighed, "It's okay A-D. Whoever you once were doesn't matter anymore. Whatever they think about you? That doesn't matter anymore. You aren't who you once were. You're A-D now. You're my friend now. Right?"

A-D shivered in her grasp as he tried to control himself. Finally, he managed to speak up in barely a whisper, "Y-y-you … p-promise?"

"Do you?" She asked him.

"YES!" He shouted out and grasped her tightly, "Please don't leave me. Please don't go! Please don't, please don't, don't-don't. I'll do *anything!*" He begged her.

She smiled and chuckled, "You don't have to beg someone to be their friend. They do it willingly. And yes. I promise."

Chapter 8: Splintered Cells

It wasn't long after the press conference finished Stephanie took A-D to his bed. It was early for sleep, but she had work to do and needed to be left alone. Plus, she was also pretty sure it didn't matter when she took him to his bed, he probably wasn't going to sleep again, even though he promised he would try. The announcement of the new second generation Angels was utterly terrifying. Not just because of the inherent meaning of them, but it was going to make her call for inaction even harder. The longer they now waited, the more likely they'd be going up against the second gen frames. She was convinced sitting back right now was still the right move, but it was going to be a hard sell to her cell.

She finished preparing her speech and quickly sent out a message to her closest friends telling them to get everyone together for a meeting in three days. She wanted to do it tomorrow, but it was difficult to get everyone together in a non-suspicious manner that quickly. Plus, there was a twenty-four-hour notice required for large gatherings and a forty-eight-hour one for people to get permission to be out and about during curfew hours. Most of her people would be able to stay the night at whosever house they chose to meet up in, but some always liked to get back home, her included, even more so with A-D now in her house.

She checked her burner phone that was tied to John's cell one last time to see if he had called her yet, but still there was nothing. If she had told her messenger her plan, she'd understand why he didn't want to call, but this worried her. All she sent them with was that she wanted to talk. Had they been captured, was John's cell disposed of quietly not reaching the news, or was he just toying with her? She grumbled to herself, either way it wasn't good.

She took a deep breath and downed the last of the water in her bottle. Then there was this whole A-D circumstance. The Archangel of Death, sleeping in her old bedroom. No memories of his past life. No signs of his powers. And so pathetic and helpless it was hard not to pity him. She'd have to tell her friends sooner or later, but how? And even if she could control him as he was, he showed no signs of having his powers the only way she could use him. If he could awaken those, if he was wrapped around her fingers the second generation Angels wouldn't matter. She could use him and take this small rebel cell into a full-blown rebellion.

Other rebel cells would flock to her and the success she could obtain with his power. She could crush everything in her path until the Empire sent another Archangel to deal with him. The Empire would have to admit he was not only still alive, but also now a traitor. Their public image would tank, hers would rise. Global contact to the countries not under their control could be established. A united warfront against the Eternal Empire… The possibilities were now endless with A-D … if only she could get him to use his powers as she willed.

She massaged her temples. One step at a time. That's how she had to look at things. And right now, the next step was addressing her cell in three days' time while slowly working on A-D in private. Possible futures would have to wait. She stood up and took a step towards her bed-

Ring … ring … ring…

The phone went off. She quickly snatched it up and answered, "John?"

"Stephanie." The low voice responded.

"What the hell took you so long? My messenger should have reached you days ago at worst!" She snapped at him.

"They did." He responded coldly, "I waited because I wanted to."

Stephanie grumbled under her breath, "You're insufferable sometimes."

"And you're a coward." John snapped back instantly, "You haven't made a single move since Eilon fell. All you've been doing is sitting in that pretty little house of yours on your hands."

Her eyes narrowed, "Oh yes because we should all be striking out when the Empire's military might is the heaviest it's ever been in our Kingdom!" She fired back, "Yes I've been keeping quiet, but I've been planning, thinking, considering, gathering information. Trying to plot the next best move for us."

"For us? Or for your survival?" He asked her harshly, "Can't be focused on living when we're rebels."

"And there won't be a rebellion if we die."

"Then at least we die like heroes, like your brother. Not like cowards scurried up underground like your parents."

John was trying to anger her. She bit her cheek but kept her tongue held back for a few seconds, "Well I was hoping to talk to you, but you obviously have something you want to say to me. What is it?" She said coldly.

"In two weeks time I'm going to strike at the main embassy of the Maynor Estate in Spoke." He told her plainly, "In one week I'll be stopping by the old car lot off route 502 to pick up any of you who join me."

"Are you insane?!" She shouted at him, "That's suicide!"

"Refuse to join me. And I'll have you branded a traitor to the Kingdom."

"Oh, like you have that kind of power you fucking prick." She hissed at him, "Even if I wanted to, Lady Love is out of commission right now. I'm working on her. She won't be back up and running for another week."

"Sounds like an excuse." He told her, "One someone who doesn't really care about our freedom would come up with. One someone who's too afraid to sacrifice their life for the cause would say."

"Sounds like a genuine reason." She snapped, "And sounds like something someone with even a modicum of common sense would say."

"I waited to call you, because I've sent your messenger back to tell your people for me."

"Well newsflash dumbass! I'll tell them my damn self when we all get together in a few days' time." She hissed at him, "I'll tell them your plan. I'll even tell them where and when you want us to meet up. And then I'll tell them my plan and why you are such an idiot who has nothing more than a death wish. Someone who's too afraid to make the tough calls and retreat when they need to. Someone who can't stand back when it's required. Someone who will always just rush headfirst into the obstacle in front of them without putting a single second of thought into it."

Silence. There was a long silence over the line.

"If my pops was still around, he'd say you really are your mother's daughter." John finally responded.

"Well, he isn't. Just like my parents. Just like my brother." She quickly said.

"No, he isn't. So, what I will say is this," John paused for a moment, "Your brother would be disappointed."

"I'd say I hope your engine misfires," She hissed at him, "But believe it or not, even though your plan is completely impossible, I hope it works."

"It'd be more likely to work if you joined me."

"And be your subordinate?" She scoffed at him, "I'd rather try to take out that embassy all alone than work for you."

"The only reason you aren't branded a traitor in this Estate is because of what your brother did." John hissed at her,

"You'd probably be more likely to walk in and bow to the praetor."

"I take it back." Stephanie snapped at him, "I hope you fucking die while taking out that embassy." She slammed the phone down on the edge of her desk snapping it in two, "You asshole… You idiot."

She was already going to barely sleep tonight, but now? A-D might even get more sleep than her.

Chapter 9: Girly Things

The next two days went by smoothly. They had acquired permission to hold a large party at Casey's house for an early birthday. Stephanie and any others who wanted it had gotten their passes to travel during curfew hours. They'd almost certainly get stopped by the Eternal Empire, even she would on her short ten-minute drive home tonight, but as long as she was on a direct path to her house, they would let her go. She had spent these last few days working hard on Lady Love.

Work on it was going well, she'd even started to get A-D to help in a more meaningful manner, only slightly as he'd help hold things out of her way or could be sent alone upstairs to grab them snacks and drinks, but it was better than nothing. A-D himself seemed to be getting slightly more comfortable around her as well. He still constantly covered his face with his hand, but his stuttering had gotten better for the most part. He still had his episodes, but those were easy to contain for her by now.

Today though she hadn't worked on Lady Love at all. The party was allowed to start at noon, and she planned to be one of the first people there. She had finished putting on her makeup, nothing too crazy, just a pink lip gloss and some blue eye shadow with liner. She put on one of her nicer dresses and came down the stairs into the living room. A-D sat on the large couch waiting, just like she had asked him to. "So … how do I look?" She asked him.

He nearly jumped up as she caught him off guard, "*Eeep*!" He squeaked as he quickly spun around to face her. The moment he laid eyes on her she could see a wave of comfort wash over him as his mouth fell agape, "*Pretty…*" He whispered softly.

Stephanie blushed and turned her face to the ground. She knew she looked good but never before had someone looked so … enamored with her. She quickly regained her composure and rolled her eyes with a chuckle, "I take it I did a good job." A-D kept staring, not even blinking as she could see his eyes through his hair over them. "Come on, anything more to say?" She teased him.

"A-angel…" He said very softly.

"Hmm?"

"Y-you look like an angel." He repeated himself, "An archangel. The prettiest of the pretty … Aah…" He kept staring at her.

She froze for a moment. She wasn't sure if he meant in general, or if she looked like one of the Archangels to him, either way she knew it was a compliment. She smiled and walked over ruffling his hair, "That's what I thought. Good boy."

"Mmm…"

She could feel him melt into the couch as she placed her hand on him. It took everything she had not to laugh.

She managed to keep it a quiet chuckle and took a deep breath, "Alright A-D, I have a very important task to ask of you."

"Mmn…" He wasn't paying any attention to her.

She shook her head and pulled her hand back walking into the entryway, "I'm going to go out again today."

That seemed to get his attention as his head snapped up, "G-go?" A hint of worry entered his voice.

"Yes, A-D. I have to go out and meet with some friends." She continued explaining as she opened one of the bags resting against the wall, "I'm going to be gone a lot longer than I was last time. I won't be home till past dark. I need to know you're gonna be okay." She pulled out a phone from the bag and turned back to face him, "You'll be okay without me for the day, won't you?"

"G-go … G-g-gone?" He started to shrink back into the couch, "No. No-no-no…"

Stephanie sighed and started walking back to him, "You remember how I came back last time, just like I promised?"

He didn't respond but nodded his head as she approached him. He was curled up into a ball trying his best to keep from shaking.

"And while I will be gone for longer than last time, I will come back. I already got my permit to come home after curfew hours. I promise."

"P-pr-promise…" He kept nodding his head, "O-okay … okay … okay-okay-okay…" She could tell he was talking more to himself than to her.

"Here, I have something for you." She held out the extra phone in her hand.

He looked up at it and carefully grabbed it.

"It will let you contact me if you need to." She sat down next to him and pulled hers out, "See?" She quickly typed a message and sent it to him.

Steph: Heyyy

A-D jumped as the phone vibrated in his hand. "Now, if you take your hand…" She slowly, carefully grabbed his hand and guided it to the phone. She used his hand to open the message she sent, "And now type something in response to me."

He carefully, with shaking hands started to type on the keyboard.

A-D: hi

As her phone buzzed, she opened the message and showed him, "See? If you need to contact me for anything, just send me a message and I'll respond as soon as I can."

"G-g-gone … bu-but can still t-talk?" He looked over at her.

"Mhm!" She nodded at him, "If you keep this in your pocket you can always reach me, no matter where I am. So, in essence, it's like a part of me is still here with you." She paused for a moment, "Can you please do this for me? Be okay while I'm out? It'd mean a lot to me."

A-D took a deep, staggered, breath before nodding his head, "Y-y-yes. I-I-I wi-will be here. W-waiting."

Stephanie stood up, satisfied she had done what she could to prepare him. "I already made that picture we took together the lock screen on it. So, if you want to look at it all you have to do it push a button on the side." Without wasting a second A-D pushed one of the buttons on the side and the picture of them holding up peace signs flashed to life. She watched as his eyes glossed over and he smiled.

She walked over to the garage door and stopped one last time, "Just like before. If anyone comes to the house, you aren't here. Don't answer it, don't make a noise, nothing. Okay?" He looked over at her and nodded his head. "Perfect, and if you get hungry, I already made you a sandwich wrap, it's in the fridge."

"T-t-thank you." He managed to whisper back, "I-I'll b-be good."

"I know you will." She said with a smile and left the house.

She quickly drove over to Casey's house and parked in the back of a nearby store's parking lot. Even an hour early she wasn't the first one there, as Jeremiah had beaten her, not that it surprised her, he was childhood friends with Casey, even before Stephanie. Stephanie raised her hand as she approached, "Been awhile since I was over last." She embraced Casey as she ran up to her, "How are you doing?"

"Oh, I've been better. I've been worse." Casey responded, "Hopefully after tonight I'll be feeling a lot better, hm?"

Stephanie chuckled and walked inside, "You're putting a lot of faith in me after that conference."

"Well, you've always been one to get our spirits high."

"Even after the incident." Jeremiah spoke up. They knew he was referring to the fall of Eilon, "You managed to get us all having fun and laughing by the end of that meet up."

Stephanie smiled softly and held back a sigh, "Well I'll try, but even I'm not feeling too confident about this one."

"Yeah, we've all heard that before." Casey told her with a smirk.

"I actually mean it this time." Stephanie told her in a somber voice, "John finally called me. It's not good. But I'll wait to explain until later."

"You two have always clashed." Jeremiah tried to cheer her up, "I think we all knew when push came to shove, you'd go your separate ways."

"That doesn't make it any easier." Stephanie responded.

"You said you'll wait and so wait we will." Casey ended that line of conversation, "But since you're here early you better help me with my last minute preparations."

Stephanie smiled at her, "Why else would I have come early?"

Slowly more and more people arrived to the fake party, but the only way to throw a party as a cover for a meeting was to throw a real party. Before long all fifty adults in her cell were there. All of them laughing, drinking, celebrating, having fun. Stephanie made her rounds greeting them all, hugging most of them, while trying to avoid getting too involved in any of the activities. She was nervous, and didn't want to get too relaxed feeling, let anything, let any knowledge of A-D slip.

Thinking of A-D she pulled out her phone and checked it, hours had passed and there was nothing from him. She halfway expected him to message her the moment she had left the house. Partly worried and partly needing to keep him convinced she actually was worried about him, she shot him a message.

Steph: Hey there A-D. Everything going ok?

A few moments passed before she saw the "..." showing he was typing.

A-D: yes. sorry. just waiting.

Steph: You're all good, just wanted to make sure.

A-D: i'm...good?

She laughed to herself, waiting a moment before texting him back.

Steph: It's a figure of speech, but yes. Stay safe.

It was weird texting him. None of his stuttering or hesitation could be seen in his text. Maybe he felt more comfortable talking like this, or maybe he just didn't spend the time to type out "I-I-I-I-I'm … g-g-good…?" She smiled and chuckled at the thought. Of course he didn't.

A-D: ok.

"*Ooo,* who you texting?" Teresa walked up beside her.

Stephanie quickly put her phone away, "Oh, just some new kid I met." She swiftly spun together a lie, "A new prospect you might even say."

"Oh?" That piqued her interest, "They just move here? Thought you had skimmed this town for everyone you thought might join."

"Mhm." She responded, "Happened to run across them while out shopping just a few days ago."

"Boy or girl?"

"Boy."

"*Oh*!" Teresa's eyes lit up, "Is he cute?"

"Is he-" Stephanie gawked for a second, "That's what your worried about?" Teresa had *no* idea who she was talking about here.

"Oh, come on it's a simple questio-" She stopped before the last word left her mouth and gasped, "Unless… Are you looking at him?"

"*No*!" Stephanie gasped, "Not even close!"

"I don't know, you sound a little defensive…" Teresa teased, "Hey Casey!" She got her attention, "Come here for a moment, would you?"

Casey quickly walked over, "What's up?"

"Need you to take the cutest pictures you can of me and Steph here." Teresa told her while handing over her phone. "Me first." She quickly popped her hip out to the side, put one hand on the inside curve of her waist, and flashed a peace sign by her eye with the other one.

Casey quickly snapped the picture and turned to Stephanie, "Alright Steph, show me what you got."

Stephanie rolled her eyes, "You have got to be kidding me…" She grumbled.

"Oh, come on!" Teresa begged her, "It's a party, we're supposed to be having fun and taking pictures remember?"

Stephanie sighed and rolled her eyes, "*Fine*."

"What's with the hesitation, Steph?" Casey asked her, "You usually aren't one to shy away from a good picture."

"It's a *boy*…" Teresa teased.

"It is not at all what she thinks it is." Stephanie responded before Casey could, "But since you've forced me into it, just know, you're the one who asked me to make the cutest picture possible." In an instant her demeanor changed from annoyed to flirty as she tilted her head to the side, lifted one leg up at the knee, put her hands in a heart shape in front of her chest, and made a small kissy face with her lips going so far as to audibly go, "Mwah!"

Casey snapped the picture instantly, "Uh oh, Teresa. You should know better than to challenge Lady Love."

"I haven't lost hope yet!" She insisted and quickly sent the pictures to Stephanie. "Now send them to him and have him tell you who he thinks is cuter!"

Stephanie quickly took back on her annoyed composure, "Just don't come crying to me when he speaks the truth." She said while sending the pictures to A-D.

Steph: One of my friends wants to know who you think is cuter. Her?

She sent the picture of Teresa.

Steph: Or me?

She sent the picture of herself.

"*So* … What's his name?" Casey asked.

Stephanie was thankfully a master at hiding her own stress. She hadn't considered someone would ask who she was texting. "He likes to go by A-D."

"That's a weird name." Teresa instantly spoke up.

"It's not his name." Stephanie was quick to think of a lie, "It's his initials. Been called it most his life so he just goes by that now." It wasn't … wrong.

"Ooo mysterious." Casey said, "Is he cute?"

"You too?" Stephanie scoffed, "Aren't you dating Thompson?"

"Doesn't mean I can't appreciate a cute guy." She shrugged.

"Ugh!" Stephanie grumbled, "He's…" she sighed, "Yes. He's kinda cute." She hated the two of them right now. She hated herself right now. Because she spoke the truth, and they had made her.

"Come on, come on! Has he responded yet?" Teresa asked her.

Stephanie looked back down at her phone just in time to see his response pop up.

A-D: friend is cute. you are an angel. archangel. prettiest of the prettys

Stephanie's face went flush instantly.

"What did he say??" Both Casey and Teresa shouted at her.

Stephanie quickly swallowed and regained her composure, still flush. He had said the same exact thing to her in the house. "He said, and I quote. 'Friend is cute. You are an angel. Archangel. Prettiest of the pretties.'"

"*Theres no way!*" Teresa quickly snatched the phone from her and instantly frowned, "*Dammit!*" She slammed the phone back into Stephanie's hands.

"She did warn you." Casey pointed out.

"It's not fair!" Teresa huffed.

"Prettiest of the pretties?" Casey added on, "He's buttering you up I think."

"He isn't." Stephanie quickly said, "He just… He talks weird."

"You can say that again." Teresa quickly chimed in, "Comparing you to an Archangel."

"Look we all want to see him dead, but even you have to admit Righteousness is one *helluva* good-looking man." Casey pointed out.

"I hate that you're right." Stephanie rolled her eyes.

"Well even if he's gunning after you," Teresa dropped her mopey attitude, "You can at least tell us what he looks like right? Do you have a picture?"

"No. And No." Stephanie responded instantly, "Not happening."

"You're no fun today." Teresa complained.

"She's not in the best of moods." Casey added on, "Give her a break. There's a lot more on her plate than all of us. And I think we all know how stressed she's got to be today, specifically."

Teresa sighed but remained silent.

"Thank you." Stephanie nodded at her.

"Just gonna say though," Casey added on, "A cute boy who calls you the-"

"I swear on my brothers grave if you even think about finishing that sentence I will break your nose." Stephanie snapped at her.

Both Casey and Teresa burst out in laughter and walked away. She took a deep breath and calmed herself down. If only they knew who they were talking about. She rolled her eyes one last time and finally responded to A-D.

Steph: Thanks~

A-D: so pretty

She smiled to herself once again and put her phone away. Soon they'd be eating, and much sooner than she liked, it would be time for a "movie."

Chapter 10: Long Live the Estates

The party continued through the evening and into the night, and finally the time for Stephanie to address them as her rebel cell came. They all crowded into the basement, putting on a movie in the upstairs living room and turning the volume up to give the appearance they were actually watching one. Stephanie sat herself up on the bar and looked out at the fifty rebels, the fifty friends, the fifty family members all gathered in front of her.

They had been through a lot together. All her pilots were at the front, including her longest standing friend trio of Teresa, Jeremiah, and Collin. They had been through the worst of it together. Multiple fights were under their belts, and thankfully none of them had died on her … yet. Every mission, every battle, became more dangerous, more deadly … more likely one of them wouldn't return.

The rest of her crew was mostly just support. Either in money, housing, food, or a very small amount of intel and mechanics. A small amount didn't offer much to her in the running of a rebel cell aspect, but she took in those that wanted to even if they had no skills to offer. All of them, no matter their history, their rank, their respect, looked to her for guidance.

She took a deep breath and slowly let it out, "I think it's safe to assume we all saw that military press conference held by Clyster, right?"

Nodding heads and a soft murmur of agreement could be heard.

"And we all know if there's one thing the Eternal Empire has always downplayed, it's their military might, correct?"

Again, they all responded in the same way.

"It's a tough pill to swallow." She paused for a moment, making sure they all could tell the weight was starting to bear down on her, "Second generation Angels. Our Mk.2's could barely keep up with them as they were. These are gonna make our Mk.2's look like Mk.1's. Completely outclassed. Which leaves us in a tough spot doesn't it?" Again, everyone agreed with her. "So I ask you, what has always been our greatest strength against the Eternal Empire? Has it been our military strength? Our ability to fight them out in the open? Our ability to go one on one and win?"

They all shook their heads at her, "I thought not. It's been their overconfidence. It always has been, even before the Kingdom fell, and always will be, even after their second generation hits our lands." She leaned forward, "But that's not so easy to believe, is it? I mean I think we all can agree … our first instinct is to strike right now, before those hit our lands, and deal as much damage as we can, no?"

Silence. They all knew she posed a different alternative, but she knew that was exactly what they were all thinking, "Well, if that's your prerogative, I've got good news for you. John is going to stop by the old car lot off of Route 502 in four days to strike at the Spoke Embassy. But, if you're willing to hear me out," she paused, "I think our best course of action is to go completely silent for a little while."

Every single one of them looked at her with anticipation, confusion, and excitement. She had them on the lure, now she just needed to reel them in, "If their overconfidence is our best weapon, then this second generation of Angel … is the best thing they could have given us. I'd be willing to bet my life that once those upgrades roll out, they cut back on the numbers that are in the Estates. The pilots within them are going to feel unstoppable and get comfortable. Too comfortable."

She jumped off the bar and paced in front of them, "The Eternal Empire's military presence has almost never been stronger in our country than right now. They know they just destroyed the last vestige of our military and all that remains are cells like us. They know that our cells are going to be getting antsy, angry, wanting revenge. They are waiting for us to strike at them right now, and are more than ready to purge anyone who does."

"If we strike right now, we are playing into their hands," she continued, "but imagine the landscape we have to work with if we wait. If we wait for other cells, others like John's, to strike out and get crushed immediately. If we wait for a sense of peace and security to fall across this land. They'll get lazy, they'll get complacent. And this world will become our oyster." She took a deep breath and stopped pacing.

"If you want to strike right now, if you can't wait, I won't try to stop you. I won't even try to tell you not to join John. Even you guys," she looked over her pilots, "but if you want to instead fight for the longevity of the Kingdom of Estates. If you want to instead fight for the endgame and just not die a meaningless death the world will forget within a day. Then I ask you. Stick with me, as you have, and together we will slowly, but surely, start a true fight against the Empire."

Stephanie stood still and faced them for a moment, before nodding at them and jumping back up on the bar, signaling she was done and questions could be asked or comments made. It was mere seconds before someone spoke up, "Stephanie," they addressed her professionally, "You've done right by us, and I want to do right by you … but we need more than just promises."

She nodded to herself as a handful of agreements could be heard, "You're right. I've been considering something massive over the past few weeks. Rumors of a hidden underground bunker that could take this rebellion to the next level…" She paused for a moment considering her words carefully. They all knew she was loyal, but still her parent's loyalty was to be questioned, "I'm just not entirely sure of its validity and haven't had the time to go check it out personally."

She sighed, but quickly continued, "Also, recently I've been working on something that has the possibility to change the landscape of our rebellion … into a war. I'm just … I'm not ready to even remotely talk about that right now as it's in the very early stages of development." A-D. If he joined them, if he could still use his powers, if he used them as she wished … it wouldn't matter if they were fifty or fifty thousand. He could wage a war for them.

"And what's John's deal?" Someone else asked her, "What's he offering us?"

"He's planning what I'd dub a suicide mission." She quickly responded, "He's angry, I get it, I am too. So, he wants to strike right now with everything he's got. He wants to reveal his whole hand on the table. To me, it didn't sound like he had a long-term plan. He just wants to try and get one last hit in." She sighed, "The Empire is dumb, but they aren't stupid. Every embassy in the Kingdom is going to be expecting an attack from rebel cells. We've all seen the news about other ones being attacked and easily defended. They are not only expecting us to, but want us to strike out."

"So, our choices are, die as martyrs for the Kingdom, or try to run a longer scale guerrilla style war against them with nothing but vague promises?" Someone asked her.

"Hey!" Collin spun around and snapped at them all, "Look, you all know me. I'm the first one of us to try and pick a fight. And I'd be lying if John's offer wasn't as tempting as a free drink, but if there's one thing I've learned, it's that Steph here has got the brains to take us to the next level." His eyes narrowed, "If you don't trust her at her word, then I'll make you trust her." He turned to face her, "On your brother's grave, do you swear these two things you are working on not only could really change the way we view this rebellion, but will come to fruition?"

She closed her eyes and took a deep breath, "I hate you sometimes, Collin." She forced a smirk, "I currently can't give you all more information on either of them, but yes. I swear on my brother's grave that in the near … ish … future this small rebel cell of ours will transform completely and entirely. I know that underground bunker will be a massive boon to us and will slingshot us from a small, meaningless cell, to an actual thorn in the side of the Empire. As for that other project I mentioned…" She shook her head, "I don't know. It will either come to nothing … or it will be unlike anything we ever could have dreamed of."

The room fell silent for a few moments before Collin spoke back up, "I'll be honest with you, Steph. I like John's idea more … but I'm sticking by your side. You … You've got everything to lose with your plan. If you wanted a nice life in the Empire, you could have had it. Instead, you choose to not only live with us, but to fight for us. John? He's a military family man. All he sees is blood, that's all he's ever seen. You see the bigger picture; you see the true battle that needs to be fought. So even though I don't like it, I don't like it one bit … me and my Knight Mk.2 are yours and yours alone to command."

Stephanie smiled at him and bowed her head, "Thank you for trusting me."

"I didn't need any convincing." Another voice spoke up, "While John's playing checkers you're playing chess. Always thinking ten moves ahead."

Her smile grew wider as more voices of agreement shot up in the crowd, "She's right, even with all of us that's a suicide mission right now."

"John's a good man, but he doesn't have the foresight you do."

"I never doubted her to begin with. She gives the word and I follow it."

"I hate that you're right. I really do."

"I don't know what she's cooking up in her mind, but it sounds more promising than anything we've heard to date!"

"We're with you Stephanie!"

"So are we!"

"Ste-pha-nie! Ste-pha-nie! Ste-pha-nie!" They slowly all started to chant her name.

She took a deep breath and smiled, "We … are the Kingdom of Estates." She said loud enough for everyone to hear.

"We will never go down without a fight." They all responded as one. "*Long live the Estates!*" They all shouted.

They all knew the importance of keeping up the party visage and instantly started to make their way back upstairs to watch the rest of the movie. Stephanie stayed behind, she always did, she was the last to leave these meetings. Collin approached her as the crowd kept thinning and leaned in close to whisper, "Look Steph, I love you, I really do, but I need more than some empty promises right now…"

She sighed as he spoke.

"What is this other thing you've been working on. I need to know."

She closed her eyes and shook her head, "Teresa." She spoke up getting her attention as she was about to leave. Stephanie opened her eyes and looked over at Collin, "I'm not ready to share it with someone like you, but would you take her word for it?"

He looked back and forth between the two of them for a few moments in anger, "Fine." He spat out.

"Thank you, Collin." She nodded at him, "Teresa, think you could stop by after lunch tomorrow?"

"You're … You're going to share this new project with me?" She asked her.

"Reluctantly." Stephanie told her, "If you want the truth, the stress from it is what has had me in such a bad mood all day."

Teresa nodded at her, "I'll be there."

"Thank you." Stephanie jumped off the bar and dusted her sides, "I'm going to go home." She said out loud

Casey, who had stuck around as well frowned, "Already?"

Stephanie nodded at her, "Be thankful you aren't leading a rebel cell in a time like this." She told her, "I feel like I'm going to have gray hairs by the end of this week."

Casey walked over and hugged her tightly, "I am forever thankful we have someone like you to lead us, Steph." She admitted, "Stay safe."

"You all as well." She said before letting go of Casey and walking out of the room, and out of the house.

Chapter 11: Like an Archangel

Stephanie was stopped for a few more short conversations on her way out, some people apologizing to her, some commending her, some just wishing her a good night. Curfew was already in effect by the time she started walking to her car. She had only parked a short walk away, but by the time she made it to the end of the block a patrol car pulled up alongside her.

"Halt there." The officer commanded.

She stopped and turned to face him, "Evening officer," She addressed him nicely, "I have my pass on me, if I may?"

He nodded at her from his seat, "Slowly."

She carefully reached into her purse and pulled out the papers handing it over to him alongside her ID, "Stephanie Maynard. I was at the party at Casey's house down the block," She told him the information on her papers as he read it over, "Most of us parked in the back of the parking lot nearby as to not crowd the street. That's the only reason I am not on a direct path home right now."

He nodded at her and handed her papers back, "Well, that all checks out, but you know I have to make sure you aren't lying about your car."

"Of course, officer." She nodded at him.

He gestured to the back seat, "Hop on in, I'll drive you there." With a push of a button the back door closest to her popped open.

"Oh! Thank you, Sir." She climbed in and sat down.

"Mhm." He mused and drove her to the parking lot in silence. He came to a stop, and more than a dozen cars were all parked around hers in the very back. "One of these yours?" He asked her while popping open her door again.

"Mhm!" She smiled and slowly stepped out of the vehicle. She pulled out her keys and pushed the button to unlock her car. *Beep beep!* Her emergency lights flashed for a second as her car unlocked, "Thanks for the lift, Sir."

"My pleasure." He smiled back, "You have a fine night now, Miss. Drive straight on home."

She chuckled, "I already have the roads memorized. You have a fine night as well, officer." She bowed her head in respect and walked over to her car to get in. As she turned it on, she quickly pulled out her phone and sent A-D a message.

Steph: I shall be home shortly.

A-D: yay

He responded almost instantly.

She smirked to herself and quickly made her way directly home. She quietly opened the door from the garage and softly announced herself, "Hey, it's me."

"H-h-hi." A-D softly responded as he still sat right where she had left him.

"Have you moved at all?" She teased him as she set her stuff down and walked up behind him. She froze as she saw what he was looking at on his phone. The photo she had sent him thanks to Teresa. "Like it?" She quickly asked him.

"S-s-s-so … p-pretty." He responded without looking away from it.

"I'm right here you know." She smirked, "Don't have to stare at a picture."

He turned around and smiled at her, "T-t-t-tha-thank yo-you."

"For?" She looked at him puzzled.

"C-coming b-back."

"I said I would and so I did. You'll learn to trust me in time. I promise." She took a deep breath and glanced around the house. It looked like he hadn't moved at all, "Doesn't look like you ate. Aren't you hungry?"

His eyes went wide, "I-I-I-I-I-"

She laughed for a moment and ruffled his hair, "Silly. I'm going to go to bed and so should you, but if you want to eat, I'll sit out here with you for a bit longer."

"N-n-no we-we can go to bed." He responded quickly, "I-I-I'm sorry!"

She sighed, "Do you wanna eat?" She asked him directly.

"I…" He turned away from her and blushed, "Y-y-yes…" He barely whispered.

She pushed herself back and walked into the kitchen, "Then first you'll eat. And then we'll go to bed."

"B-b-b-b-but y-you wanted to-

"Shush." She held up a finger towards him, "You need to eat, A-D. And I've already left you alone for long enough today. I can easily stay up a bit longer with you. It's no problem." She came back out with the wrap she had made him and handed it over.

"T-t-t-too k-kind." He squeaked as he carefully grabbed the plate from her. "I-I-I-I failed y-you."

"And how did you fail me?" She asked while sitting down next to him.

"D-d-didn't eat-t." He responded before taking a small bite.

"Well considering you get a little … hm, panicked when alone I can't say I'm surprised." She told him, "But, you did well today."

"I-I did?" His eyes snapped up to her in shock.

"Mhm!" She smiled at him, "Doesn't look like you had a full mental breakdown. You managed to use your phone to message me, without constantly spamming me with messages, and you helped put Teresa in her place."

"T-T-Teresa?" He took another bite.

"Yeah, that was the other girl I sent you a picture of. Shoulda seen the look on her face when I told her your response." She laughed, "Serves her right for thinking she's cuter than me. Everyone knows I'm the prettiest girl around."

He nodded his head at her, "Y-y-yes!"

She rolled her eyes at him, "But I should warn you. Staring at a girl's picture for hours on end is a bit…" She sighed, "You're perfectly good A-D and fine, I understand you don't know better, but others might find that a bit … creepy."

"Oh." He quickly dropped his eyes away from her, which had been staring.

"No, no, no! It's okay. It's okay." She reassured him, "You've got a lot to learn. It's okay.

She sighed heavily and shrugged, "Plus, if you were going to be staring at a girl, I'd rather it be me at least, hm?"

"S-s-sorry." He whimpered, "Ju-just so pretty… S-so per-perfect. L-like an-an Archangel."

"You keep comparing me to an Archangel," Stephanie pointed out, "Yet when you saw one of them on the TV you panicked. I'm sorry, but I don't understand."

He set down the plate with a shaking arm and started to curl up, "I-I-I … I-I just … I just…" The tears started to flow down his cheeks.

She quickly leaned over and pulled him into a soft hug, "Shh, it's okay. It's okay. You don't have to."

"*No*!" He shouted and spasmed in her arms, "I-I … y-you d-d-deserve t-to know."

"Know what?" She tried her best to hide her excitement, and fear. What was he keeping from her?

A-D tried his best to keep himself calm through the tears as he spoke, "I-I … always … w-wanted to b-b-b-be one. T-t-they were s-su-suppose-supposed to b-be p-perfect."

She slightly increased her grip on him and started petting his hair as his shaking started to get worse.

"B-b-b-but I-I-I w-wasn't good enough! N-never g-g-good enough!" His sobbing started to take over. "*They hated me!*" He cried out before being consumed by sorrow.

"*Shh, shh…*" She softly comforted him, "It's okay, A-D. It's okay…" She could feel him start to relax as she continued to scratch his head, "You're here now… I've got you now." If what he said was true, and she was inclined to believe it was, it only cemented her idea that he was an outcast not by choice, that he wasn't welcome in the Eternal Empire, that this fear and pain came from before the Chaos Bomb and it made her wonder. Did he even want to fight for the Eternal Empire while he was there, or was he forced to?

After a long few minutes, he finally started to calm down and pulled away to look at her, "B-but y-you?" He said softly while nodding his head, "C-caring … k-k-kind … l-l-loving…" He stopped and took a deep, staggered breath, "Real Archangel."

Stephanie's eyes locked with his. There was so much fear and pain behind his, but still he looked at her with joy. She was … terrified. This was exactly what she needed him to believe for her plan to work, but she was just playing him like the Eternal Empire did. What would happen if he saw through her lies? She took a deep breath to calm herself down and forced a soft smile while blushing, "I… Thank you." She shied away from him, "I don't know what to say to a compliment like that. I've never … gotten one like that before."

A-D smiled to himself, proud. "C-can … w-we g-go to b-bed now?" He asked her softly, "V-v-very h-hard t-t-to share th-that."

She nodded at him relieved, "That sounds good me." She smirked, "I've had a long day as well."

Chapter 12: A-D

Ding-dong. The doorbell to Stephanie's house went off and A-D jumped in surprise, "*Eep!*" He squeaked as he quickly grabbed the blanket off the couch and covered himself in it.

Stephanie couldn't help but laugh, "It's okay, A-D. That's just a friend of mine." She pulled out her phone and quickly checked the cameras. Teresa. She started tapping her foot, anxiety slowly starting to take over as she grit her teeth and whispered to herself, "Shit…"

"F-friend?" A-D asked her, still hiding in the blanket.

She put her phone away and placed her hands on her face rubbing the bridge of her nose with them, "Yeah." She responded with as much confidence as she could. She had no idea how to tell Teresa she had the Archangel of Death in her house. She had no idea how she was going to justify it to her. "Why did I agree to this…?" She asked herself.

"T-t-to what?" A-D popped his head out of the blanket just to his eyes and looked over at her. Seeing her stressed demeanor he instantly jumped out of the blanket and ran over, "A-a-are you okay?" He asked her frantically. Her head snapped up in shock as he hugged her, "P-p-please b-be okay!"

She took a deep breath and nodded her head, "I'm fine, A-D. Just a bit stressed." She paused and placed a hand on his shoulder, "Think you can handle meeting someone new?"

"P-p-p-p-people?" He asked her fearfully.

"Just one." Stephanie told him, "And old friend of mine. Actually, the cute one in the other picture."

His body started to shake, and he let go of her.

"It'll be okay. I'm sorry I didn't tell you last night, but I invited her over."

"N-n-n-no, no-no." He took a few steps back and lowered his head, "I-i-it's okay!" He tried his best to sound confidant and started to nod his head, "D-d-don't be s-s-s-sorry!"

She genuinely smiled at him, and it caught her off guard for a moment. He was trying his best to be strong … for her, "If you want you can go hide in your room, but … she'll want to meet you."

"N-no-no i-i-it's okay." He managed to respond, "I-I-I…" He took a deep breath, "I-I-I'll be okay."

"Thank you, A-D." She ruffled his hair, "I'm gonna go talk to her for a moment outside before I bring her in, okay?"

He nodded his head at her repeatedly, "Okay." He muttered.

"Go sit down, get comfortable." She told him while walking to the door, "Stay strong, A-D. For me. Please?"

"I … I…" He took another deep breath and managed to calm his breathing a little bit, "For you." He barely managed a whisper but didn't stutter at all. He forced a smile at her and went back to the couch letting his hair completely cover his eyes and raising his hand to cover his face.

Stephanie smiled at herself and stepped outside to greet Teresa, closing the door behind her and donning a much more serious look.

"What's up?" Teresa instantly asked her. She was always just invited in directly. This was new.

Stephanie took a deep breath, still unsure how to address the circumstance, "Teresa." She addressed her very formally, "I need to know I can trust you."

"What?" Teresa was taken aback in disbelief, "Of course you can! We're besties!" She paused for a moment, "What's going on, Steph?"

Stephanie took her right hand and started to massage her temples, "It's … It's not easy to explain." She sighed and whispered softly, "And not fit for outside." She went back to her normal volume, "I've got A-D over right now." She held up her hand silencing Teresa as she went to speak up, "He's very skittish, very…" she sighed, "pathetic and terrified. I need you to maintain your composure and stay calm no matter what you see, or think you see. Understood?"

"Woah, woah, woah." Teresa took a step forwards, "Steph, you can always talk to me you know."

"Not here." She hissed back, "Okay. Please just … trust me … and stay calm. No sudden outbursts or anything?"

"Why would I…?" Teresa looked at her utterly confused, "I don't understand."

"You will." Stephanie told her sternly, "You will very quickly. I *need* to know you can stay calm."

"Okay." Teresa took a deep breath and nodded at her, "I don't know what you think might make me freak out, but you got my word."

"Thank you." Stephanie said with a hint of relief, as she grabbed the door handle, she stopped one last time, "One more thing. Please uh, try to have an open mind. I have a plan. I promise."

"When do you not?" Teresa chuckled.

"Ha!" Stehpanie scoffed as she led Teresa into the house, "Hey, A-D! I let Teresa know in advance you were here. Wanna say hello?" She announced as they walked into the living room.

"H-h-h-hi…" He said softly. His back was towards them as he sat on the couch.

"Hey there, kid." Teresa responded quickly. "Steph really wasn't joking when she said you were shy." She continued as the two of them walked around to sit down. The moment Teresa got a look at A-D's front side she stopped in her tracks though, eyes going wide.

There were only a few promotional pictures ever released, but anyone could recognize the pitch-black hair blocking the eyes and right hand covering the mouth instantly.

The Archangel of Death. Her eyes quickly shot over to Stephanie who calmly sat down, right next to him. Stephanie looked up at her and forced a very fearful smile, "See, I told you he was cute." She said with a little giggle. The pleading, the begging, in her eyes was palpable.

Teresa glanced back and forth between them for a few seconds, gritting her teeth. She could tell Stephanie was desperate for her to maintain calm, and A-D … he started to slightly shake as she hesitated. She flashed a quick loathsome glare to Stephanie and composed herself as she promised, "Ah, well, not quite my type, but I can see what you mean." She took a seat across from them, her heart racing.

"C-c-cute?" A-D flashed a glance at Stephanie.

"What?" Stephanie looked over at him, "Think I'd let you stay here if you weren't?"

"*He-*" Teresa quickly caught her raised voice, "He's staying here?" She asked as calmly as she could. Her blood pressure rising with every passing second.

"Mhm!" A-D nodded his head repeatedly, "S-S-Steph-ph-phanie h-h-h-has b-been nothing-thing b-b-but kind."

"Yeah," Stephanie admitted, "I found him about a week ago in the woods outside of town. He doesn't really remember anything from before that though. No idea who he is, how he got there. Nothing."

"N-nothing g-g-g-good a-at least." A-D started to curl up slightly.

"That's ok, A-D." Stephanie comforted him and placed a hand on his shoulder, "You're safe now."

Teresa's eyes and mind raced as she tried to grasp the situation, "You … you're serious?" She finally asked.

'Y-y-yeah..." A-D muttered. He curled up even more.

Teresa took a deep breath, it failed to calm her down, "So, where'd the name A-D come from?"

"Stephanie gave it to me!" He excitedly said and quickly looked over at her with a smile. "S-s-s-she's the best!"

In that fraction of a moment where his hair swished Teresa caught a glimpse of his unique eyes, "My god…" She whispered.

"Aw…" Stephanie smiled at him and blushed, "Thank you."

Teresa had had enough of this. "Steph," Teresa quickly stood up, "We need to talk. Alone." She hissed. "Now!" The anger rose through her voice,

Both Stephanie and A-D froze. She closed her eyes and balled her hand into a fist out of stress, it shaking slightly. "Teresa, please."

"No!" She hissed again and walked past her, grabbing her by the arm and pulling her out of the chair.

Stephanie gasped and struggled to not fall over as she got dragged away keeping her eyes on A-D who started whispering to himself, "No, no, no, no-no-no-nonono…" His whole body shook. "Let her go! Let her go, let her go, let-her-go-let-her-go!" He jumped off the couch screaming, "*Let her go!!!*" He turned to face them, his hair flying away from in front of his eyes and slowly started to reach out with the hand covering his face.

Stephanie's eyes went wide in panic. She had seen him do this before. In that video … where the Archangel of Death… In an instant she broke free of Teresa's grasp, "What the-" Teresa spun around to face them.

"*A-D no!*" Stephanie screamed as she quickly tackled him to the ground, his arm halfway outstretched towards Teresa.

Teresa stood and stared in shock as they collapsed to the ground. A-D instantly cried out in pain and shock, convulsing violently, "*I'm-sorry! I'm-sorry, I'm-sorry-I'm-sorry!!!*" He pleaded as the tears streamed down his face, "P-p-p-please don't h-hurt me, hurt-me-hurt-me! No-no-no-no-nononono…" His tears overcame his ability to speak.

Stephanie quickly sat up panicked, and grabbed him into a tight hug, "No, no, no, no A-D. It's okay, it's okay, it's okay!" She quickly tried to calm him down, "I'm sorry. I'm so sorry. I didn't mean to hurt you! I'm so sorry A-D!" He kept crying in her arms as she started to scratch his head, "You're okay A-D. I'm not mad. I'm not mad. I'm sorry. I'm sorry. Please be okay, A-D. Please be okay…" She pleaded with him.

Finally, he started to speak, but barely, "I-I-I ju-just wanted to-wanted to pro-protect you." He slowly wrapped his arms around her, still crying profusely.

"I know. I know, I know." She rested her head on his, "I know you did." She took a deep breath, "Remember what I said about friends? How sometimes they make you wanna punch them in the face, but you don't?" She asked him. He faintly nodded at her, "That's all this is. That's all this is." She assured him, "Teresa would never hurt me. She's just a little mad right now I didn't tell her about you, okay?"

"O-o-o-okay…" He whimpered. "I-I-I-I-" His voice got caught worse in his throat with every stutter.

"Shh, shh, shh…" She silenced him, "It's okay. You don't need to be sorry. You were just trying to protect me. It's okay." She flashed a quick glance back to Teresa who was still standing in utter awe … and disgust. "Thank you, A-D. Thank you. It's nice to know you want to keep me safe."

"I … it-it is?" A-D asked her hesitantly, his crying finally calming down.

"Mhm." She responded, "Just like how I want to keep you safe and … I am so sorry for jumping on you like this."

He hugged her tightly, "I-i-i-it's okay." He mimicked her comforting of him.

She let out a sigh of relief and pulled back slightly, "Are you okay, A-D? Did I hurt you at all?"

He shook his head at her, "N-n-no." He let go of her and scooted back a bit.

"Oh, thank heavens." She smiled at him, "Now, I do need to go talk with Teresa, okay? I promise. I'll be fine. Plus," She glanced back at Teresa again, "She couldn't hurt me if she wanted to." Teresa maintained silence, merely looking at Stephanie in a mixture of anger, disgust, and confusion. "We'll be back up in no time, okay?"

"O-o-okay…" He whispered softly looking down at the ground.

Stephanie smiled at him and ruffled his hair, "Don't worry A-D. I'm coming back. I always do." He didn't respond and she slowly pulled herself off the ground. She glared at Teresa and walked past her, "Come on, let's go down."

"Let's." Teresa finally spoke up following her.

They travelled down the elevator in complete silence. The moment they stepped out and the door closed behind them Stephanie spun on her heel and slammed her hand on the wall pinning Teresa against it, "*One thing!*" She screamed, "*I asked you one thing!!!*"

"*You have the Archangel of Death in your home?!*" Teresa screamed back, "*And you expect me to maintain calm?!*"

"*He just about killed you right there!*" Stephanie screamed back in her face. Teresa froze, "I've seen that look on him before. In the video where he killed my brother. That's the *exact* same pose he struck, Teresa. I needed you to remain calm because he's…" She couldn't think of the words she wanted.

"You're … you're actually serious?" Teresa asked her calmly, "He…"

"*Yes!*" Stephanie screamed, desperation entering her voice. She let her arm drop to her side, "Fuck…" She whispered to herself and dropped down to the ground throwing her head into her hands and letting the tears fall freely.

"Steph I…" Teresa stopped herself and slowly sat down as well. She had never seen Stephanie like this, "Alright. We'll play this your way. What's the story?"

"Thank you…" Stephanie barely managed to say as she let her head hit the wall behind her and her hands dropped to the ground, "I…" She took a deep breath, "I found him in the woods on the day of … well his own memorial. And…" She threw her hands up for a moment, "Shit, what was I supposed to do? Leave him for the Empire to find and use again? Kill him?" She scoffed, "He survived a Chaos Bomb! That's impossible! So … so…" She coughed to hold back tears.

"You took him in…" Teresa finished.

"Yes." Stephanie sighed, "He remembers nothing. Nothing at all. That's not a lie. I had to teach him what food and drink were. I had to show him how to bathe! His memory is completely gone! I think … I think the Chaos Bomb wiped it."

"And… the…?" Teresa just kinda gestured unsure of how to word his being so pathetic.

"I don't know." Stephanie responded instantly, "But … but I," she sighed, "I don't think that's from the Chaos Bomb."

"What?" Teresa snapped at her.

"Yeah…" Stephanie groaned, "It seems ingrained in him. Always apologizing, always fearful, never thinking he's good enough or did anything right. He had a mental breakdown when he saw Lady Love." She weakly gestured to her mech, "He freaked out when Righteousness showed up on that press conference. It's like he remembers emotions, but no details."

"What do you mean?" Teresa asked her.

"The sight of Lady Love brought him pain." Stephanie explained, "Rambling about being crushed, endless pain, his flesh turning into steel…" She paused for a moment, "I don't think The Scythe had a cockpit. I think it relied on his immortality."

"My god, you're serious." Teresa remarked.

"Yeah…" Stephanie weakly smirked, "When Righteousness came onto the screen, he hid himself under the blanket pleading for mercy about how he didn't mean to be seen and was begging not to be hurt." She paused again, "I … I…" She sighed.

"Just tell me Steph." Teresa responded defeated, "We're already screwed."

Stephanie started to laugh and shook her head, "What if … what if I told you I don't think we were? What if I told you…" She grumbled to herself, "A-D is the project I mentioned. And you just showed me that it's starting to show fruit."

"*What?*" Teresa shouted at her.

"He just about killed you … to protect me." Stephanie finally rose her head and faced Teresa, "I've got him wrapped around my finger tighter than a noose after the body has dropped. Imagine what we could accomplish if he … if he did my bidding."

"You're insane…" Teresa was astonished.

"Yeah." Stephanie smirked, "That I know, but I'm in way too deep now to back out."

"Steph!" Teresa shouted, "We're talking about the guy who single handedly conquered our Kingdom. We're talking about-"

"*You don't think I know?!"*" Stephanie shouted at her, "*He murdered my brother!* So how do you think I feel? *Huh*?"

"I…" Teresa stopped, "I … shit." She sighed, "I hadn't considered that."

"Of course you hadn't." Stephanie snapped at her, "It's not your fault. I try not to make you guys worry about me, but right now? Teresa, I need your help. I need your support."

"On … with *him*?!"

"I don't want you to help control him." Stephanie explained, "I just need you to let Collin and the others know I have a plan. That I'm working on something massive. Because as much as I hate to admit it, if we had the Archangel of Death on our side…"

"We'd be an actual threat." Teresa finished her sentence.

"Yes." Stephanie nodded at her. "What else would you have me do about this? What else should I have done differently?"

Teresa sighed, "I really wish I had something I could tell you."

"So do I." Stephanie chuckled for a moment, "For once I wish I was wrong."

"You're never wrong though." Teresa chuckled with her, "And now we're all in deeper than we ever thought." They sat in silence for a while, "So what happens if he remembers everything one day?"

"We either die, or he joins us." Stephanie said plainly, "But, I think if I play my cards right here? I think we have a chance." She paused, "Let's just hope he doesn't though, hm?"

"Dammit, Steph!" Teresa grumbled, "If you were anyone else."

"I know … I know…" She said softly.

"I'll play along with you on one condition."

"What?" Stephanie asked her.

"Don't lie to me about him. On anything." Teresa spoke with a sense of severity, "You have to trust me. We've been friends since kindergarten."

Stephanie sighed, "You got a deal."

Teresa stood up and offered her a hand, which she reluctantly took and got up as well, "You haven't uh … done anything have you?"

"*No!*" Stephanie shouted at her, "Are you out of your mind?"

"I mean, you said you had to teach him how to bathe." Teresa pointed out, but it was obvious she was teasing her. Payback for … this.

"Teresa, I swear on all that is holy in this world…"

Teresa burst out in laughter, "You know I had to."

"Please don't." Stephanie pleaded with her, "You really don't understand how hard it is on me. Do you know what he did when I sent him those pictures of us yesterday?"

"What?" Teresa asked.

"He seriously spent the rest of the night staring at that picture of me until I got home!" Stephanie nearly shouted, "*Hours!*"

"I think he lik-"

"Don't. Please." Stephanie begged her.

Teresa started laughing, "Alright, alright. I'll stop. I'll think of some way to get Collin calmed down."

"Thank you." Stephanie said sincerely, "Any bit of relief is more than welcomed, but no one else can know about A-D, Teresa. No one." She emphasized, "They aren't ready yet."

"I wasn't ready yet." Teresa smirked.

"And neither am I still." Stephanie responded, "Not a word, promise?"

"I promise." Teresa nodded at her, "You're right. They aren't ready to accept this kind of thing yet."

"I've no idea when I'll tell everyone." Stephanie said softly more to herself than anything, "But I'll figure it out. Don't have a choice."

"I'll be the first to say," Teresa told her, "I don't think this is a good idea, but if anyone can pull it off. You can."

"Heh…" Stephanie forced a smile.

"Are you going to be okay, though?"

Stephanie shrugged, "Don't have a choice." They shared a few moments of silence as the severity of it all kicked into Teresa's mind, "Let's get back to him."

Teresa looked at her worried for a moment, but knew not to push her any further and sighed, "Alright."

"He's probably barely keeping it together right now." Stephanie chuckled, "And thanks to that stunt of yours I'm probably going to have to spend the next few hours just letting him lay his head on my lap."

"Wait." Teresa stopped them as they stepped onto the elevator, "Just how far are you willing to take this with him?"

Stephanie stopped and thought about it for a moment before taking a deep breath and letting a hunger enter her eyes, "If he starts showing results? Using his powers for us? I'll go as far as I have to."

"Maybe don't tell me if it ends up going that far." Teresa teased, "You've got a stronger heart and will than the rest of us. That's for sure. I don't think anyone else would have even considered this."

"They wouldn't have." Stephanie agreed, "That's why I'm the leader." She hit the button and they started to ascend. As they got back upstairs A-D was still curled up where they had left him. "Come on, A-D." Stephanie called to him as she walked over and sat down on the couch. She patted her legs lightly and A-D, head hung low, walked over and laid down with his head on her lap as Teresa sat across from them.

Stephanie rolled her eyes at Teresa and glanced down at A-D for a second. Terese merely shook her head in response. "I-I-I-I'm sorry." A-D said as Stephanie started to play with his hair.

"No that's my bad, kid." Teresa responded before Stephanie could, "Steph warned me you're a bit jumpy and I caused that to happen."

"Y-you're … n-not-t mad?" A-D asked her even though he was facing Stephanie.

"Nah," Teresa told him, "Steph and I just go *way* back so … I was a little upset that she had a boy living in her house and didn't tell me."

Stephanie glared at her for wording it that way. Teresa merely smiled back in response. "W-w-why w-would that m-matter?" he asked

"Oh, come on everyone knows that a boy and a girl who aren't family living together is…" Teresa stopped for a moment, "You don't know anything about anything do you?"

"N-n-n-no." He twitched slightly, "S-s-s-sorry."

"Well don't worry about it then." Teresa could see Stephanie give a sigh of relief, "She's been living alone ever since her brother died. Might be good for her to have some company."

"Died?" A-D froze for a moment, his eyes going wide. Stephanie could feel his whole body tense up, "S-s-s-so much death… S-s-s-so much blood … hurt … p-pain…"

"Shhh…" Stephanie worked on keeping him calm, "You're here now. With me. With friends." She comforted him, "You aren't there anymore."

He sighed softly and cuddled up into her, "N-n-no. S-s-safe here. S-s-s-s-safe with you."

"Dammit, Steph! I take it back." Teresa grumbled, "He is kinda cute."

A-D squeed a little bit and grabbed Stephanie's hand. She merely glared at Teresa once again.

Chapter 13: The Tough Calls

The next week and a half went by smoothly. Teresa had held up her end of the deal and managed to get Collin to back off, not a single one of her people had left to go join John thankfully, and A-D was slowly starting to act a little bit more like a normal person around the house. She was able to get him to genuinely help with the dishes, do laundry all by himself, help with some cleaning … and most importantly he was getting quick with handing her whatever tools she needed on Lady Love.

All she had to give him was some simple positive reinforcement and basic affection. He was like a puppy who just wanted to be involved, help, and make her happy. Two nights ago, work on her mech had finally finished, Lady Love was ready to fly again. This time hopefully at full capacity. For celebration they spent yesterday watching movies together and eating junk food.

She was terrified though. Not of A-D, but of herself. They had passed out on the couch while watching movies late into the night … and she had woken up … to them cuddling. Thankfully she fell asleep last and woke up first, and A-D showed no signs of realizing what had happened, but she had curled up around A-D, one arm draped over him in her sleep.

She was angry, livid, pissed at herself. How could she? How could she let herself cuddle him for … for nothing? What scared her even more though, terrified her to her core was she could remember the first few moments of waking up, before she had realized what was going on … and she enjoyed it.

Today though. Today was a new day, an important day. She was going to get A-D to come on a test flight with her. Make sure everything in Lady Love was working perfectly. It was a little bit of payback for last night, but mostly because she needed him to be comfortable in the cockpit. If she wanted to use his powers for the rebellion, she needed him to go with her into battle and this was the first step.

Stephanie looked over at her jumpsuit which hung up by all the computers. It was crème colored with bright pink snaking lines running along all the seams. She glanced over at A-D who was wearing his black hoodie and jeans still. She sighed, turned back around, and started to take off her clothes, keeping an eye on A-D who was, as per usual, staring at her.

She smiled to herself as she tossed all but her bra and panties to the side and turned to face him. She had spent enough time around him by now, she could tell when he liked what he saw. "Hey there," she addressed him, "You know it's not polite to watch a woman change."

His eyes went wide and he gasped quickly turning around, "S-s-sorry!" He squeaked, "You-you're just-"

"So pretty I know." She finished with a laugh. "I'll let you watch on two conditions."

He perked up and turned back around, "Mhm?" He asked her.

"First," She told him, "I'm gonna want your help with the zipper on the back of the jumpsuit."

"Okay!" He said excitedly.

"And secondly…" She paused and looked over at her mech, "I want you to come with me."

"I-i-i-in that?" He asked her in a worried tone looking over at it.

"Mhm!" She smiled at him. "Please?"

"I-I-I-I-I…"

"Oops." She said sarcastically as she undid the hook on her bra and let it fall down to the ground. A-D spun around and froze as he stared at her. She slowly rose her hands up to cover herself, "Well either turn back around or come with me."

"I-I-I'll come!" He said, staring at her still.

"That's what I thought." She dropped her hands to her sides and slowly continued to undress. Her heart beat faster with every passing moment. She was using her body to get A-D into her mech. No, no she was using it to get him to fight. Then why did it excite her? After sliding off her panties she stretched her arms into the air, interlocking her fingers and moving her back from side to side getting it to crack a few times. She then turned around and leaned forward, away from A-D, holding her arms out in front of her repeating the process, focusing on her moving her hips for her lower back to crack. "I am pretty, aren't I?" She asked A-D as she stood back up and faced him.

A-D nodded his head at her, "*Mmn…*" He couldn't even form a word as he was nearly drooling.

She giggled at him and booped his nose, "Shows over for now, kid. Time to get suited up." She quickly grabbed her jumpsuit and slid her legs in, one after the other. She snapped her arms down, slotting them into their holes and quickly pulled the skin-tight suit up over her breasts. She popped her arms straight out and now all that was left was the zipper up her back. She reached behind her and pulled it up halfway before turning her back to A-D and jingling it. "Can you get the rest for me please?" She asked him.

He nodded his head again and walked over slowly raising his hands to her back. One of his cold fingers brushed her skin and she gasped. A-D jumped back instantly, "S-s-s-sorry!"

"No!" She quickly responded, "No, it's okay. I just … I wasn't expecting it to be so cold. Please, continue." He slowly walked back up and grabbed the zipper with one of his hands, but softly placed a finger on the back of her neck with the other one. He lightly ran it down her spine and she closed her eyes enjoying the moment, letting out a sigh of relief.

What. Was. She. Doing?

That was the question running through her mind repeatedly, consuming her every thought.

"Done!" A-D said proudly as he took a step back.

Her eyes shot open and she gasped lightly. She hadn't even felt him pull the zipper up. She quickly cleared her mind and turned around to face him. "Well, what do you think?" She asked while striking a few poses. The suit was completely skintight, like a second layer. It showed every single curve on her body, hiding nothing but the color of her skin and body parts. Flight suits were made to be as flexible as possible. Offering no protection. It was for quick entry and the fastest reaction times possible. It did have some benefits though. While female pilots were gawked at more often, it hid nothing of male pilots as well.

His mouth dropped open again, "V-v-very … p-p-pretty."

"That's what I thought." She ruffled his hair. "Now come on. It's already getting late. I'll show you how to get in and strapped in. And then it's time for a little joy ride."

\ \

"I don't need your damn help anyways." John grumbled to himself as he sat in his mech, the only Knight Mk.2 under his command. Around him thirty-six Knight Mk.1's prepared for combat. Half were in the more combat oriented fighting stance, half in the jet configuration. He had a plan. Him and the eighteen others in fighting stance were going to move in first and draw the Angels protecting the embassy out, while they fought, the jets would come in and blast the Angels out of the sky. Then, with the main defense force gone they would move in, and he would eliminate the embassy.

It wasn't a perfect plan. Half of them, if not most, would probably die, but it was a plan. One with a high chance of success. He had some contacts on the inside that gave him the normal patrol routes, guard rotations, and even a hack to obscure them from the long range and on-board sensors. Alongside that 55 men within the city were prepared to start a riot once they struck, to split up the remaining Angels.

Stephanie didn't even have half the Knight's he did, but she had three Knight Mk.2's, and Lady Love, assuming it was operational. Those would have been a great boon. The rest? Well, they would have hopefully soaked up a few bullets or missiles, but she was a coward, a traitor to the Kingdom, just like her parents.

"Assault team?" He addressed them all, "Ready check!"

"Ready!" They all responded to him as one.

"Support team? Ready check!" He called out.

"Ready!" Again, the other eighteen responded as one.

"Today marks the day where the Empire will learn the Kingdom of Estates is not yet dead!" He rallied them, "Today we will destroy the main embassy in the Maynor Estate and claim it back as our own!" He paused for a second, "*We are the Kingdom of Estates!*" He shouted as loud as he could.

"We will never go down without a fight!" They all shouted as one, *"Long live the Estates!"*

"Assault team! Move out!" John commanded them and took off from their hiding spot.

A-D didn't hesitate once getting into Lady Love. He climbed into what was once the second pilot's seat, now just a passenger's seat, and quickly followed her instructions on how to strap himself in. The most fear he showed was the hyperventilating and the small squeak as the hatch closed above her. She had been terrified about trying to convince him it was okay and safe, this easiness made her little strip show more than worth it. He was useless to her if he refused to get inside.

"I-it … it d-doesn't hurt?" He asked her, slowly opening his eyes once again.

"Nope!" She chuckled at him, "Just like I told you." She turned on the mech and it roared to life. A-D squealed in fear as the loud engine turned on but calmed down as it started to quiet. "Sorry about that." She glanced down at him, "I don't even notice the noise anymore. You'll get used to it." She leaned down and was barely able to scratch his head, "You're doing great, A-D."

"T-t-t-thanks…" He whimpered as she pulled her hand back up and disengaged the docking locks.

"Now, it's gonna get a little bit bumpy." She warned him, "Nothing too crazy. I need to check and make sure everything is working as I want it too before I really take her out for a spin."

"I-I-I-I'll b-be okay!" He shouted back at her, "I-I-I-I promised!"

"I know you will." She smiled to herself and pushed the button to open the large steel doors which led into the intricate underground tunnel system her parents had built. "Ready?" She glanced down at him as the doors finished sliding open.

He paused and looked up at her. Locking eyes with her for a moment he forced a hesitant smile, "Y-y-yes!"

She smiled back and snapped her eyes in front of her, "Here goes." She sent the mech flying forward.

\ \

"We've passed within their long-range senor line," one of John's men informed him.

"Still no sign of movement on our scanners," another one said.

"Looks like that hack worked." John smiled to himself. While even in fighter form, they flew just above the ground faster than any car could hope to drive. "You all know your groups and which patrol to hit. Split off now and keep to the plan." What was once one large group of nineteen Knights quickly split into three groups of six, with his having seven. "Once your patrol is dealt with meet at the secondary staging zone."

"Yes, Sir!" The two squadron leaders he had appointed responded.

"Five minutes till intercept." John announced. "Support group launch the moment we engage." With each squadron having six Knights, and the element of surprise, they could each easily take on the patrols of three Angels. After contact it would take about five minutes for backup Angels to arrive. His plan was that his backup would arrive right around the same time.

"Yes, Sir." The leader of the jet group responded. Even though John and his Knights had launched thirty minutes ago, the jets would make it to the intercept points in five. The speed Knights could achieve while in jet stance was almost ten times that of fighter stance. The speed came at the cost of fighting prowess, and it took fifteen immobile seconds to change from one stance to the other, but it undoubtably had its benefits and uses. And this was one of them.

Stephanie went easy on A-D, at first at least. She slowly ramped up the severity of the moves she was testing out. Her hands flew across the command console as she piloted Lady Love. Her maneuvering thrusters and jetpack were working perfectly in fighter configuration. She even tested her massive gun, its aim, and her ability to snap shoot at anything. Everything was working better than she could have hoped, and a whole two days sooner than she had expected.

"Hey A-D. Wanna see something really cool?" She paused, hovering her mech in the air.

"W-w-what?" He was still terrified but was also faring far better than she had expected. Had … had stripping worked that well? Or was he already that dedicated to doing what she asked? She prayed for the latter.

"It's about to get really loud." She warned him, "But for most mech's, this takes a full fifteen seconds to complete." Her hands flew across the control panel in a blur and at once Lady Love's form started to shift. The sound of metal sliding across metal filled the air and A-D covered his ears letting out a slight shriek of fear, yet within moments though the sound stopped.

"Open your eyes." She told him.

As he slowly opened his eyes he gasped as her chair was right in front of his now. He lurched forward and hugged her from behind the chair. Stephanie grabbed one of his hands tenderly and laughed. Looking down at the console she let out a sharp whistle, "2.476 seconds while stationary. I'll take that. I will take that." She mused to herself and patted A-D's arms. "Sit on back now. Time to test out just how quick this baby is."

A-D slowly leaned back into his seat.

"Oh, and it's going to get a *lot* bumpier. I'd suggest grabbing onto those straps tightly."

"O-o-o-" She didn't wait for him to finish as she shot Lady Love off forward. If he wasn't grabbing the straps before, she knew he was now.

"Red 1, 2, and 3." John addressed the men in his small squadron, "Spread out a bit. As soon as all of you are in range, fire one missile at each target a piece."

"Yes, Sir." Red 1 responded, "Linking targeting now … Targeting linked."

"Red 4, 5, and 6. As soon as you see those Angels move; scramble and engage."

"Yes, Sir." They responded as one.

"With some luck though they won't be able to dodge three surprise missiles." John smirked. This was the plan for all three of the squadrons. He specifically chose the one that went right down the middle, the closest to the city. Where there was the most danger, he wanted to be found. Soon he could barely make out the lights of the Angels up in the sky.

"Entering range in five ... four ... three ... two ... one ..." Red 1 counted down, "All Knights locked on targets. Missiles away." Each Knight shot off three of their missiles and they soared into the night sky.

John kept his eyes on the Angels. Within seconds they quickly split, but it was too late for one of them as one of the missiles collided with him in an explosion. The other two spun above firing their guns at the incoming missiles. One gone, two gone … another target hit. Another Angel down. Right as the final Angel shot the last missile out of the sky John put full power into his jetpack and shot into the night sky, his sword raised high. The Angel turned down just in time to see John's sword go right through the cockpit. John ripped the sword out and let the Angel fall.

Calls came in from the other groups. They had been similarly successful. "All squadrons, move to staging ground B! Support squadrons, be prepared for immediate combat."

The spotlights from the city turned from white to red as the alarm went out.

They were under attack.

John and his cell would soon be entering the close range scanners they were *not* invisible to, which the Angels could connect to, overriding the in-frame scanner hack as well. The element of stealth and surprise was gone.

The real battle was about to begin.

A-D held onto the straps for dear life as Stephanie whipped about through the tunnels. All this work had been more than worth it. Lady Love was more responsive than ever, and she finally had her maneuvering thrusters working in flight mode as well. She was glad she had turned off the terrain proximity alarm as it would have been going off this whole time. The walls were scorched in multiple places from how close her engines got to them as she could turn on a dime.

She could easily see why this prototype was discontinued. The two pilots would need to practically share a brain to really use it to its full capacity and she was the only pilot skilled enough she knew to even attempt this. She loved zipping around the tunnels as fast as she could. Her years and years of practice down here gave her insane maneuverability at high speeds in battle.

She slowed to a stop, a grin spreading from ear to ear on her face as she did so, and held back a hand towards A-D, "A bit rough, but safe." She told him, "You okay?"

He quickly grabbed her hand and gripped it tightly, "I-I-I-I p-p-promised-ed!" He squeaked.

She rubbed his hand a bit and chuckled, "You're doing amazing, A-D."

"I-I-I-I am?" He leaned his head into her hand.

She scratched the top of his head, "Mhm! I really need you to get okay with being in here as I'll be in here more and more as time goes on. I want you to come with me."

"M-m-m-more?" He asked terrified.

"Yeah, this is how we fight the Eternal Empire. From inside of here. Don't worry. I'll keep finding ways to thank you."

"N-n-no!" He shook his head, "I-I-I-I'll do it!" He grabbed her hand and pushed his head against it, "I-I-I w-w-want t-to pro-protect you!"

"Thank you…" She mused at him, "You are very kind." They sat in silence for a bit before she spoke up, "Wanna see something special? A secret? One Teresa hasn't even seen?"

His eyes lit up and he nodded, "Yes!"

"Sit on back then." She pulled her hand away from him, "I'll take it a bit easier than I have been though. Stress test is complete. Lady Love is functioning perfectly." She glanced back and waited for A-D to sit all the way back in his chair before smiling at him with soft eyes. He nodded at her and she looked back out front before taking off again, this time delving deep into the cave system.

John had been hoping to regroup with the other squads before reinforcements arrived, but his hope had been a fever dream. Six Angels had come to intercept each group of his men. They still had a small element of surprise since their Knight composition was unknown, but this wasn't good. All they needed to do was hold out for a few moments longer before his support team entered the fray. If they could deal with these Angels that would be a majority of the frames that would have been airborne at the time of their attack, but he knew every single frame on the ground was currently getting prepped and ready for combat. They had five minutes at worst until more would join the fray, twenty at best before all one hundred Angels would be in the sky.

"*Scramble and engage!*" He shouted across their connected radios, "*Defeat them as soon as possible! Victory is more important than survival!*" As soon as the first Angel came into range, he unleashed a trio of missiles at it. He was running on half the normal amount of missiles as usual since he had replaced his left shoulder missile silo with a singular large one to destroy the embassy. All he needed was one good shot.

The Angel quickly shot down his three missiles, but John was already firing his bullets. His aim was nigh unmatched in the rebel cells and the Angel quickly went down. He swiftly flew behind a building, using it to absorb the missiles that had been locked onto him. The rest of his men scrambled and engaged immediately. He watched as one of them exploded from a missile and another was shot out of the sky, a cloud of dust kicking up from where they landed.

They were outclassed. The Knight Mk.1's stood no chance against the Angels in fair combat. The radio chatter became filled with the sound of combat. The other two groups had engaged the enemy as well. He shot back out the other side of the building and let loose. Even with the sound dampening padding of the mechs, the sound of massive gunfire rang in his ears. Another nine missiles shot out from his right shoulder silo. He was halfway to empty now, but his quick flank made it worthwhile as two Angels exploded in the night sky.

Two more of his men had fallen as well. Sweat dripped down his brow. How many would he even have left by the time they reached the second staging ground?

"Sorry for the wait, boys."

He heard his support leader come in over the radio and looked up just in time for the other three Angels to get shot out of the sky.

"*Damn* good timing!" John shouted. His radio chatter now filled with the sounds of cheering. Looked like his plan worked, "*Everyone to staging area B!*" He shouted at them all, "Our timing window runs short before we are completely overwhelmed!"

"We'll fly ahead and shoot down any late comers to the party, Sir." The support leader said as their Knights shot by above, "Let chaos be our greatest ally."

Stephanie slowed Lady Love down to a stop and turned on the spotlights on the front. There in the rock wall in front of them was a small steel door sealed shut. "See that right there?" She pointed to it.

A-D leaned forward a bit and nodded, "Mhm!"

"That right there is my parent's legacy. They built this massive underground bunker for us rebels to use as a last resort."

"W-w-why is i-it cl-closed?" He asked her softly.

"Because we aren't yet at our last resort." She explained to him, "These doors will unlock for you and I to enter into, alongside three others hidden about these tunnels when I signal for an evacuation, and only then." She turned back to face him, "I wonder to myself often what's behind those doors. What was so important that they'd sacrifice their lives for it? Why they said I should only use it at the last possible moment?"

"D-d-d-desperate times … c-c-call for d-d-desperate m-m-m-measures?" A-D pointed out.

She sat back slightly and blinked at him in surprised, "You … you might be right, A-D."

He blushed and smiled at her.

"Well done!"

He rocked side to side in his seat smiling, proud of himself.

"I've never shown anyone this. You're the first. I can't trust them."

He stopped instantly, "B-b-b-b-but y-you tr-tr-trust me…?" He hesitantly asked.

"Everyone else would insist that we open it up right now and see what's inside." She sighed heavily, "They wouldn't understand waiting, but you? I knew I could trust you with it. Because you trust me."

He nodded at her, "Y-yes! Y-you are kind!"

"I wanted to show you this so that you know I trust you." She explained, "Because I do, A-D. I trust you." She was trying to convince herself as much as she was him. And while he was far easier to convince than she was… She could feel a small, minuscule, hint of truth in it. She could trust him, but how far, how long, and with what?

"I-I…" Tears started to form in his eyes, and he dropped his head down.

"No one's ever trusted you before, have they?" She asked him.

He shook his head aggressively, "*No!*" He shouted letting the tears flow, "I-I-I only l-let e-e-e-every-everyone d-down-wn…"

"I know you won't let me down, A-D." She reached back and grabbed one of his hands, "You haven't yet, and I know you won't." He grabbed her hand and tried to speak, but the words kept getting caught in his throat.

"Shh … shh…" She comforted him, "It's okay. It's okay…" She smiled softly, "Look at me." He shook his head and kept his eyes down. "Look at me, A-D. Please?" She begged him. He slowly opened his eyes and looked up at her, greeted with her warm smile, "You won't let me down. Not as long as you put your heart into it and try your hardest. I know you will make me proud. I promise." She stretched over as far as she could and wiped some of the tears off his cheek.

"I … I…" He started crying more, but she could tell, this time it was tears of joy, "I won't let you down!" He shouted, "I … I'll make sure!"

She ran the back of her hand down his cheek and slowly pulled it away, "I know. Come on. It's been a long night for you. Let's get on home."

He nodded at her, but remained silent as she slowly turned Lady Love around and started to head home.

The three squadrons had barely gotten back together before the first of the Angels lifted off and engaged them. Bullets, missiles, and mechas tore up the night sky. John's support team had been a massive boon at first, but now they would have been much more helpful in their fighting stance, but there wasn't time to transform. They dove in and out of the battlefield, using their limited access to missile munitions as best as they could, but soon Angels came soaring into the night sky in their own jet form.

It was a battle on all fronts. And while they were doing far better than they should have, they didn't have the numbers. Half of his men were gone, and they weren't any closer to getting to the embassy. An entire skyscraper collapsed from collateral damage. Every building in a miles radius was littered with bullets or partially destroyed from explosions or falling Angels and Knights. He couldn't even consider the civilian casualties. If the Eternal Empire didn't care about them, how could he and still dream of a chance at a won fight?

The barrel of his gun was a bright red from continuous fire. He couldn't count how many Angels he had shot down, more than the rest of his life combined. His one missile silo was completely empty. His sword was dulled and dented, his armor scratched and cracking…

One shot. One opportunity. That was all he needed. And he was going to get it one way or another.

"*All operating Knights!*" He shouted over the radio, "*Clear a way to the embassy! I repeat! Get me line of sight to that embassy no matter the cost!*

"*Yes, Sir!*" They all responded as one. In an instant they all broke away from their engaged targets and started to drive a hole through the defenses directly towards the embassy. A handful more of his men fell as they tried to disengage and join on him. He was down to just a handful left in fighting form, and only slightly more in jet.

"Blow a hole straight through this building!" He shouted at them as he focused all his firepower on the skyscraper directly in his way of the embassy.

"Sir we're all out of missiles!" One of them responded.

"I've got you covered, John." One of his men in a jet responded. *"For the Kingdom of Estat-!"* The Knight blew past them and tore right through the skyscraper. The radio went to static as it exploded after blasting out the other side of it.

John said nothing as he rushed forwards through the hole. As soon as he was on the other side, he was finally within range. The second his screen flashed the words "Target Locked" he fired the special made missile. It was made to obscure all targeting abilities. There was no chance it was getting shot down.

He didn't even hear the radio calls from his men as they fell. He smiled as he watched the missile head directly for the embassy. He would die here, but at least he wouldn't be dying without reason.

A golden light flashed down from the sky … as the missile exploded only halfway to the embassy. Weapons might not have been able to target it, but an Angel had just dove out of the sky and took it out with its own self. His mouth dropped open and anger welled up within him. He let out a guttural scream throwing his Knight Mk.2 into full speed forward. He could do the same… He stopped only moments after starting as the dust from the explosion faded.

The Angel. It hovered there directly in his path. Sword in one hand and its massive gun pointed directly at him. It looked like no Angel he had seen before. A small energy sphere around it shattered and faded into nothing. There was only one thing this could be.

A second generation Angel.

As Stephanie and A-D neared the entrance back into her basement she spoke up, "Alright, I might have lied a little bit to you, there's still one more thing to try out." She glanced back at him for a second and smirked, "But it's pretty complicated and I've never successfully done it before."

"Y-y-y-ou c-can do any-ny-thing!" He shouted back at her.

She smiled, even with who it was, having someone who believed in her was nice. Every time she had tried this before she only had her doubts, but now, even though it was an amnesia ridden Archangel of Death who was the most pathetic excuse of a man she had ever met … it was nice. "Just how much faith do you have in me? Cuz if this fails, we're gonna crash and have to spend another week just on repairs."

A-D's eyes went wide, and he whimpered for a moment, "*No*!" He shouted to himself, "Y-y-you can do i-it! I t-t-t-trust you!"

Her smile grew wider, "Well now I have to pull it off." They neared the largest open cavern, and she took a deep breath, "You got this, Steph." She whispered to herself. Changing configuration in seconds was unheard of already, but just shy of three seconds was still three immobile seconds. In combat that meant death. The main draw, the main idea behind this prototype Knight was not for that … it was for changing stances while still moving.

There were a million things that had to go perfectly. Stabilizers needed to keep her pointed forward. There needed to be enough space at all times for her mech to shift forms. She needed to properly execute the order in shifting forms. She needed to do it fast, as this cavern allowed for, in her estimate, a maximum of ten seconds to change before she'd slam into the wall. She needed to do it all manually, automatic transformation in Lady Love still took fifteen seconds. And she had failed at every single one of these at one point in time in the past.

She closed her eyes. She knew these tunnels like the back of her hand, she knew she had fifteen seconds until she reached the cavern. She knew exactly where every button was she needed to push. She knew the order they needed to go in. She knew she could do this … she just never had succeeded before. But now? Now A-D trusting her relied on her pulling this off.

"Hang on tight." She warned him just moments before her Lady Love entered the cavern. Her hands flew across the control panels and the mech instantly started to shift its form while keeping its forward momentum. Not enough upwards thrust, her left foot lightly tapped the vertical thruster just a fraction of a moment before it went inoperative.

The cockpit went vertical as it turned into the chest of the fighter form and the head rotated to the front. The wings moved back into their positions as arms while her shoulders unfolded from around the cockpit, The main engines of the jet shifted down the back wings and turned into Lady Love's lower legs and feet.

The moment control of the mech came back to her she spun around and put full power into the engines, throwing their bodies against the back of their seats and slowing them to a stop. She let out her held breath and opened her eyes finally.

She had done it.

She had done it!

"*I did it!*" She shouted at the top of her lungs, "*I did it!*"

"*Eee…*" A-D squeaked in fear.

"I can't believe it! *I finally did it!*" She continued to shout. She glanced down at her control panel. 8.756 seconds. "*In under nine seconds!? A-D, I did it!*"

"Y-y-y-y-y-y-ye-yea-yeah." He barely managed to stutter while shaking in his chair.

She spun Lady Love around in the air in joy, "A-D, we are going to celebrate tonight!" She still shouted as she finished flying them home.

"Say hello to the second generation of Angels." A female voice came over the open radio channel. John was frozen in fear, "Comes equipped with a single use energy shield that makes us immune to all damage for an entire second." The voice was haughty and prideful, "Oh, it can also be replaced during maintenance."

John's rage bellowed within him, "*Go to hell!*" He shouted.

"No can do." She chuckled, "I'm an Angel. And to think. We didn't even need our backup." Within seconds his radar flooded with pings of dozens upon dozens of more Angels, "Seems we heavily overestimated your ability."

"I'll kill you." John hissed at her, "I'll kill all of you."

"You and what army?" The Angel pilot asked him with a chuckle. He glanced back at his radar. None of his men were transponding. "Truth be told I just wanted to show off this new frame a little bit." The pilot started to laugh, "You and your kind are utterly hopeless."

"You and me!" John shouted at her, "Right now! A duel!"

The pilots laugh turned hysterical, "You're joking right?" She paused, "Oh my God Emperor he's not joking. You've got armor barely holding itself together, no missiles, a half-melted gun, and a sword that could barely cut warm butter."

"*Raaahhh!*" John let out a guttural scream while charging forward.

"Have it your way." The pilot calmly responded before firing one single shot. John could feel the force of the bullet rip through his Knight right below him. The control panel flashed and went dark. The lights went out. He continued to scream as his mech lost all power and fell freely into the city below.

They were no more than thirty seconds away from home. Stephanie quickly landed Lady Love and powered it down, "Home again." She undid her straps and held her hand down to A-D, "Come on. Let's get out of here."

He nodded at her and undid his straps with his shaking hands. He reached out and she helped him up the ladder and out on top of the mech. Climbing up after him she slid down the front of it and landed down on the ground. She looked back up at A-D and gestured for him to come down.

"N-n-n-no l-l-ladder?" He asked her in fear. She hadn't landed back in the docking clamps. She didn't even think about it. She only ever used those when she was working on Lady Love, but this would be another good lesson for A-D.

"Gotta get used to jumping down sooner or later." She smiled at him, "Come on. I'll catch you." She held her arms out towards him.

He nodded at her mumbling to himself, convincing himself it was safe, for a few moments before speaking up, "O-o-okay … h-h-here I … I c-come." He slowly pushed himself down the face of Lady Love towards her and fell. She quickly moved and caught him in her arms.

The moment he was in her arms she stood up and spun around, "*I did it!*" She shouted again, "I can't believe it! Thank you!"

"F-f-f-for…?" He held onto her as she spun around the room.

She stopped and looked down at him, her hair landing on his face, "Believing in me. I don't think I could have done it without you." She set him down and he stood up on his own, "*I did it!*"

"I-I-I-I … k-knew yo-you c-cou-could!" He curled slightly where he stood watching her excitement.

"Thank you! *Thank you!*" She shouted while grabbing him in a tight hug, "No one else actually believed I could pull it off. They all thought it was impossible." She let him go and he staggered back a little bit. She spun around in an instant, "Zipper?" She asked him while pointing at it on her back.

He nodded at her, "O-o-of c-course." He walked up and slowly unzipped the back of her flight suit.

"Thanks." She smiled at him and quickly took off the whole thing. She grabbed her clothes in her arms and turned back around to face him. He had been staring, but instantly shot his eyes to the ground as she turned. She smirked and rolled her eyes, "I'm too ecstatic to care right now, A-D, plus I plan on putting on some pajama's when we get upstairs. You can look."

He looked back up and gasped as she was already right in front of him, most of her body covered by the clothes she held in her arms, "Come on." She used her head to gesture at the elevator, "I've got some ice cream and beer to celebrate. Tonight was a wonderful night."

He nodded at her and mused happily to himself. She grabbed him by the wrist and started to pull him across the room, he offered no resistance. They rode the elevator up, both beaming with joy, for very different reasons. As the doors opened, she let go of him and started to make her way up the stairs, "I'm going to get changed and then I'll be right back down to dish us up some celebratory dessert. Okay?"

"O-o-okay!" He nodded at her and slowly made his way to the living room couch.

Within minutes she was back down in the kitchen, wearing her soft pink pajama pants and an oversized crème t-shirt, "So A-D," she addressed him while she dished them up and pulled out a pair of cans, "Lady Love isn't that bad now is she? Think you could get in her again?"

"Y-y-yes..." He responded softly, "As l-long a-as you-you're there t-t-too!" He quickly added on.

"Well good news for you then." She smiled, "I'm the only one who can pilot her."

"I … I … understand t-t-that." He said softly.

She paused for a moment as he looked down in sorrow. The Scythe. He did understand being the only one that could pilot a mech.

She walked up to him and set down his bowl of ice cream and a can, "Wanna turn on the TV? We can see if there's anything worth watching." She went back to grab her own.

"Mhm!" He nodded at her and spent a few seconds finding the remote.

She plopped down next to him as the TV sparked to life. "We're here, live, outside the Spoke Embassy."

She froze in her seat. Destruction could be seen all across the city … The part that was supposed to be inhabited still.

"A rebel cell launched an attack earlier this night on the city itself. Hundreds are dead and thousands are injured as they got caught in the crossfire."

John. What the hell had he done?

A-D saw her fear and his eyes opened wide for a moment. Her eyes were so focused on the TV she didn't even realize he had slowly reached his arms out around her and pulled her against him, "I-i-it's … o-okay." He said, mimicking what she did to him.

For a fraction of a second she wanted to scream at him, but she instinctively leaned into him and sighed heavily. It felt

… nice. His arms were shaking and his hold on her was weak at best, he was scared as well. He was always scared, but he was trying to comfort her instead of the other way around.

"The Praetor is currently not taking questions, but we can personally assure you he is safe and sound. It appears that he was their primary target. Here's a clip of his only response to us so far after this attack."

The screen cut to a shot of the Praetor, "Right now we are focused on helping those who were injured in the attack and making the roads safe to travel on again." He said with a hint of stoicism, "Tomorrow I'll give a proper address about the whole circumstance. Just know, the insurgents have been dealt with, but the roads still may not be safe. Please call the corresponding departments for any injuries, damaged buildings, or other possible dangers. We are working overtime to bring peace back into this city."

The screen cut back to the reporter, "While details and numbers are unknown. It is confirmed that every rebel has been killed, and that some Angels were shot down as well." She paused for a second, "We will be continuing this report through the night giving you any updates as we get them."

"Shit…" Stephanie whispered to herself as she turned off the TV. She had forgotten. Today was the night John was planning on striking. She knew how it would end, but still she couldn't help but ask herself… What if?

"I-i-it's okay…" A-D repeated himself while trying his best to comfort her.

She sighed heavily and looked up at him, "Thanks, A-D. You know, you're not a bad guy." She let her head rest all its weight on him for a moment and closed her eyes sighing again, "We came up here to have a good night. To celebrate our success below. Come on." She pulled away from him and took a long drink from her beer.

He let her go and smiled at her, a sparkle of genuine joy in his eyes. "Y-y-yes!" He grabbed his bowl of ice cream. She watched him while they ate and drank. With every passing day she found it harder and harder to believe just who he was exactly.

Chapter 14: Consequences

Stephanie, Jeremiah, Teresa, and Collin met in the basement of the abandoned mall again. The praetor's press conference was going to be this evening during dinner. They met up just before it started to watch it together and catch up. The four of them, the four original members of their, her, rebel cell hadn't properly met up since the memorial for the Archangel of Death … who was currently living in her house.

"Well," Stephanie sighed as they all sat down, "Want me to start with some good news?"

"Sounds good to me." Jeremiah responded, "Got a feeling that the press conference is going to leave us feeling as defeated as Clyster's military one."

Collin smirked, "Oh come on, it can't be that bad."

"For once I agree with him." Teresa said, "Nothing can top the information he dropped right now I think."

"Anyways…" Jeremiah ignored them, "What's the good news, Steph?"

"I got Lady Love up and running again. Took her out for a spin last night." She told them.

"That fast?" Collin exclaimed, "That's at least a day ahead of schedule."

"She was working two nights ago actually. Better than ever before." Stephanie smiled, "But that's not even the good news."

"How quick did you do it?" Jeremiah quickly leaned in. She had all of their attention.

She eyed them over mischievously for a moment before responding, "2.476 seconds." She told them. All three of them recoiled back in awe, mouths a gape.

"No way!" Teresa shouted.

"That's impossible!" Jeremiah followed.

"That's got to be a world record." Collin shook his head in disbelief.

"2.4 something seconds?" Teresa asked her, "You serious?"

Stephanie laughed heartily, "That's still not even the good news."

"*What?*" Collin shouted.

"*How?*" Teresa nearly screamed, "What could be better than that?"

Jeremiah eyed her over for a bit and shook his head, "You didn't…" He barely whispered.

"Bet your ass I did." She leaned forward and they all went still, "Transformed. In motion. In 8.756 seconds." Their mouths all dropped to the floor. They were utterly speechless. "Not even a slight scratch on her." She said back and smiled proudly as she gawked at her.

"I-I mean." Jeremiah stuttered, "I always knew you could do it one day, but this soon … and that fast?" He shook his head, "Steph, you're insane."

"Amazing is more like it." Teresa chimed in. "I can only imagine the thrill of that moment. Wish I was there to see the look on your face."

"That would have been a sight to behold." Collin commented, "I call shotgun next time."

"*Hah!*" Stephanie nearly coughed on her laugh, "You'd go insane having not a single control in arm's reach."

"She's got you there." Jeremiah nudged him with his elbow.

"Worth it to witness something like that." Collin shot back.

"He's got you there." Teresa nudged Jeremiah with her elbow, and they all shared a laugh for a moment. "I can't believe it. So not only is Lady Love up and running earlier than we thought? You got a record-breaking transformation time? *And* you pulled off a transformation while in flight?"

"*Yup*." Stephanie chuckled at them all, "So at least last night wasn't all bad for us."

"Really had to kill the excitement with that, huh?' Collin asked her.

"You know me." She responded, "I try to keep things realistic."

"Yeah…" He mumbled to himself.

"John's really dead." Jeremiah stated, "It's hard to believe."

"That loose cannon had it coming." Teresa quickly responded, "He's caused so much trouble for all of the rebel cells in the area."

"He had the Knights to do so." Stephanie commented, "And he thought he was doing what was best. While I don't agree with his methods, his heart was in the right place, and we lost a good soldier … for nothing."

"We all saw the shots of the city." Collin spoke up, "They had cleared a path to the embassy. Think we could have made the difference…?" He asked the question on everyone's mind. They all remained silent and looked to Stephanie.

She took a deep breath in and sighed, "I don't know if we would have succeeded in destroying the embassy. Maybe we would have." She admitted, "But I do know something," She quickly added on. "We'd all be dead right now. And that victory would have been for naught." She paused for a moment, "I've considered all sorts of attack plans for that embassy. Destroying it would be a massive milestone for us, but there's no victory I can see that doesn't come at too great of a cost."

"We need to get the rebel cells to work together." Jeremiah said, "It's the only way we have a chance."

"Yeah, but none of the leaders are willing to give up their leadership." Teresa added, "Not without some massive feat from another leader. If we could destroy that embassy every single cell in the Maynor Estate would flock to us."

"But we can't destroy it unless we work together." Jeremiah grumbled, "Stuck between a rock and a hard place."

"And it's only going to get harder I imagine." Stephanie added on, "I'd bet this press conference will be a call to peace and unification. Alongside an announcement of new rules to help keep us under control."

"She's right." Collin said solemnly, "I'd bet my Knight that she's right on the money with it."

Teresa and Jeremiah glanced at each other for a second, "Sorry," Jeremiah said.

"No counter bets from us." Teresa finished for him.

Stephanie sighed deeply, "Anyways," she changed subjects, "it's been awhile. How are things going for all of you?"

"Same soup different spoon." Collin responded instantly in a monotone.

"Good!" Jeremiah piped up and smiled, "Teresa and I have been hanging out a lot. I mean, helps we live in the same apartment complex, but we've been having a lot of fun just hanging out."

"I swear to god Jeremiah, I will beat you in that racing game one day." Teresa glared at him.

"Not a chance." He responded with a chuckle.

"What about you, Steph?" Teresa asked her. "I know things have been a bit … stressful lately."

Stephanie glared at her for half a second before rolling her eyes, "I keep on keeping-" She stopped as her phone vibrated multiple times in a row.

She quickly pulled it out and her eyes went wide seeing the notification. Multiple texts from A-D all sent at once. With the last one reading, help

Her eyes snapped to Teresa as she stood up, "Speaking of stress…" They had a silent understanding, "I'll be right back."

"Got it." Teresa responded and Stephanie quickly walked away while opening her phone.

A-D: someone is here

A-D: they won't go away

A-D: calling for you

A-D: i am scared

A-D: help

She quickly shot a response to him.

Steph: One moment.

She opened up the app on her phone that connected to her cameras. On her front porch was a very well dressed man sitting on one of her chairs smoking a cigarette. Next to him was a box. A delivery. She wasn't expecting anything. And why was he waiting at the door and not just dropping it off?

She went to a separate room and closed the door behind her calling A-D. The first ring didn't even finish before he picked up, "H-h-h-help…" He whimpered.

"Shhh it's okay A-D. It's okay." She quickly told him, "I need you do to me a HUGE favor, but it's going to be a lot for you. Can you do it for me?" She could hear him hyperventilating over the phone, "Please? We can sit down and play some games all night long." She needed to know what this was about, and didn't have the time to rush home, even if she got one of her friends to drive her, "You can cuddle up to me all you want A-D. Please."

"O-o-o-okay…" He whispered, "I-I-I-I'll do it. I'll b-b-be st-strong."

"Good boy." She smiled to herself, "Are you wearing your hoodie?"

"Mhm." He responded.

"Good. Pull the hood up and over as far as you can." She told him. She heard the sound of clothing moving around and continued, "Make sure your hair is covering your eyes, but don't cover your mouth. Just look down at the ground instead. Okay?"

A few moments of silence before he responded, "O-o-okay…"

"Now. I need you to put me on speaker phone." She told him, "It's the little speaker button on the bottom left of the screen. Tell me when it's green."

A few more moments passed, "I-i-it's g-green…"

"Perfect." She comforted him, "You're doing wonderful."

"T-t-thank-nk y-you." He whimpered.

"Now, here's what I need you to do." She told him, "I need you to be strong for me and go to the front door … and open it."

"W-w—w-what?" He shouted.

"*Please.*" She begged him.

She could hear him take a few short, staggered breaths trying to calm himself down, "O-o-o-okay…"

"Once that door it open, I'll handle everything. Okay?" She told him, "I just need you to open the door and hold the phone by your chest. I'll be watching everything through my cameras."

"O-o-okay…" He responded again.

She put him on speaker as well and switched so she could watch her camera. She heard as A-D opened the door and watched the man quickly stand up putting out his cigarette with his fingers, "Greeti-" The man stopped short as he saw A-D, "Well you don't look like a Stephanie Maynard to me."

A-D put the phone near his chest and she quickly spoke up, "Hey there! Sorry, I'm not home right now." She had to think of a quick lie to explain A-D … and she hated that Teresa had the right idea, "And I apologize for my boyfriend. He's got some past trauma from when the Maynor Estate fell, and news of last night's attack sent him into an episode."

"Ah, no troubles there, Miss. The war's been hard on all of us." He politely responded, "I must apologize as well, but I can't leave until I've ensured this package has been delivered."

"What is it?" She asked him, "I haven't ordered anything."

He shrugged, "No idea, Miss." He responded, "All I know was that I was paid to stand out here all day and night if I had to. Special order request to ensure it reached your hands, but I think in your home would suffice." She paused for a moment. This was suspicious at best, but the longer that man stood in sight of A-D, the more likely he might make the connection. She needed to get him away, and fast. "No offence to the boyfriend here, but he looks a little ... meek, and this box has got some heft to it. If I can just set this inside your entryway, I'll be on my way."

"That works perfectly." She instantly responded, "Thank you, good Sir. And again, apologies for not being there."

"Oh, it's no problem to me, Miss." He said while picking up the box.

"It's okay." She told A-D, "You can move out of his way." A-D nodded and stepped to the side remaining silent. "I'm sorry, sweetheart. I'll be home soon. You know I had to go to this important work meeting."

"I-i-i-it's okay…" A-D barely whispered as the man set the box right on the inside of the entryway and stepped back outside.

"Hopefully that work meeting goes quick." He said to her, "Your poor boy is utterly terrified."

"Agreed." She responded, "My boss hasn't heard the half of what I have for him to hear about this."

The man laughed for a moment and bowed before A-D, "Well you have a fine day, Miss. And you as well, Sir."

"Thank you. May the rest of your day go smoother than this." She replied. The man then turned away, got in his vehicle and left. "You can close the door now, A-D. And relock it please." A-D almost instantly did them both and he let go of the breath he was holding and started hyperventilating again. "Shh … shh…" She tried her best to comfort him over the phone, "You did amazing, A-D. I'm proud of you."

He slowly collapsed onto the floor whimpering and shaking, "Hey, hey, hey…" She sighed to herself. She … she felt bad. And there was nothing she could do for him from here. Her eyes opened wide and she bit her cheek as she thought of something to calm him down. Scent was a powerful tool. "Hey, A-D. You like how I smell?"

"M-m-m-mhm-hm…" He barely managed to make the sound.

"As long as you promise not to touch anything besides my bed," She silently grumbled to herself, "You can go on up to my room and crawl into my bed. I'm sorry I'm not there right now, but that might help remind you of me."

"O-o-o…" He couldn't even form a word, but she could hear over the speaker phone as he slowly got up.

"I'm proud of you, A-D." She told him again, "I'm so proud. Okay? Remember that. Remember my voice. The touch of my hand on your head. I will be home as soon as possible, okay? I'll get one of my friends to give me a ride making it much quicker even."

"O-o-o-o-okay…" She could hear him walking up the stairs.

"Once you're in my bed and you close your eyes it should almost feel like I'm right there with you." She told him, "I promise. I'll come home. I'll come pick you up and bring you downstairs. Make some popcorn and we will just relax for the rest of the night together. I'm so sorry. I know yesterday and today has been a lot for you."

She heard him crawl into her bed and instantly a sigh of relief came from him, "Mmm…" He mused.

She smiled for a moment and then gritted her teeth. The Archangel of Death. Was in. Her bed.

And her gut reaction was … relief?

She quickly composed herself, "I … I need to get back to this meeting, A-D. Will you be okay? Can you promise me you will be okay?"

"Mhm…" He muttered as she heard the blankets wrap around him, "I-I-I-I'll … b-be okay-y."

She let out a heavy sigh of relief, "Thank you, A-D. Thank you. I'll be home before you know it. I promise." She finally hung up and rested her body weight on the wall next to her. This was too much. How long could she keep this up? She really did have to treat him like a boyfriend. A broken, hurt, and pathetic one, but a boyfriend, nonetheless.

She stayed out there in utter silence for another minute. Purging all her thoughts and just … accepting reality for what it was. She needed to pull herself back together before she went back. The last thing she needed was any of those three doubting her, and Teresa already knew too much for her liking. At least she could trust her. She felt bad about keeping anything from them, but Teresa and her had been through everything together. While it was a risk, and a never-ending aspect of stress knowing that she knew the truth… She was glad she had shared it.

She finally pushed herself off the wall and took a deep breath. The conference was starting soon. She needed to get back, and she was feeling as ready as she possibly could. She walked back through the door and headed over to the table her friends sat at, only to freeze as Jeremiah and Collin were glaring at her while Teresa shied away in her chair. "I'm so sorry,

Steph." She squeaked out, "I'm sorry but you know how they can be!"

Stephanie grumbled to herself and walked up to her chair, "What on earth did you tell them?"

"*You have a boyfriend?!*" Both Collin and Jeremiah shouted at once.

Stephanie flashed a glare at Teresa and growled to herself. The stress never ended. "One job." She said to Teresa, "You had *one* job!"

"I'm sorry!" She shouted refusing to make eye contact.

"Goddammit." Stephanie grumbled and sat down. She had to think of multiple lies … and fast. "We aren't actually dating." She quickly told them, "We just hang out a lot and happen to probably be interested in each other."

"That's not what Teresa said." Jeremiah quickly replied.

"Yes well, Teresa doesn't know how to keep her mouth shut." Stephanie again glared at her and mouthed "I will kill you," to her, "I thought girl talk was … I don't know. Supposed to stay between us *girls?*"

Teresa shrunk farther into her chair, "I didn't know what else to tell them!"

Stephanie sighed heavily. "You're dating someone who's not in our rebel group?" Collin asked her, "Teresa said we wouldn't know him. That he was new to town."

"No, I'm not." Stephanie quickly responded. Collin was going to be trouble about this, "But he's only not been officially introduced to the group. He's got a lot of trauma from the fall of the Maynor Estate. He's terrified of people, especially crowds, and might be the most skittish person I've ever met. Teresa can attest to that."

Both Jeremiah and Collin slowly turned their heads to Teresa, "You … *met* him?!" They shouted as one.

Stephanie smiled and winked as Teresa looked at her in terror, "I-um-I-uh…"

"Yes." Stephanie responded for her, "When she came over last, he was also over." Their heads snapped back to Stephanie, and then back to Teresa.

"Y-yes…" She admitted and caught Stephanie glaring at her. If looks could kill… "Yeah…" She admitted, "He was super shy and afraid of me." She finally spoke up a little, "But god, the two of you were so cute!"

Stephanie silently let a wave of relief wash over her. Teresa was finally playing along. She was a damn good friend, the best. "Look, maybe unofficially we are." She sighed, "But I was slowly going to get you two to meet him as well first before I went public."

"*When?*" Jeremiah shouted as the two of them snapped their heads back to her.

"And how long have you two been together?" Collin added in.

"I don't know when." She said exasperated, "You've no idea how hard and stressful it was to introduce him to Teresa. And we've been kind of dating for about a month now. Not even."

"Seriously." Teresa added on, "He refused to speak to me unless he was right by your side. And even then, it was full of stutters."

"Oh, that's just normal A-D." Stephanie chuckled.

"A what now?" Collin asked her.

"A-D." She clarified, "That's what he likes to be called. It's his initials."

"Huh." Jeremiah mused out loud, "That's kind of a cool idea actually."

"He's just used to it." She told them, "Feels more natural than his real name."

"And what is it?" Jeremiah asked her. It was obvious he had started to get excited for her. Excited for a lie.

She smirked at him, "Now that's a girlfriend secret."

"You're telling me!" Teresa shot forward in her chair, "I practically begged her for hours to tell me his real name!"

"Hey," Collin interrupted them looking at the TV, "The conference is about to start."

That silenced all conversation about A-D as Stephanie quickly turned up the TV just in time.

"And now we're headed to Praetor Gallenhall, with his address to the entire Maynor Estate." The reporter said right before the screen cut to the praetor standing behind a podium with a massive crowd in front of him.

"I think we call can agree, both Empire loyalists, and Kingdom sympathizers, that the destruction caused by last night's attack was..." he sighed, "Horrible. A confirmed 137 dead, 2259 injured, with 54 civilians still missing." The crowd was completely silent, "When fights against rebels happen out in the open field, only Angel and Knight pilots are injured, only those actually in the fight, but when they happen over a city like this..." He sighed and shook his head, "The ones who lose the most are the civilian's just trying to live their lives."

Stephanie and her friends were dead silent. They all hated to admit it, but he had a point.

"While we are all thankful to our Angel pilots who stopped the attack, now is not the time to honor them. Now is not the time to rub salt in the wound of the other rebels out there. I get it, I understand. Many of you, many even not partaking in this rebel activity, aren't fond of the Eternal Empire, and you have the right not to be.

"We came into this Estate, into this Kingdom, and conquered it." He continued, "Many of you have lost friends and family to the war, but that war is over now. You haven't even given the Eternal Empire a chance to show we can be gracious leaders. Now is the time for us to come together. To work towards and build a better future together."

He paused for a moment and sighed, "That's why I'm offering the first olive branch to you all. Any rebel who ceases all activity and lives a peaceful life under the Eternal Empire's rule will be cleared of all past crimes. Cease all rebel activity now, and you can live a peaceful live with us here." Gasps rose through the entire crowd.

Even Stephanie was taken aback. Such an offer was unheard of.

"I've been advised to implement very strict new rules on the whole of the Estate." The praetor continued, "But I have chosen to go against such advice and only update one new rule. For the safety of my citizens, I can't just sit back and do nothing, but I'm being exceptionally lenient as I want to give each and every one of you a chance at redemption. Curfew will now take effect at 8pm instead of 10pm and it will last until 6am instead of 4am. I feel as if this update will still give early morning and evening businesses the chance to survive, while securing our safety.

"If you are the owner of a business who thinks you will be negatively affected by this change of curfew, we are also offering aid to you." He added, "Please go to your city center and ask for a meeting to see if you qualify for aid in keeping your business afloat and your workers paid." He stopped and took a deep breath, "This is a tough time for all of us, but if we work together, we can achieve a better future. A better future for the Eternal Empire, but more importantly, a better future for the Maynor Estate." He bowed his head, "Thank you, I will now be taking questions."

Stephanie muted the broadcast and turned back to her three friends, "Well I guess we are halfway obliging him." She tried her best to sound lighthearted, "With an offer like that, assuming he's serious, we just lost half of the remaining cells in the area."

"Yeah…" Collin said quietly.

"There's no way he's serious right?" Teresa asked them.

"I think he might be." Jeremiah spoke up, "All he wants is the fighting to stop and for Empire control to be accepted. A deal like that furthers his goal."

"We stick to the plan." Stephanie addressed them formally, "We lay low for a while, let this blow over, and then we come back with a vengeance." A grim seriousness entered her voice, "Demanding blood for those we've lost. Demanding freedom for us, our country, our people. We aren't going to go about it the way John wanted to, but when we come back, we won't stop. Never again. We will not let them forget who we are."

"Now that's the Stephanie I know." Collin smiled at her.

"Damn right!" Teresa added on, "They won't see us coming!"

"While this is all good and dandy." Jeremaih spoke up with a worried tone, "Stephanie, don't you have a two hour walk home? It's six right now. And curfew is now in effect at eight."

"Shit." She cursed quietly to herself, "Think one of you can give me a ride?" She asked them, "I should probably get home soon anyways. A-D is having a rough day."

"I'll take you home." Collin responded before anyone else could.

"Thank you." She smiled at him before looking over at Teresa, "You share with Jeremiah the promise I'm working on something big as well?"

"Oh yeah." She responded instantly, "Hell, I told him before I told Collin even."

"Whatever it is you got cooking in that head of yours Steph," Jeremiah looked over at her, "You know I'm with you 100%."

"I know." She smiled at him, "Thank you." She turned off the TV.

"Well," Collin slowly stood up and looked over to her, "Guess we should get you home, eh?"

Stephanie sighed and stood up. "We all should get home." She told them. She could tell from the tone in Collin's voice. He was about to make this car ride a nightmare.

Chapter 15: An Old Flame

An awkward silence filled the car as Collin drove her home. The tension could be felt in the air. Stephanie nervously tapped her foot as she rode in his passenger seat. All she could do was pray that the silence would remain. Her hope was crushed about halfway home, "So…" Collin spoke up softly.

"Don't." She shook her head, "Just don't."

"Couldn't even tell your friends?" He asked her.

"I'm allowed to have a private life." She quickly responded.

"We don't even know the guy." Collin continued ignoring her.

"And?" She snapped at him, "You don't have to."

Collin took a deep breath, "So just uh … gonna ignore-"

"If you know what's best for you, you aren't gonna finish that sentence." She cut him off.

Collin ignored her, "What we once had?" He finished the question.

Stephanie shut her eyes and clenched her first, "You really wanna do this, Collin? Really?"

"Yeah!" He snapped to look at her, "I do. Because I actually care."

"About yourself, maybe." She sighed, "That was three years ago, Collin, and we weren't even together for two months."

"Happiest two months of my life." He shrugged, "But you know. Doesn't matter."

Her eyes snapped open and she flicked her head over to glare at him. "Oh yes of course. Happiest two months of your life because you were sleeping with me!" She shouted. He opened his mouth, but she cut him off, "*No!*" She yelled at him,

"You wanna hear it? You want to really do this? Then fine! I'll do this!" She slammed her fist on his dashboard, *"You took advantage of me!"* Her words turned into daggers.

"You saw a pretty girl who was in an insanely tough spot mentally and played your part perfectly to get what you wanted! You started by just caring and going above and beyond to try and comfort me, but what was it. A *week*? Not even I think!" Her voice kept raising louder, "And then you started to work your way into getting in my pants. Then affection towards me quickly became reluctant if you didn't think I was going to put out afterwards.

"You should be thankful I chose to still be your friend!" She continued, "Jeremiah and Teresa were ready to cut you out. I convinced them not to! I convinced them it would be fine!" She punched the dash again and sat back in her chair, "Happiest two months of your life? Grow the fuck up." She shook her head, "This is exactly why I didn't want to tell you. You haven't changed one bit."

"I…" Collin stuttered as the words cut into him deeply, "That was…"

"Brutally honest?" She finished for him.

"Not the words I would have used but…" He sighed, "Come on Steph…"

"Don't you 'come on' me." She hissed.

"I do care…" He whispered.

"Good." She snapped, "And I care about you, and Teresa, and Jeremiah, and Casey, and … the list goes on."

Silence filled the car for a few moments, "So … I'm supposed to believe you have a boyfriend and he isn't trying to get in your pants?"

"Mhm." She responded. "How many times do I have to say we aren't actually dating? Haven't even kissed. We're just kind of … together."

"I find that hard to believe…" He rolled his eyes.

"Find that hard to believe all you want." She smirked, "I really don't care."

"You've changed, Steph." He said quietly.

"You try leading a rebel cell for years on end while our Kingdom falls around us and tell me the stress doesn't get to you." She sighed heavily, "Then I'll hear your complaints about how I've changed."

Collin shifted uncomfortably in his seat and took her the rest of the way home in complete silence. As he pulled up in front of her house she spoke up, "Look, Collin. I'm sorry. I'm stretched thin as it is and I just don't have the patience to deal with this right now. Maybe I went a bit far, but god you can be so dense sometimes."

"It's fine." He responded in a low voice.

She looked over at him, "Thank you for the ride. Truly."

"Mhm." He muttered.

She sighed and shook her head. He was going to be in a bad mood for a while. She got out of the car and as she closed the door, she heard him getting out with her. "What are you doing?" She asked him.

"I'm going to go meet him." Collin eyed her over coldly.

"No. You're not." She narrowed her eyes.

He shook his head, "What? You gonna try and stop me?"

"Collin…"

"Don't you 'Collin' me." He hissed and took a step forward.

She quickly took a step in front of him and pulled out her phone, "This is my private property. If you refuse to leave, I'll be forced to call the cops."

His eyes narrowed, "You wouldn't."

She maintained a cool gaze on him, "Try me." She quietly hissed.

He grumbled while glaring at her, "I should have gone with, John." He finally hissed, "Then at least I could have died a meaningful death."

"And lived a meaningless life." She instantly retorted, "We all live with regrets, Collin, don't make that one of yours." She paused and shook her head, "And don't make sleeping with you one of mine."

Collin quickly got back in his car and slammed the door shut before speeding off. Stephanie shook her head and sighed, he was going to be a problem.

Chapter 16: Mysterious Package

Stephanie waited a few more seconds outside before entering her home and collapsing against the door. All she could think about was how Collin was mad over a complete lie, but he'd be even more livid if he knew the truth. He was bloodthirsty, but the best fighter she had, probably now one of *the* best left fighting for the Kingdom of Estates. His skills in the Knights jet form could use some work, but he could go toe-to-toe with any Angel pilot in their fighting stance and come out unscathed.

She hit her head against the wall lightly and chuckled away the tears that wanted to fall. How the hell was she going to explain the truth to him, to everyone? Most of them couldn't see the bigger picture. They only saw what was right in front of them and nothing more, but that's why they looked to her as their leader … but this was pushing their trust in her too far, and she knew it.

She sighed heavily and opened her eyes looking at the box that was right next to her. "And now this." She said softly to herself. "Just what I needed."

"S-S-S-S-Steph?" She heard the soft voice of A-D and quickly looked up to see him looking down at her from the top of the stairs. He was wrapped up in one of her soft blankets with it held over his nose.

She couldn't help but smile at him. He was … adorable. "Hey there, A-D." She responded while slowly getting off the ground, "Sorry, I just needed to destress a bit. I didn't mean to disturb you."

He shook his head at her, "Y-y-y-you're-re o-okay!" He silently walked down the stairs towards her, "Y-y-your p-plan worked-d." She couldn't see his face, but could tell he was smiling, "I-I-I f-feel much better n-now."

"I hoped it would." She walked over and ruffled his hair, "Only so much I can do to calm you down when I'm away."

"T-that's okay!" He rubbed his head against her, "I-I'll b-be okay. F-f-f-for you!"

She let out a sigh of relief, "Thank you, A-D. You've no idea how much that means to me right now." Any bit of respite was a welcome one. Even if it came from him. "Shall we see what's in this 'oh so special' box?"

"Mhm!" He nodded at her.

"Come on. I'll carry it to the living room." She nodded her head that way while picking it up and following him in. She set the hefty box down on the coffee table. "Can you grab me a water?" She asked him right before he sat down.

"O-o-of course!" He dropped the blanket on the couch and quickly went to the kitchen, grabbing her a glass of water.

She drank nearly half of it the moment he handed it to her. Setting it down she pulled out a knife and carefully cut the tape while he propped himself up on the couch on top of her blanket. "I don't know about you, but I wasn't expecting anything to be delivered."

He shook his head, "S-s-s-should I b-b-be worried…?" He asked her carefully.

She looked over at him and smirked giving a shrug, "Let's find out." She pulled back the straps. On the very top was a letter, but it was what was below that made her eyes go wide. It was a part for a mech. Looked like the base of a scanner module, but heavily modified like she had never seen before. She very carefully grabbed the note and sat next to A-D while reading it.

Greetings,

Enclosed is a special-made module for your Knight, Lady Love. It is a scanner/scrambler combination module that should keep you invisible to most of the Eternal Empire's sensors while picking up any of their frames using a scrambler as well... Theoretically. Hopefully.

Stay alive.

~ A Concerned Sympathizer

This was suspicious at best. Someone knew her name, her address, her Knight, meaning her involvement in the rebellion, and she knew nothing about who they were, but on the off chance this was real…

She quickly came up with a plan, "Hey A-D, I know I promised you a night of gaming or movies, but can I make you a different deal?"

He nodded at her.

"How about we spend tonight in the basement checking this thing out, and I'll let you keep that blanket until it doesn't remind you of me anymore? Sound good?"

"*Deal!*" He instantly shouted, eyes going wide for a moment before quickly retreating back into his timid self, "I-I-I-I mean…"

Stephanie laughed and ruffled his hair again, "Adorable. Come on, let's get this downstairs then, hm?" She picked the box up again and for once followed him as he picked up the blanket, wrapping himself in it again and walked to the elevator.

As soon as they got to the basement she quickly hooked the module up to a secure system that didn't connect to anything of importance in her house and ran a full diagnostic on it. Every piece of tech, every bit of code, anything and everything within this module was displayed before her eyes across all twelve of her monitors. It was … clean. It was real. There was no suspicious tech within it, no funny looking code. By everything she could tell … it was legit.

That raised even more questions than answers. Who was watching her? How did they know so much about her? How did they get their hands on this module, or did they make it, and if so … how? Why send this now? What did it all mean? She had no answers, but she wasn't about to look a gift horse in the mouth.

She pushed her chair away from the desk and turned to face A-D, "Well A-D." She smiled at him, "Looks like we've got some work to do tonight."

"I-I-I'll help!" He excitedly said.

She winked at him, "You know exactly what I like to hear."

Chapter 17: Signs of an Archangel

Stephanie was worried she had played her hand too far with A-D. Giving him a strip show, letting him have a blanket purely because she slept in it. She had been terrified he might start to … well, do what any other guy would do in his shoes, but instead what he did surprised her, and relieved her. Over the past two days A-D had become even more friendly and outgoing with her, being more willing to help, more excitable, more conversational … and not a single move she feared was made.

To her, it seemed like it didn't even cross his mind. It made some sense, as she had to teach him what a friend was, what *food* was, but still. Human instinct was human instinct. And she knew she was effectively grooming him to be her boyfriend. Not that that's what she wanted, but it was practically what she was doing.

She shook her head and gritted her teeth as she lay in bed, she was doing to him exactly the same thing Collin had done to her. Very different end goals in mind, but the method was the same. How long until she needed to do more to keep his attention? How long until he tried to ask for, or take, more? How would she respond when the time came?

She was in far too deep to back out now, not that she had anywhere to back out to if she wanted. If he was anyone else, *anyone* else … she might be okay with the idea. But he was the Archangel of Death. He was what they feared the most. He was death incarnate. Destruction. Desolation…

She chuckled as she imagined the scolding her brother would be giving her if he heard what she was doing. He was strong-willed, stubborn, hard-headed, but kind and caring. Soft when he needed to be. Willing to back down when the moment required, but he wasn't here now. She was. And she was alone.

She sighed and closed her eyes. Only time would tell what time would bring. In the meantime, a good night's rest would be hard to come by, but she had to try.

A sound. A-D heard a sound. He slowly crawled out of bed, Stephanie's blanket tightly wrapped around him. His whole body shook as fear gripped his heart tightly. He froze in an instant as he heard the sound again. Footsteps. Quiet, but they carried a weight far beyond the sound they gave off. He could tell they weren't Stephanie's. Hers were soft and comforting, warming, but these… They brought nothing … nothing but terror.

He slowly, silently, walked outside his room and looked down the open hallway towards the stairs. More footsteps. Multiple sets. Someone was coming up. He gripped her blanket tighter and took a deep breath. He could almost hear her voice in his head as her scent filled his nostrils, *"Stay strong for me, A-D…"*

He nodded to himself and managed to work up the courage to speak, even it *was* barely just a weak squeak, "H-h-h-h-hel-hel-lo-o?" He asked as the first figure stepped up onto his floor.

Instantly the figure turned to face him and pulled the trigger.

Bang! The gunshot made Stephanie jump out of bed.

"Not the target I repeat, not the target!"

She could hear yelling from a floor below her.

"Move! Move! Move!"

A-D! Her heart dropped for a moment. She quickly blinked and shook her head, pulling herself together. *No*, there were more important things than him right now. She grabbed her phone, unlocked it in an instant, and sent out the evacuation alert. Maximum level, immediate effect. If the Empire knew about her, she could only pray they came for her first.

She grabbed the pistol she kept loaded in the nightstand and quickly moved to the secret hatch on the other side of her bed. That level of evac alert would start wiping her hard drives and transferring anything she needed to keep to Lady Love's hard drive. Now she just needed to survive. She quickly slipped into the hidden passageways between her walls and closed the hatch behind her.

\ \

Jeremiah and Teresa sat in their Knights after a long day of working on them. They weren't like Stephanie, who knew these things inside and out, but they could do some basic maintenance, and both of theirs were more than overdue for that.

"Been awhile since I slept in one of these." Jeremiah commented as he sat on top of his Knight drinking a beer, "I am going to be *so* sore tomorrow."

"Tell me about it." Teresa scoffed, "I'm going to look like an utter mess. Didn't even get to clean up after working on her all day." Teresa sat on top of hers, which was right next to his, also drinking a beer.

"Hey," he smiled at her, "you're kinda hot after a long day of work." He winked at her.

"Oh, shut it." She rolled her eyes at him and failed at hiding a blush, "I can feel the sweat making my flight suit stick to me. I am going to be disgusting in the morning."

"I don't know about you, but I was planning on taking mine off after climbing in for sleep." He shrugged at her, "Not like you'd be able to see me unless you came crawling over here."

"Utterly shameless!" She laughed at him and took another drink, "But not a half bad idea." She looked over at him, "But if I even think I catch you trying to get a glimpse…" She left it unfinished and laughed.

"Oh, come on!" He laughed with her, "You know I'm *way* too polite for that."

"More like you don't have the balls." she continued laughing.

"Oh, you asked for it." He leaned back and glared, "Like I haven't caught you staring."

She instantly stopped and went completely flush.

"Yeah that's what I thought."

"You!" She pointed at him, "You shut your damn mouth ri-"

Both of them froze as their phones started blaring a loud alarm. They both went pale. They knew what that meant. They quickly checked to see how bad it was.

Emergency Evacuation. Ultimate Level.

They locked eyes for a moment before quickly diving into their Knights and turning them on.

"We need to help evacuate everyone else!" Teresa quickly shouted at him.

"Agreed!" He replied, "With curfew being so tightly enforced the police are all over the streets."

"There's four Angels in our city," She said, "With eight more maybe ten minutes away."

"At best. If we can get our other pilots into their Knights, we might be able to get a majority of people out safely."

"You'd better be praying Collin is near his." She added as their Knights fully came to life, hovering off of the ground, "We could really use him right now."

\ \

Collin was flying low to the ground in the open fields around their town. His eyes were narrowed, his blood boiling. He wouldn't – he couldn't – accept what Stephanie had said, even though he knew deep down there was some truth to it. What he needed right now to calm down, to think straight, was a good fight.

So why the hell were there no Angel patrols?

There were always some Angel's patrolling this area. Always on the lookout for rebel activity. But nothing. Nothing on his scanner, no far off lights he could spot. The night was completely … dead.

He instantly came to a stop as his phone started going off. The screen showed on his control panel.

Emergency Evacuation. Ultimate Level.

He slowly smiled to himself and chuckled while spinning around and speeding back home. This was perfect. A fight was to be had. And he already had a plan.

\ \

"She's not here!"

She heard the voice coming from up in her room. She had barely gotten out in time.

"Search the entire house!"

She heard six different sets of footsteps running out across her home. Her heart was racing. Panic but a mere moment away from taking over. She took a deep breath and quickly thought everything over.

Six men were in her home. They wanted her dead. She could hear the hum of Angels outside; they were ready to ensure she was gone at all costs. Cleanly or not. A-D was de- no, he wasn't dead. He was just…

She nearly started to hyperventilate. She couldn't let them get him. If they took A-D everything would be lost. She could theoretically escape on her own, the passages didn't lead all the way down into the basement with Lady Love, but they got right by the elevator. "Shit." She whispered to herself. She couldn't leave him, she couldn't. If they got the Archangel of Death back… Who was she kidding? She couldn't leave him because she didn't want to lose him. Because she actually cared about A-D.

Twelve bullets. One extra magazine of twelve more. Her .45 pistol. And there were six fully armed men in her house. This was suicide. She opened a hatch hidden in the kitchen wall and slowly peaked out. There was one thing she had over them. Home ground advantage.

She heard a set of footsteps coming from the living room and knew exactly where to aim. *Bang! Bang! Bang! Bang!* Four quick shots and she could barely see the body drop. Footsteps coming down the stairs, *Bang! Bang!* She heard the body stumble and fall.

She quickly dove behind a counter, and bullets flew past her head. More bullets flew aimlessly into the kitchen. Her heart felt like it was going to fly out of her chest. She was used to combat inside Lady Love. This was … a far more visceral feeling. She could hear a gun reload and held her gun up over the counter shooting aimlessly. *Bang! Bang! Bang! Bang! Bang! Bang!*

She heard a cry of pain followed by another body hitting the floor. She quickly dropped her empty magazine and loaded the new one as she heard the other three sets of footsteps reach the bottom floor. "We've got you cornered." The leader said as she saw three laser dots appear on the wall directly opposite of her, just barely above her head. "Your friend sold you out in exchange for a quick death. You rebels are all the same. Any last words?"

"S-S-S-Steph…?" She heard the meek voice of A-D.

A rain of bullets followed by A-D's scream pierced her ears. She dropped her gun and raised her hands to cover them. The remaining men also started to cry out in pain.

"*What the-*"

She slowly stood up and turned. She could see the blood pouring from A-D's body … staining the blanket she had given him. "A-A-A-A-D…" She barely managed to whimper as tears fell down her cheeks.

He slowly looked over to her, his whole body shaking as he cried in pain. "I-i-i-it … it … it h-h-hur-hur-hurts…" He whispered. The leader managed to gain his composure and saw Stephanie standing up straight. He quickly raised his rifle, "*Noo!*" A-D's scream pierced her very soul. She pressed her hands as hard as she could against her ears and watched in horror as the three men turned into a red mist.

A-D dropped down to the ground engulfed in tears.

"Infiltration team, report."

The call came over their radios. Stephanie fought to move, but was frozen in place. Both from the fear running through her veins, and finally seeing the Archangel of Death use his powers first-hand. Where there once was three men, now nothing but red puddles on the floor. No bodies left at all.

"Report!" The voice yelled at them.

"S-S-S-S-Steph…" A-D faintly called out.

She screamed gutturally and forced herself to move, shaking with every step. She quickly sprinted over to him and grabbed him as tightly as she could, "Oh A-D … A-D…" Her tears fell onto his face. "I'm here, A-D, I'm here."

He slowly reached his arms out around her and gripped her back tightly. She couldn't tell who was shaking more. Her or him. "I-I-I-I-I'm … sc-sc-sc-sc-scared…"

"Angel's. Prepare missiles."

"Wait!" Another voice called out.

She recognized it. Police Chief Hollander.

"I'm moments away with a whole swat team. Let us go in and do it cleanly!"

"No can do, Sir." The first voice responded. "Her death is far more important than how it gets done. Plus, we've got three Knight's coming in on our radar. All units, engage them as soon as we're done here."

"A-D…" She quickly pulled back and looked at him, "I … I…" She shook her head and focused. Their lives, no, just her life, was seconds away from ending. "There are Angels outside our house right now. I need you to do whatever you just did to those men to them."

His eyes went wide, "No! No-no-no-no-nonononono…"

"A-D *please*!" She begged him, "If you don't, we're both going to die!"

"I-I-I-I-I *can't!*" He screamed out, "It hurts! It hurts, it hurts-*it hurts!*" The crying took over.

"All Angels are locked on target." The voice came over again.

"A-D please, please, please…" She continued to beg him through the tears.

"Firing in five … four … three…"

"*Fuck!*" She screamed before grabbing A-D's face … and kissed him.

Instantly her hair rose in the air as she could feel the air about them sparkle with life. And then-

BO-BO-BOO-
BOO-BOO-
BOOM-
BOOM-
BOOM-
OOM-OOM-
OM-OM!!!!

The whole house shook violently as the twelve Angels surrounding it exploded at once. She slowly pulled her lips away from his and looked into his eyes … and for once, they were at peace.

"What in the God-Emperor's name...?" Chief Hollander's disbelief could be heard over the radio.

She stuttered as a smile slowly formed on her lips, "Y-y-yo-you … you did it!" She exclaimed and hugged him tightly, "*You did it, A-D!*"

He whimpered in her arms, but smiled.

She quickly caught her breath and started thinking straight again, "Okay. Okay, okay-okay… We need to go. Now! Okay? Okay!" Her heart was beating faster than she thought possible.

He nodded his head at her as she stood and pulled him onto his feet. He had let go of the blanket that was now completely stained with his blood, and she could see the holes in his clothes where he had been shot … but the wounds were … gone.

She blinked a few times and hugged him again tightly for a few seconds. He had just saved her life, twice. She didn't have the time to comfort him though. She had to pray he was in good enough shape and could pull it together well enough seeing her this panicked, to get inside Lady Love. She grabbed him by the wrist and quickly dragged him down into the basement where Lady Love should already be running.

Chapter 18: Civilized Men

"That can't be..." Jeremiah stared in awe at his sensor as they neared the city. Twelve Angels were all gathered in one area. *Twelve.*

"That's..." Teresa gasped, "That's every single one nearby."

"They're all in the northern edge of the city-" Jeremiah stopped short.

"*Steph.*" Both of them said at once, their eyes going wide.

"Hey, Teresa..." Jeremiah said calmly, quietly, solemnly over the radio, "Before we go to die..."

"Don't." She begged of him, "You wanna tell me something like that? It better be face to face."

Jeremiah sighed, "Fine ... it's been a pleasure."

Teresa sighed as well, "Same..."

They could see explosions off in the distance and suddenly all twelve Angels disappeared from their radar. They stopped in their tracks, "*What the hell?!*" Jeremiah shouted, "They're ... they're ... gone!"

"Oh ... my ... god..." Teresa stared in awe as the smoke rose in the distance. There was only one thing that could do that, "She did it..."

"*Did what?!*" Jeremiah shouted at her.

"She... Her plan." Teresa could barely believe her eyes, the words coming out of her mouth, "It worked."

"What plan?!" Jeremiah shouted at her.

"This is Collin," His voice came in over the secured open channel, "What the hell just happened?"

"Steph..." Teresa took a deep breath and refocused, "Steph just destroyed all twelve Angels. Takes about thirty minutes to get here from Spoke, but they might have some patrols closer. We've probably got about twenty of air dominance."

"*How?*" Collin shouted.

Teresa shook her head, "No time for questions we don't have the answers to. Police are out in force and our people are running."

"We have total air superiority if they have no Angels." Jeremiah added on, "We can save everyone."

"Let's split up!" Teresa said, "Cover more ground!"

"I've got a plan." Collin told them, "Need one of you to find Chief Hollander. Think we can end this without bloodshed."

"On it." Jeremiah nodded at him and took off, "Teresa?"

"I'll start … encouraging them to back off our people." She chuckled.

"We may yet live the night…" Jeremiah mused to himself as he quickly started searching the city for the chief. He had to have been out on a night like this.

\ \

"*Get out of the car!*" The police officer screamed at Casey, Thompson, and the two others that were in her car. Five other cops quickly jumped out of their cars and pointed their rifles at her and the group. She looked over at Thompson and grabbed his hand tightly, "So, this is it eh?" She asked him.

His knuckles turned white as they gripped the pistol he held in his lap, "Not without a fight." He shook his head, "Not without a fight." He repeated.

A mech frame came into sight and lowered itself behind the cops. Casey quickly placed her hand over his gun and held it down, "Wait."

"Finally, some backup." The police officer said in an annoyed tone.

"I suggest you let them go," Teresa's voice came over the speakers on the outside of her Knight, and she raised her gun to the officer's head, its barrel as wide as his head. He very, *very*, slowly turned around and went pale as the sight of a Knight Mk.2 was right in front of him. Teresa cocked her head to the side, "Now."

His whole body was trembling in fear as he slowly dropped his gun to the ground, "I-I-I uh … t-think there's uh … been a misunderstanding…"

"Mhm…" Teresa mused.

"That's my girl." Casey smiled as everyone in her car relaxed.

"Now, you've got two options…" Teresa pushed her gun forward slightly.

The cop leaned back and raised his hands, "I-I-I, uh, think, uh…" He looked around at his comrades who were all frozen in fear, "Think our uh s-shift just ended. Right, boys?"

"Y-y-yeah!" One of them shouted.

"Oh man lost track of time!" Another added on.

"O-o-our apologies, Miss!" A third one commented.

The officer took a step back from her, "We'll, uh … uh be on our way, Miss."

Teresa nodded her head to the side and flicked her gun, "Well, go on then."

They all broke off in a sprint away from her. She quickly flew up to the car, "Y'all okay?"

"We are now." Casey shouted at her, "It's like this everywhere in the town! I've no idea why there's no Angels, but you need to help others! We'll be good from here."

Teresa nodded at her, "Thank Steph for the lack of Angels. Stay safe." She didn't wait for a response before flying off to the next group of friends she saw.

Jeremiah flew across the town. It was going to be a nightmare to find Chief Hollander in this mess. Below him he could see patrol after patrol of police roaming the night. Stopping anyone and everyone they ran across. Even with their air superiority, they needed to broker a deal to let everyone go. Otherwise, it'd take long enough for backup to arrive from Spoke … or they would have to kill a lot of people.

He quickly spun to the side as he saw Hollander's sports car speeding down the road in the distance. He was headed for Stephanie's house. He was in the middle of two swat vans. "Got eyes on the Chief." Jeremiah announced over their radio connection.

"Perfect timing." Collin responded, "Tell him that he should be answering his phone for me, would you?"

"Got it." Jeremiah quickly landed in front of them and the cars all came to a screeching halt.

As the fully armed men jumped out of the vehicle and took aim a voice stopped them just short, "*Halt*!" Hollander shouted as loudly as he could as he got out of his car. Not that their small arms fire would have done anything more than scratch his Knight.

Hollander slowly approached Jeremiah, "You want me?" He challenged him, "Here I am."

"Actually," Jeremiah replied. "I've been told you should answer your phone."

"How in the hells…?" Chief Hollander grumbled to himself as he sped down the roads to Stephanie's home. Twelve Angels … just gone. In an instant. As if an Eternal Empire Military operation within his town wasn't stressful enough, they had done so without notifying him, and now twelve Angels had just been destroyed. He had his suspicions about Stephanie, but for the EEM to retaliate in such an extreme manner was overkill to him … and now their operation had gone haywire and he was left to clean up the mess.

"Sir," one of his escorts came in over the radio, "Knight approaching. Head on."

"I can see it." He grumbled, "Full stop." He slammed on the brakes and his sports car came to a screeching halt, with the two armored vans coming to a stop around him. Before the escorts had even come to a full stop the men inside jumped out and pointed their rifles at the Knight. Hollander rolled his eyes and sighed, "Idiots…" Those wouldn't do anything except annoy the pilot.

He quickly got out of his car, "*Halt!*" He shouted as loudly as he could while holding his hands up. He turned to face the Knight as it came to a stop in front of them. It was a Mk.2. Had to belong to one of the rebels' best pilots. He took one final deep breath and slowly approached it, "You want me?" He challenged the Knight, "Here I am."

"Actually," A voice he recognized spoke from within the Knight, one of Stephanie's friends, Jeremiah, "I've been told you should answer your phone."

Hollander froze for a moment, and quickly pulled his phone out, picking up the call from his wife, of which he had already missed five, "Darling?" He asked her.

"S-s-s-sweetheart?" His wife responded in tears, "Y-y-you need to stand down."

"W-what-"

"You should listen to her." Another voice spoke to him from across the phone, another one he recognized, another one of Stephanie's friends. Collin.

"You bastard!" Hollander yelled.

"Honestly, to me your family was just a way to get your attention." Collin chuckled, "Let's talk."

"What do you want?" Hollander responded coldly.

"We've got three Knight Mk.2's in the air right now, with more on the way as we speak." Collin explained, "You've got nothing. Let our people go peacefully, or we'll kill every, last, one of you."

"You're insane."

Hollander heard the Knight on the other side of the phone move slightly and his wife whimpered in fear, "You're in no place to negotiate. So, I ask you one last time. Shall we handle this like civilized men, who go their separate ways, or shall we continue this cycle of bloodshed? Because if I find out that a single one of my friends has been taken, I will burn this whole fucking city to the ground right now."

"Shit!" Hollander shouted over the phone, "Shit…" As if the night couldn't get worse. He grabbed his radio and made a call over it, "All units. Stand down. I repeat, all units stand down."

"Sir?"

"What?"

"We've got them!"

"Those lights you see in the sky aren't Angels. They're Knights." He told them, "They've got this whole town held hostage right now, and if we don't let them leave, they've promised to burn it to the ground."

"Shit."

"You've got to me kidding me?"

"No Angels?"

"Stand. Down." He repeated, "That's a direct order."

"Understood."

"Yes, Sir."

"As you command."

"Do we let any go that we've already arrested?"

"Yes." He responded instantly, "Let them all go. Don't follow, don't attempt to track them or slow them down. Everyone's life in this city depends on it."

"God-Emperor dammit!"

"Happy?" Hollander hissed over the phone.

"Only if you're good on your word." Collin told him, "I've known where you lived for years, but waited to do anything until now. Remember that."

"You going to let my family go?" Hollander asked him.

"Civilized men." Collin responded, "Have a good night." The sound of a Knight flying away could be heard.

Chapter 19: Lady Love

Either A-D was still in a trance from the kiss, or he understood the severity of their situation. She was easily able to get him downstairs and into Lady Love with minimal commands. She didn't have time to change, but she was not about to leave her flight suit behind as she gave it to A-D to hold in his seat. She lifted her Knight off the ground and turned it back towards her technical setup.

"It's been fun." She mused softly to herself as she pulled the trigger and blew everything to bits. Any information she needed was now stored within Lady Love, and she couldn't risk the Empire getting any of it. She needed to move, and fast. She quickly switched to jet configuration and took off into the tunnels.

Turning on her radio she called out, "Anyone there?"

"Steph!" Teresa shouted back instantly.

"You're alive!" Jeremiah added.

"Thank god." Stephanie let out a sigh of relief, "How is it up there?"

"I just brokered a deal with Chief Hollander." Collin responded, "He's letting us go."

"Good work, Collin." She smiled. This was the Collin she could rely on.

"We've split up." Jeremiah told her, "Each heading to a different evac point."

"Good." Stephanie responded, "Wait until everyone is accounted for before you move out from there."

"Understood." Teresa responded.

"What the hell happened?" Collin asked her.

Stephanie shook her head, "John." She said, "They got my info out from him."

"No..." Jeremiah softly said.

"How do you know that?" Collin asked.

"They told me." She replied.

"How the hell are you still alive then?" Collin responded.

"I…"

"A-D." Teresa responded for her, "He saved you, didn't he?"

"Yes…" Stephanie said softly, "He did."

"Your plan…?" Teresa carefully asked.

"He's with me right now in Lady Love." Stephanie ignored the question. "We're currently underground."

"Where you headed?" Jeremiah asked her.

"You all just keep heading towards the evac zones." She told them.

"Steph…?" Teresa cautiously questioned her.

"I've got a plan. I'll meet you all at the bunker." She told them, "Going radio silent. Stay safe." She quickly turned off her radio and pushed Lady Love as fast as she could through the tight tunnels.

She knew that every single Angels was going to be headed towards here. While her people should have the time to get on their way to the bunker safely, she needed to make sure the Empire wasn't going to be tracking them immediately. Spoke was going to be left nearly undefended. And these tunnels connected there. Now was her best chance. She could use this commotion to her advantage. They'd never be expecting an attack there now.

She flew as fast as she could, faster than she should. She had to shut off the proximity sensor once again as every corner would set it off as she came within inches of the walls. The fear had turned into adrenaline that pumped through her veins. She reacted to every single twist and turn instantly. On sharp corners she gritted her teeth as she pushed through them, barely slowing down, and jolted in her seat as Lady Love lightly scraped against the walls.

Time was of the essence. Every second wasted increased their chances of being found. The Angels could fly in a direct line to their town. They would arrive before her no matter what she did. She needed to draw their attention away from it as soon as she could. She pressed Lady Love forward even faster as she weaved her way towards Spoke.

\ \

Hollander stood as tall and proud as he could as the lead Angel slowly lowered itself in front of him. He knew he had been defeated, that the Empire would not approve, but in his mind, the citizens' safety came before everything else.

"What the hell are you doing?" The female pilot of the second generation Angel snapped at him as she landed.

"Saving lives." He responded, "They held this entire city hostage in exchange for the handful of them to escape. I made the call."

"*You let them go?*" She screamed at him.

"And now the city stands." He said with a grim determination, "We had no Angels and they had multiple Knights. They could have burned this city to the ground if they wanted to, but they said if we stood down, they'd leave us alone. And they did."

"Did you follow them?" She glared at him.

"No." He glared back, "I wasn't about to risk all of our lives on some small rebel cell."

"*Idiot!*" She shouted, "You should have let them level this whole town!"

"It is my job to protect the people of this town." He told her, "Not wage war."

\ \

Stephanie didn't want to think of how scratched up and dented Lady Love's paint job was. With every passing minute she pushed forward, faster and faster. Cutting the corners closer and closer, scraping the sides more and more, but she had made it. She slowed to a stop, "A-D," She quickly spoke up for the first time, "Hold on tight. It's about to get even more bumpy."

She had the entire map of the tunnels in the Maynor Estate in Lady Love's navigational data. She was in the center of Spoke, and directly above her the tunnels came dangerously close to the surface … dangerously close to the embassy.

She took a deep breath and focused herself. It was now or never. She snapped her engines to full power and shot upwards. Spinning, she launched the six missiles she could in jet form while firing an endless barrage of bullets. It was as she hoped, that was just enough to make a hole to the surface above. She blew past the rubble as it crashed off Lady Love and shot up into the night sky.

It was now … or *never.*

As soon as she entered the air above her hands flew across the control panel as she started to change stance. Nine seconds … nine seconds… She knew her momentum from going full speed would keep her going for a bit. As Lady Love changed form, she simultaneously started manually locking her missile's on to the embassy no more than four blocks away. Sweat dripped down her brow as she finally got the notification that Lady Love had finished transforming. Right as her it reached the apex of its rise she got the lock on, and fired the remaining forty-two missiles in her silos.

The moment they all left Lady Love the momentum she had faded away and she started to fall back to the ground. Wasting no time she got to work switching back into jet mode. She wouldn't fit in the hole she made in fighter form, and she needed to get out of here now as her sensor showed dozens of Angels taking to the sky through the city.

She didn't have the time to look as she heard the explosions from her missiles ring out through the night sky. Her hands kept moving in a blur as she neared the ground. At the last moment possible she got the notification her transformation was complete, and her engines kicked in once again as Lady Love scrapped against the side of the hole she had blown.

She pulled up as hard as she could and put the thrusters to full power as she flew down into the tunnels below. She wasn't out of it yet; she still needed to stop the drop. Lady Love quickly flicked to a horizontal position and she hit the engines to full power. She was thrown about in her seat as they bounced off the ground, sparks flying all about them. A-D screamed in fear as she continued to grind across the ground for a few more moments before getting back into the air.

Half of her screens were flashing red warning messages, multiple systems were down, structural integrity was barely holding, engines were now at half capacity … but they had lived. And she had just performed a double transformation while in motion.

As she finally gained semi-control of Lady Love, she glanced down at A-D. He was completely stained with blood, "You okay A-D?" She shouted at him. He whimpered in fear, his knuckles white around her flight suit. He was okay … enough. She nodded at him and took off back towards her private entrance into the bunker.

The Angel rose its gun towards Hollander, "Rebels let town stand as they flee for their lives…" She hissed at him, "*That only incites sympathy!*" She screamed at him.

"*What?*" He snapped at her, "You'd really rather have this whole city be destroyed?"

"We'd have war." She chuckled at him, "That's all we ever-" She stopped mid-sentence. An awkward silence filled the air. Suddenly she started to shift back into jet form, "Remove this traitor from command and lock him up!" She ordered everyone else around him, "The Praetor will deal with him."

Hollander shook his head and turned around, holding his hands up to his fellow cops, "So, this is how it is, hm?"

"Sorry, boss." His second-in-command walked up, "We'll do what we can for you."

"Don't." He shook his head, "Save yourselves." They locked eyes, both filled with sorrow, "Keep my family safe, would you?"

"On my life, Sir." He responded while putting Hollander in cuffs.

As soon as the Angel was done transforming it took off, alongside the dozens of others in the night sky above them.

Chapter 20: Last Resort

None of them knew what to expect at the evac points. But a small computer gave them directions. A hidden door opened to an underground tram. They had waited until everyone was accounted for and either on board or in their Knights nearby, while Collin. Teresa, and Jeremiah stayed in constant communication. With everyone inside they gave the go signal and followed the trams deep into the underground tunnels.

Tunnel after tunnel, corner after corner after corner. The three of them knew these tunnels well, but even they were getting lost. As the tram went down the track, the parts behind them started to fall apart. This was a one-way trip. Finally, they each arrived at hidden steel doors that opened and let everyone inside before closing behind them, and not long after that the three tracks finally met up.

"Any idea where the hell we are?" Jeremiah asked over the open radio comms.

"Nope." Teresa responded, "Never been this deep in the tunnels."

"Same." Collin responded, "And you're telling me Stephanie was keeping this secret from us this whole time?"

"Guess so." Jeremiah responded, "She really does have a lot of tricks up her sleeve." They all stared in awe as a gigantic cavern opened up before them. In the center a massive concrete bunker dominated the scene. Even still, the cavern was so large a formation of six Knights could fly around the smallest of the corridors with ease. Three large open docks reached out from the compound, and the three trams were headed all to the nearest one.

"She once mentioned to me a last resort." Teresa flew up ahead and landed, "I'm guessing this is it."

"This is insane..." Jeremiah stated in awe as he landed next to her. "How in the world was this built?"

"Her parent's ran a whole underground smuggling operation." Collin reminded them, "I'm sure this once belonged to them."

Jeremiah tried repeatedly to ping Stephanie's personal radio, "Steph, come in. Steph!" He shouted.

"She said she was going radio silent." Teresa responded, "We won't be hearing from her until she decides." Teresa climbed out of her Knight as the trams docked and quickly got to work getting everyone out, making sure they were all safe.

Jeremiah and Collin also jumped out of their Knights. Jeremiah got to work helping Teresa as Collin walked up to the large TV screen in the room and hit the power button.

"It ... it appears the Spoke Embassy has been utterly destroyed..." The sound of the TV filled the whole hanger, and everyone immediately turned to look at it.

A live feed of smoke rising from where the embassy once was filled the screen, "We're still trying to put together what just happened," the reporter continued, "but in the mean-" He stopped, "Wait. I'm getting word we've got footage of the attack. Viewer discretion is heavily advised."

The scene snapped to a shot from earlier recorded on a phone. Someone was recording a friend on top of a building doing flips that happened to be facing the embassy. Multiple explosions clip the audio repeatedly as rubble goes flying into the air from the ground behind them. "What the- *get down!*" The man in the video drops to the ground, but the video quickly zooms in on a Knight, painted in crème and pink soaring into the night sky. In seconds it changes form, launches a whole barrage of missiles, and changes back while diving back underground. In an instant the entire embassy explodes as the missiles collide with it and finally the video cuts to the ground as the person holding it drops to the ground.

Everyone's mouth dropped as they watched the video. "No way…" Jeremiah said out loud.

"Impossible." Someone else stated.

"*That's…!*" Another person shouted in awe.

"Stephanie!" Teresa shouted at the top of her lungs and jumped, "That's my girl!"

Cheers erupted from everyone.

"Did…" The reported stared in awe, "Did that Knight just … transform in flight?"

"Sure looks like it." The anchor responded.

"How?" His mouth dropped.

"Perfect timing!" The anchor smiled, "We've got our specialist calling in from home right now. Put him on."

"Hey there, Delilah." He quickly greeted the anchor, "Kevin here. I … I…" He caught his breath as the excitement could be heard in his voice, "I mean I've just now seen that footage like the rest of you, but that right there? I believe that to be a prototype two pilot Knight that the Kingdom of Estates cancelled."

"A two pilot frame?" Delilah asked him in shock, "Is that even possible?"

"Apparently so." Kevin responded, "It's the only mech frame I know of that was meant to transform while in motion. Looks like the rebels got their hands on one and figured it out."

"Is there anything else you can tell us about it?" She asked him.

He let out a heavy sigh, "I mean, the video is pretty blurry, but the color scheme matches a well-known rebel Knight in the area. Although we had no idea it was one of these prototypes."

"Really?" She asked excitedly, "Whose?"

"No one knows the pilot's … or two pilots' names," He corrected himself, "But it goes by the name of Lady Love. I'm afraid I don't have much more until I can analyze this footage."

"Well, thank for your input." She quickly responded, "Alex," She addressed the reporter on the scene again, "Do we have any word as to why all of the Angels quickly left the area only half an hour before this attack?"

"Actually, we do!" He quickly responded, "We've yet to get someone on scene out there, but it appears there was an attack in one of the outlying towns that left twelve Angel's destroyed. Now I don't have any connections into the military, but I'd be imagining that attack was just a diversion for this surgical strike."

"This is..." The anchor shook her head, "This kind of coordination is unlike anything we've seen in ages out here. What does..." She stopped, "Wait ... wait. We're getting in reports..." Her face went pale, "Oh my God-Emperor..." She whispered, "It..." She took a deep breath, "We've got confirmation that Praetor Gallenhall was in fact ... inside the embassy at the time of attack. Teams are currently searching through the rubble to find him."

Alex shook his head, "And right after he gave a call to peace. An olive branch, promising to forgive any past transgressions..." The anchor was silent as she raised her hands to her face in horror, "I think it's quite clear the rebels have given their response." The on-site reporter quickly took over, "They don't want peace. They don't care about saving lives. All they want is bloodshed and war." He shook his head, "With this attack they can kiss any chance at living a life out of prison away. The Eternal Empire will not stand for such an assault."

Everyone stopped watching the TV as the sound of a Knight slowly approached. Just from the sound alone everyone could tell it was heavily damaged. They all turned to face the entrance to the bunker and shouted in joy as Lady Love slowly flew in. "Hey there." Stephanie announced over her speakers with a smirk, "Sorry, transmitter got damaged on my escape."

Lady Love was constantly spitting out sparks as it hovered above them. It was barely still functioning. No one below seemed to care in the slightest as they all cheered at her, "I've got myself a private dock in front of my suite." She told them while slowly hovering to a door that opened above her, "I'll be back down in a minute."

"We'll be impatiently waiting!" Teresa shouted back at her over all the cheering.

"Oh," Stephanie stopped before continuing up, "One last thing. Whole ground's about to be shaking a bit. Don't you worry, just properly placed explosions to hide our tracks." She then continued up into the small passageway, the door closing behind her.

Stephanie landed Lady Love while it was still in its jet form, she wasn't convinced it could even transform back right now. She'd have to hook it up and run a full diagnostic on her. Sending out the ultimate evacuation alert had some unforeseen side effects. A ton of information was added to her mech about the bunker and displayed the moment she passed through the door towards it.

She confirmed to the computer that everyone was inside, that the evacuation was complete, and almost instantly the whole ground started to shake. Her parents had set this up decades ago, and yet it was perfect. The tunnels they had taken to get here were all collapsed, multiple false tunnels were destroyed as well, and this bunker was deep enough in the ground to be obscured from even the strongest sensors. The Eternal Empire would have to spend a year alone just searching for this place now.

Information about her private suite and dock were also given to her, alongside so much else she didn't have the time to look at. She had two priorities right now: addressing her people … and that required her to get A-D settled in, and fast. As the cockpit opened she quickly jumped up on the side and turned to face him. He was frozen in fear, well, aside from his shaking and shivering. He was utterly terrified.

She quickly unlatched the straps holding him in place and hugged him tightly, "It's okay, A-D. it's okay…" She tried her best to reassure him, but even she could tell it was unconvincing at best, "I'm sorry, I didn't want any of this to happen." Those words were the utter truth.

She took a deep breath and placed her forehead on his, closing her eyes, "You … you saved my life. Twice." She told him, "I won't forget that. Ever."

He whimpered in her arms and slowly grabbed onto her,

"Can you hold on tight to me?"

He only whimpered again and grabbed her tightly.

She slowly pulled him out of his seat "Come on…" She whispered softly while jumping down to the ground.

Her suite was even better set up than her basement. There was a full Knight diagnostic system, another twelve screens, docking locks, repair tools, even some spare parts in the far corner of the dock. It led directly into her room which was fully furnished. Nothing was nearly as fancy as in her mansion, but it would make do. She set him down on the couch and laid down next to him. "You … you, okay?" She carefully asked.

He shook his head and latched onto her arm, "N-n-n-n-n-no." He squeaked, "S-s-s-so m-much b-b-blood. Th-th-th-the v-v-voices!" He started to cry and convulse. "M-m-m-m-monster! A-a-ab-ab-abom-abomination! *That's all I am!*" He screamed out in horror.

"Shh, shh…" She placed her head against the back of his, "No … no…" She told him, "You just saved my life, A-D. You are the only reason I'm still alive. And that's good, isn't it?"

"Y-y-y-y-yes…" He barely could speak, "D-d-d-death." He said, "Th-th-th-that's al-all I br-bring. Death … death … death … death-death-death-deathdeathdeath." He repeated, over and over and over.

She sighed heavily and sat up, "Look at me, A-D." He shook his head violently and whimpered. "Look. At. Me." She said in a more commanding manner, slowly turning him over to face her. He finally turned over, and locked eyes with her. They were shaking again. His eyes. It was just like when she first found him.

She used the back of her hand to wipe away some of the tears and leaned towards him, "I'm not going to leave you." She told him, "I'm not scared. I'm not angry. I'm not…" She sighed again, "I'm sorry. I didn't … I didn't mean to boss you around so much. I just … I just want you to be okay." She placed her lips on his forehead and kept them there until his shaking started to slow down.

"O … O-okay…" He finally whimpered at her.

She took a deep breath and sat back, "It doesn't get better, yet." She told him, "And unless you want to meet fifty some new people, I need to go for a bit."

"*No!*" He shouted and grabbed her arm.

"A-D…" She said softly, "Have I ever not come back?"

"N-n-n-no…"

"I'll come back. I promise." She told him, "And I'll spend the rest of the night right next to you, okay?"

"I-I-I … I d-d-don't want y-you t-to go." He pleaded with her.

"I honestly don't want to either," she smirked as she confided in him, "but I have to. I've got a lot of other people relying on me right now, and I need to show them that we are safe." He slowly released his grip and she stood up, "A-D?"

He looked over at her, "Y-y-yes?"

"Thank you…" The words were honest as they left her mouth, "You saved me. Never forget that." She slowly walked away, making sure he remained … as calm as she could get him right now, and left the room.

Chapter 21: The Enemy of My Enemy

As the door into the hanger bay opened, Stephanie could hear the chants start immediately, "STE-PHA-NIE! STE-PHA-NIE! STE-PHA-NIE!" Everyone pumped their fists into the air as they shouted in joy. She smiled and raised her hands waving at them all. It had been ages since they were all this excited. A reminder, that even in the darkest part of life, there was a light to be found.

"I live!" She laughed at them all and finally got them to start calming down, "We all live. Thank god…" she took a deep breath. "So, how's it looking out there? I honestly don't even know if I hit the embassy."

"*What?*" Teresa shouted, "How the hell do you not even know when you fired the missiles?"

Stephanie laughed again, "I was a bit busy trying to transform back in time to not crush myself into the ground. Or the tunnels I came out of," she chuckled. "Cut it a *little* bit close. You all saw how Lady Love looked."

"It's gone." Jeremiah told her, "Report is the Praetor was in it as well." He shook his head, "You just accomplished what John's whole team died trying to do. And you did it *solo*."

She shrugged and smiled at them, "Don't ask me how. No idea how I'm standing here right now. I should be dead thrice over."

"But you aren't." Collin walked up to the front of the crowd and smiled at her, "That's the Steph *I* know, right there."

She sighed and gave him a nod of respect, he was back on her page … for now at least, "Well, guess you all want to uh, know what the hell just happened?"

"You got that right!" Teresa snapped at her.

Stephanie leaned up against the wall, "John sold me out."

Gasps filled the air.

"They must have captured him and tortured it out of him. I woke up to an infiltration team already in my home."

"Oh my god…" Murmurs stirred throughout the crowd.

"I'll get back to how I survived that," she looked over at Teresa, "but once I was in Lady Love I knew that every Angel in Spoke was going to be headed our way. Leaving it utterly defenseless. Honestly, I went there because I wanted to make sure you all had the time you needed to escape here, destroying the embassy is just a lucky plus."

"Where … exactly … is here?" Jeremiah asked her.

She took a deep breath, "Look, I know some of you at least question my parents' loyalty, but this is proof they were loyal until the end." She pushed herself off the wall and walked towards them a bit, "They made this. For me. For us. Was meant to be saved as a last resort to keep us safe. I'll be the first to admit, I don't all know what's in here. All I know is that it was built to be not just a safe haven, a bastion, but a whole center of command for the rebellion."

Everyone glanced around the room at each other. Some were excited, others wearisome, most somewhere in between, "I can see some of you wondering why I've kept it a secret, wondering if you can trust it." She paused for a moment, "I've got some worries too, but honestly? We don't have much of a choice. After that stunt I just pulled, we'd be dead for sure on the surface."

Everyone agreed with her, some albeit reluctantly, "So what's the plan then?" Jeremiah asked her.

"And how'd you survive?" Collin asked her, "I saw twelve Angels outside your house on my radar."

Everyone stopped to stare at him.

"And then I saw them all disappear at once. Not leave, but disappear." He continued.

The room went silent as they all slowly turned to look at her now. She took a deep breath and grumbled to herself. She glanced over at Teresa who nodded at her. It was time. She pulled out her gun and held it up, "Alright, this is going to take some explaining to do and I don't want to be interrupted." She told them, "So, as long as this gun is in my hand. Silence. Understood?" They all nodded at her in confusion and concern. "Perfect."

She closed her eyes and shook her head for a moment, how was she even going to approach this? She was far from ready, but she didn't have much of a choice. Finally, she sighed heavily and spoke up, "Right now, in my suite, is the most pathetic, scared, skittish, weak, terrified excuse of a person I have ever met. And he's the only reason I'm alive right now. Twice over." A few gasps came over her people.

"Shit, he's the only reason I was able to send out the evac alert." She forced a smirk. How much time could she buy? How long before she had to say who it was? "This… This is about to get really confusing, but it will all make sense in the end, I promise." She paused again, trying to buy more time, "I found him out in the woods about a month ago. During the memorial for the Archangel of Death. He was terrified. A crying mess. Didn't know who he was, where he was… Didn't even know what food was."

She stopped and groaned to herself, this story was fucking impossible to share without saying who it was, "Fuck…" she said softly to herself before speaking out loud again, "Right now in my suite? The man responsible for us being here right now, the man who killed the people in my home, and destroyed the Angels outside my house?" She took one last deep breath. This was it, "Is the Archangel of Death."

Gasps and shouts immediately erupted from them all. All except Teresa, who looked at her with pain, Jeremiah, whose eyes just went wide, and Collin, who glared. She held her gun out towards the end of the dock into the cavern around them and pulled the trigger firing a shot off, "*What did I say?*" She roared at them. In an instant they all silenced.

"I recognized him out in the woods," she explained, "and I had to make a choice. Leave him for the Empire to find sooner or later … or take him in." She smirked knowingly, "And no, obviously we all know killing him wasn't an option considering he somehow survived the Chaos Bomb." She started to pace. She needed to keep the stress down. She needed to address them as calmly as she could. It took everything she had to keep her hands and voice from shaking.

"So, I took him home, and I've been slowly caring…" she stopped, narrowed her eyes and turned to face them, "No. I've been grooming him." Her voice lowered, a sinister undertone creeping its way into it, "I saw the Archangel of Death broken. Utterly and completely broken. Helpless. With no knowledge of anything. Like a lost starving puppy. So, I gave him food, I gave him a name, I gave him a home. And I've been working on turning that lost little puppy into the fiercest fighting dog ever."

Everyone stared at her in disbelief … with a hint of horror.

She leaned over on a railing as a smile started to creep on her face, "I've got him wrapped tighter than a tourniquet around my fingers. He comes when I call, he stays when I tell him to … he kills when I ask him to." She chuckled, "Actually, he killed the men in my home without me telling him to. He did that on his own, to protect me."

Mouths were still a gape as she spoke, "And I plan on continuing to use him for our rebellion. Because let's be honest. We really don't stand a chance against the Eternal

Empire." She pushed herself off the rail, "We're like gnats to them. Annoying, but not a real threat. Him, on the other hand?" She pointed at the passage she had taken to her private suite, "He's a threat to them on multiple fronts. Not only can he kill swathes of them with just his mind, but he's going to be a PR nightmare." She shook her head, chuckling, "Imagine their news hosts trying to explain that. It's impossible."

She paused for a second and eyed them all over, "So that's how I survived. That's the big project I've been working on. And it is only because of the fruit that it has borne that any of us are here right now." She set down her gun loud enough for the click to echo about the completely silent room.

Silence filled the air. A long, deafening, tense, tangible, silence. Teresa was the first to speak up, softly, "Did … Did he really…?"

Stephanie nodded at her, "Yes. In fact, the only reason I woke up is because they shot him first. Right in the head. Could see the blood still pouring out when he came to save me."

"He really is … immortal." Jeremiah said in awe.

"I watched him get peppered with I don't even know how many bullets." She stopped for a moment as she remembered the exact moment. She could see it in her mind. She could feel her… She quickly forced herself to stop thinking about it. Not now. She needed to stay strong in this moment, "By the time I got to him thirty seconds later… The wounds were all healed."

"*What?*" Multiple people shouted all at once.

"I watched as he screamed…" Again, she pushed the memory away … *A-D…* "And turned them into nothing but a red mist."

"Holy shit…" Jeremiah scoffed, "How…?"

"Hell if I know." Stephanie laughed for a second, "All I know is he did it. And he did it because I've been grooming him to trust me."

"What the hell happens if he remembers who he is?" Collin asked in a very accusatory tone. His glare was trying to see behind her eyes; see what secrets she held. She wouldn't let him in.

"Well," Stephanie sighed and shrugged, "we're either all dead, which we would be right now without him, or he joins us." Shock rippled through the crowd, "Which I think there's a decent chance he would."

"What?" Collin snapped at her.

She smiled at him, it was a teasing, proud, try me, smile, "I've reason to believe that he wasn't willingly working with the Empire."

More shouts of confusion came from the audience.

"Without boring you all with endless details of his mental breakdowns, which he has at least once a day, multiple times a day when I first found him, it seems he remembers feelings from his past, but no *actual* memories. And every single feeling he has … are ones of pain, regret, torture, depression, terror, sorrow, fear…" She took a deep breath, "As he's told me, that's all he knows."

"You're actually serious right now?" Collin asked her.

"Deadly." She coldly responded, "Take the Scythe for example. I'm 99% certain it didn't have a cockpit and instead relied on his immortality."

"*What*?" Multiple people shouted again.

"When I first brought him to Lady Love he had a full-on panic attack." She told them, "Begging me not to make him get inside. That it caused him pain. I believe his exact words were something along the lines of, 'Crushing pain. Flesh. Blood. Bone. Gone. Pain… Body turned to dust, turned to steel. No body left, but the pain remains.'"

Everyone stared at her in horror as she coldly recited his words.

"Oh my god…" Teresa shook her head, "What the hell?"

"Of course, I cut out all the repeating and stuttering and crying he did." Stephanie continued, "But to me? That doesn't sound like he enjoyed working for them."

Jeremiah shook his head slowly, "You're insane, Steph…" He sighed, "But she's got a point." He turned to address the rest of them, "As much as I hate to admit it, she's got a point. And frankly, we're all in too deep now to back out."

People started to begrudgingly agree with him.

"She's got us this far. And while this…" he forced a smirk, waving his hand in a circle, "this thing with the Archangel is utterly insane. I don't even think she'd disagree with that."

She laughed and nodded at him.

"I still trust her with my life. I still know she's the best damn leader we've got. And I still plan on following her wherever she takes us."

"Same." Teresa instantly said and walked up next to Jeremiah. "Plus, for those of you who aren't so convinced," She glanced over at Collin who was still brooding, "What other choice do we really have, hm? In for a penny, in for a pound." Those who weren't agreeable before started to agree now.

Jeremiah turned around and faced Stephanie, "So, Steph, what's the plan?"

She nodded a thanks at the two of them and flashed a smile, "First things first. Get settled in, pick your rooms, and, well I'd say unpack but you all look like you brought about as much as I did. Nothing." A few chuckles came from the crowd, "I want a full inventory of everything in this bunker.

Ammunition, food, water, rooms, beds, computers, anything and everything. I've honestly no idea what's in here."

"Yes, Ma'am!" They all responded at once.

"Rest up first though," she told them. "I don't know about you all, but I've had a long night and am utterly exhausted. Teresa. Jeremiah. Collin." She nodded at them all as she addressed them. Hanging her eyes on Collin for longer than the rest, "You three make sure everyone gets as comfortable as possible."

"And what are you going to go do?' Collin asked her.

She let out a long sigh, "I've got A-D in my suite right now, and I'll be surprised if I don't walk in on him crying on the floor." She stopped for a moment, "A-D is what we all are going to be calling the Archangel of Death." She told them, "Get used to it now and not later. That's an order." She then went back to what she was saying before, "So I've got to calm him down, check out the control panel in my room, run a full diagnostic on Lady Love to see if she's even still functional, and maybe, if I'm lucky, catch some shut eye." She waved at them all and left before another word could be spoken.

Chapter 22: Is My Friend

Stephanie marched all the way back to her suite. She got about halfway down the last hallway before she finally slowed to a stop and let her head hang down. She took a deep breath and placed a hand on her head, barely holding back the tears as stress ran through her veins. She had gotten everyone on board enough, with some help from Teresa and Jeremiah, but at what cost? Now she had three different versions of her relationship with A-D she had to uphold.

The cold, cruel, manipulative once she told everyone about, the one she planned from the start. What Teresa knew about it, how stressful and hard it was to keep up the façade of caring and how taxing it was to maintain the relationship with him was … and the real one she kept to herself. She closed her eyes and let the images play out in her mind of what had just happened.

Her first thought when she shot out of bed, worry for A-D. Her refusal to leave him behind – not because of what the Empire would do with him, but because she didn't want him to go back to whatever torture they had put him through. Tears formed in her eyes, the pain she felt in her heart as the bullets flew into him…

The line between pretending to care and actually caring had been blurred completely. And now it was too late for her to back out because, well she actually did care about him. She cared about the poor, pathetic, broken, barely able to function man she had found out in the woods. He wasn't the Archangel of Death to her, he was just … A-D.

But A-D was a ticking time bomb, and she had left him alone in a bad state.

She quickly recomposed herself. She had to be strong for him, so he would be strong for her. One day all this stress and hurt she was bottling up would come back to bite her in the ass, but not today.

She froze and her eyes went wide as she could hear A-D scream out violently all the way from within her room. She instantly sprinted down the hallway and burst into the room, "*A-D*?!" She cried out in a panic.

"*Shut-up!* Shut-up-Shut-up-shut-up!" He shouted to himself as he slammed his head backwards into the far wall. Blood stained the floor all around him, it dripped down the wall, it flowed down the back of his neck soaking his clothes. His hands were pressed as hard as they could be on the sides of his head as his whole body shook and he rocked back and forth, "No-no-no-nononono! *Stop!*" He pleaded with tears streaming down his face.

Stephanie was halfway across the room before she even realized she had moved. She dropped down to her knees beside him, sliding in the pool of blood, and quickly grabbed onto him as he went to throw his head back into the wall again. The tears of fear flowed down her face just as much as his own, "No, no, no-no-no-no!" She pleaded with him holding his head tightly against her chest. The back of his skull was completely shattered as the blood now started to completely soak into her clothes as well. "I-I-I'm here A-D…" She could barely speak through the knot growing in her throat.

"The-the-the-the voices. The voices, the voices, the *voices!*" He whimpered in her arms, shaking with every sound he made, "They won't stop … they won't stop..."

"No, no, no…" Her hands tightened their grip on his body, "I'm here now, A-D. I'm here now. I'm here now." She struggled with every word. "Pl-please come back to me. Please, please, *please*" She begged him while rocking him back and forth.

"No one could ever like me. No one could ever like me." He convulsed violently in her arms, "No one could ever care, ever care, ever care about me! I-I-I-I'm a m-m-monster! A-abomination! H-h-h-hated! Death, death, death, death, death-*death-death-deathdeathdeath!*" A sudden strength from him she wasn't expecting burst out as he tried to throw his head against the wall again as hard as he could. She was barely able to move her hand behind his head in time and cried out in pain as it was crushed between his fractured skull and the wall.

She gritted her teeth and quickly pulled him back against her, the pain burning through her hand. At least some of her knuckles were broken, "I like you. I like you, I like you." She started convulsing as she cried in desperation, falling to the ground and bringing him down next to her, "Please, A-D please, please, please, come back. Come back, come back, come back."

A-D didn't fight against her, but kept shaking and sobbing as he finally went silent.

Stephanie had no idea how long they laid there in his blood crying. A minute, five, fifteen, thirty … an hour? She'd believe any of them. She couldn't form a single coherent thought as she lay with her head on the ground. A-D had stopped… A-D had stopped… That was all that mattered… That was all the mattered.

She felt A-D suddenly grab onto her clothes and pull himself up a little bit, "S-S-S-S-Steph…?" He meekly asked as his eyes leveled with her.

She opened her eyes, tears still flowing down from then, "A-D…" She said his name tenderly, "Oh, A-D…" At once they hugged each other tightly.

"I-I-I-I'm … s-s-s-sorry-ry…" He whispered.

"Shh … shh … no..." She told him while holding onto him tightly, "All that matters is that you're okay. That's all that matters to me right now."

"It … it …" He coughed for a moment. She wrapped one of her hands around his head. It had already healed back over, "It hurt…" He barely managed to speak, "Pr-protecting you … it hurt … and the-the-the voices … they … they screamed and screamed and screamed."

Stephanie pulled his head, so their foreheads were touching.

"B-b-b-but then … y-y-y-you … silenced them." He let out a sigh of relief and suddenly felt…relaxed, "Gone … calm … peace…" He pushed his head against hers a little bit. "And … and I … I felt … free." His stutter got better with each passing word, "I … I saved you. I saved you. And … and it didn't hurt! The voices weren't there!" He shook as he started to cry, "That's … that's never happened before!"

She closed her eyes and sighed as well; he had to have been talking about when she kissed him. She could vividly remember that moment. The air itself around her had felt alive in that moment. Not just around her though, but within her as well. She felt a spark. Like she had been floating.

"But…" A-D continued, "But th-they returned… They returned, they returned, they returned… W-w-w-with a vengeance!" He wept, "N-n-n-no one c-c-could ever l-l-like me … c-c-c-care f-f-for me. N-n-no-not-ot after w-w-what I've done!" His shut his eyes as tightly as he could and gripped her tightly, "Over and over and over and over and over and over and-over-and-over-and-over…"

Stephanie waited for him to stop repeating himself before speaking up, just as softly as he was, "I do." She told him, silent tears falling down her cheeks, "My first thought when I woke up to the gunshot … was of you." She told him, "I stayed in my home … because I couldn't bear the thought of leaving you behind. When they shot you?" She choked on her words, "Pain…" She told him, "I felt pain…"

She held him against her tightly, "And when I came into this room. I was already at your side before I even knew what I was looking at." She didn't know if she was telling him this, or herself this. She smiled to herself. In that way, she was

just like A-D right now. "I care about you, A-D. I do." Instantly it felt like a massive weight had been lifted off her shoulders. Admitting that, to herself.

"I…" He relaxed in her arms, "I care about you too, Stephanie."

"I know you do…" She relaxed in his grasp, "I know you do…" They laid there in silence for a while longer before she spoke back up again, "We should uh…"

"C-clean up?" He asked her.

She smiled at him and chuckled, "Yeah. Let's pray there's a washing machine in here as well."

"T-t-t-there is." He told her and weakly pointed down the small hallway to the left. "B-b-b-by the bath."

"You looked?"

"I…" He took a deep breath, "I t-tried to be st-strong and l-l-l-looked around. B-bed. Bath. W-washer-d-dryer combo. P-p-p-package on desk with c-c-computer."

She sighed and finally let go of him. They locked eyes for a moment, and she crawled up off the ground. He followed suit, "You did amazing, A-D." She smiled at him. "Everything else can wait. Let's just … get out of these clothes, shower, and go to bed."

"T-t-t-there's only one bed." He told her.

"Oh, shut up." She said while walking to the bathroom taking off her clothes, "We'll share."

He quickly followed her stripping down as well, "W-what?" He asked her as she took her clothes and threw them into the washer.

She grabbed his from him as he finished stripping down and tossed them in as well. His might have been naught but scraps at this point, but they were better than nothing, "You heard me." She told him, "Now get in the shower. I'll start it for it us."

Chapter 23: Their Final Message

Never in Stephanie's life had she imagined she would be sleeping naked next to a man and that she wouldn't be having sexual relations with them; and that if by some strange turn of events that was the case, that that person wouldn't try anything, but A-D was different. They had washed themselves off in the thankfully stocked shower and gone directly to bed. She didn't even pretend to herself anymore as she wrapped her arm around him being the big spoon as they both nearly instantly passed out.

As she woke up A-D still laid next to her and … nothing had happened. She checked her phone and glanced at the messages. All of them were from last night … all of them she had missed. Teresa, Jeremiah, and Collin had all sent her multiple messages. She sighed and opened her phone starting a group chat,

Steph: Sorry, the exhaustion was worse than I had thought. Passed out almost instantly. How're things?

As none of them responded instantly she assumed she woke up before the rest of them. Every single one of them had an incredibly long night, and she probably passed out before they did. She looked over at A-D who still slept peacefully and smiled. "The hell are you doing, Steph?" She whispered to herself as she lightly played with his hair. He let out a soft moan and rolled over happily, still asleep.

She got out of bed and looked down the hallway considering grabbing her clothes, but stopped herself short. It didn't matter. The door to her suite was locked, and A-D had already seen everything. Plus, on the off chance he woke up in moments, she knew she needed to be in this room. He needed to know she hadn't left.

She sat down at the desk and turned on the computer. The two screens flashed to life and displayed a myriad of information. Too much for her to take in in her half-asleep state, but she did take note that there was an inventory of everything that was supposedly in the bunker. She looked over at the package on the desk. It was labelled to her and signed "From Your Loving Parents."

Dust covered it, they must have put it down here when they built it, knowing that one day she would be here. She shrugged to herself and ripped it open. There were only two things inside. A phone, and a letter. She pulled the phone out and set it on the desk before opening the letter.

"Our dearest princess,"

Her eyes went wide. She hated it when they had called her that. That was something she… She sighed and continued,

"We can only hope you are the one reading this, as only you had the key to access this vault we built. If you are reading this, then we are long since gone, dead. We're sorry we couldn't spend more time with you, but we never gave up hope on the Kingdom of Estates and always looked forward. May this bunker become the base for your rebellious activity, and may it become the spark that lights a fire across our whole Kingdom which has now most certainly fallen.

We already know of the rumors about us. That we are traitors, that we stopped supporting the war effort. The latter half of that is correct, we did stop supporting the war effort. Instead looking towards the longevity of our beautiful Kingdom, our beautiful daughter.

Instead, we built this. The war was going to be lost no matter what we did, but there was hope to be had for after it. This phone, this phone is the key. It's attached to only one number, the man who helped fund this bunker.

You must call him Stephanie. It is your only hope in waging a true rebellion against the Eternal Empire. He has intel the likes of which you could never believe. And while he will refuse to share his identity with you, we both promise you this. He wants the God-Emperor dead more than anyone else on this planet, and he is willing to do whatever it takes to achieve that goal.

He is waiting. He will be waiting for as long as it takes for you to get here.

Our princess, our darling, our hope.

Stay safe our love.

Stephanie took a deep breath and slowly let it out. Tears did not fall, but they formed in her eyes. After all these years … and her parents were still looking out for her. Their final message, the final words she would ever read in their voice…

"Mmn…" A-D moaned softly as he woke up.

"Morning sleepy head." She turned around and smiled at him as he sat up.

"M … mor … morning…" He grumbled as he crawled out of bed, "I … I…"

"No more about last night A-D." She told him, "We're okay. That's all that matters."

He nodded at her, "O … okay…"

"I don't know about you, but I could use some coffee, and I saw a fully stocked pot in the kitchen." She stood up, "Come on."

"Mhm…" He barely mumbled as he followed her out to the main area.

"Can you hook Lady Love up to the diagnostic machine for me?" She asked as she got the coffee started, "I'll see if there's any food in here for us."

"Mkay…" He sleepily walked over to Lady Love and slowly pulled out the cable. She had shown him how to hook it up before and was honestly surprised he remembered.

"Thank you!" She called out while opening the pantry. MRE's. Lots of them. "Smart." She mused to herself as she pulled out a pair of breakfast ones. Hashbrowns with eggs, bacon, and cheese. She quickly opened them up and got them cooking as the coffee finished right when A-D did. "Perfect timing." She smiled at him and pulled down a pair of mugs pouring them both one, "Didn't see any creamer. Sorry."

He walked up and grabbed his mug lifting it to his nose, taking a long smell of it. He looked up at her and … brushed his hair away from his eyes and smiled, "T-thank you."

Her mouth dropped as she stared at him. "O-of course!" She stuttered before drinking her whole mug and pouring another cup. Never had he moved his hair out of his eyes on his own before. But there he stood, opposite of her. Sipping from his mug … hair brushed to the side.

"How are you feeling?" She asked him as she waited for the MRE's to finish cooking.

"I … I'm okay." He sat down on one of the stools, "No." He snapped his eyes up to her, "I … I … I'm good."

She could feel the smile beaming on her face. Not only did he move his hair, but for the first time since she met him, he said he was doing good! "Sleep well?"

"N-never better!" He looked up, closed his eyes and smiled at her, "C-c-can we do that … e-every night?"

"There's only one bed." She reminded him with a smirk.

He cocked his head to the side confused.

"That means yes." She explained.

"Yay!" He said softly while taking another sip. "Oh!" He spoke up again, "I-I…" He took a deep breath, "I started the … the … d … di…"

"Diagnostic?" She leaned forward and asked him.

"Mhm!" He piped up, "I-i-it showed up on the-the screens. S-s-so I clicked it f-for you."

She ruffled his hair, "Thank you, thank you, thank you!" She quickly repeated herself, "That in itself is going to take an hour or two at least. So, getting that started as soon as possible is wonderful."

"Mmm!" He mused to himself.

As the MRE's finished cooking she poured them out on some plates, "Well they may not look like much, but I've had some of these before and they aren't half bad." She slid a plate over to him and sat down on a stool opposite him. "Eat up."

As they ate, she felt her phone *finally* vibrate. She pulled it out and opened the message,

Teresa: No worries, Steph.

Jeremiah: We got it all figured out. You earned some rest after that stunt you pulled in Spoke."

Steph: Ha! Not even the most exhausting thing I had to deal with last night.

Teresa: A-D?

Steph: Yes. It...was bad.

Jeremiah: Everything good up there?

Steph: Mhm. Actually far better than expected.

Collin: I want to meet him.

Steph: No chance in hell. We all know you're mad about it.

Collin: You aren't actually dating him right? That was just a cover?

Teresa: My bad! I met him earlier and so you all know how terrible of a liar I am.

Steph: Yea... Thanks for that.

Teresa: Sorry!

Collin: Well at least there's that. But that doesn't change the fact I want to meet him. Jeremiah should as well.

Steph: I agree. But...well, Teresa you tell them.

Teresa: She wasn't lying about him being pathetic and shy. If anything she under described it.

Jeremiah: You're kidding, right?

Teresa: Nope.

Steph: Jeremiah. If you want to come up in an hour to meet him you can.

Steph: Collin. I need you to calm down first, but yes, you should meet him."

Collin: Fine. But I want us all to meet up afterwards.

Steph: Deal. Looks like there's a small conference room at the end of my corridor. You and Teresa can wait in there while Jeremiah comes here.

Jeremiah: I'll be available in 2 hours or so.

Teresa: Sounds good to me!

Jeremiah: Should...I be worried?

Steph: Just...stay calm.

Teresa: Oh...and don't make any aggressive moves towards Steph. He does NOT like that.

Collin: I'll be waiting.

Steph: One last thing. I found a manifest of what we should have in the bunker, but it's from when it was built. Would still like us to update that.

Jeremiah: We'll get people started on that before we come on up.

Steph: Thank you.

Stephanie looked back up from her phone and saw A-D was already done eating, while she still had half of her plate left. "T-t-tasty." He said.

"Better than I expected." She chuckled and went back to eating, "Hey, A-D. So … my friends kind of all know about you now. Is it okay if one of them comes up in a bit to meet you?"

"J-just one?" He asked.

"Yep." She responded, "Jeremiah. Him and I go way back to second grade. He's really chill, less … excitable than Teresa."

He nodded at her, "O-okay!"

She finished her plate and put the dishes in the sink, "Guess we should put on some clothes then finally. Think I spotted some spare clothing in the closet. With some luck there will be something that fits you well enough."

"O-oh yeah!" He got up and started to head towards the washer-dryer combo. She stayed back for a moment and looked at the blood on her floor.

She sighed and pulled out her phone sending a private message to Jeremiah

Steph: Huge favor. Don't ask about or mention the blood on my floor.

Jeremiah: HUH?

Jeremiah: Teresa is asking if it's A-D. I'm asking if you're okay.

Steph: I'll be fine. THAT was the most exhausting thing I dealt with last night.

Jeremiah: So A-D. Got it. Not a word.

Steph: Thank you.

She quickly followed A-D and got dressed with him before walking back into her room and looked at the phone. She had just over an hour. She had to know.

Chapter 24: Mysterious Stranger

She sat down at the desk and picked up the phone, turning it on. The screen showed only one button. Call. She sighed and glanced back at A-D, "Have to make a call. Can you try to stay quiet please?"

"Q-quiet?" He asked before nodding at her, "I-I'm good at that." He sat on their bed and curled up.

She smiled at him, "Thanks." She turned back to the phone, shook her head, and hit the button.

Ring.

Ring.

Ring…

Ri-

Click. "Stehpanie Maynard, no?" The voice that answered was being put through a changer, making it impossible to try and recognize. "I pray you had time to install my gift before the fiasco last night."

"How do you know my name?" She asked him.

"I knew your parents quite well." The voice responded, "Told me once you hated it when they called you Princess."

Her eyes went wide and she gasped. He really did know them, "I'd ask who you are, but they left me a message saying you wouldn't share."

"Correct." He replied, "Unfortunately I operate best anonymously."

"Well, that makes this a tenuous start." She grumbled, "You sent that scrambler to my home?"

"Yes," He told her, "Once I learned that your … comrade," he used the word loosely, "had been taken alive, I knew it was only a matter of time."

"You knew he had been taken alive?" She asked him.

"I have eyes and ears everywhere within the Eternal Empire." He answered.

"You're one of them." She accused him.

"Obviously." He responded with an annoyed tone, "I hope that is no problem to you."

"Great…" She said sarcastically, "Well, I called. What's the deal?"

"Straight to business. I like you already." He smirked, "As I'm sure that note they left informed you, I want to help your little rebellion."

"Why?"

"The God-Emperor took my family from me." He told her, "I have the resources and time to pay him back for that one day."

"Yeah…" She rolled her eyes, "I meant why help me?"

"Because I've been assured that you could bring the Kingdom of Estates back from the grave." He replied, "And your recent escapade has only proven that you have the spark. I was planning on testing you before offering my aid by asking you to destroy that embassy, but you've already done that for me."

"I did what I had to." She told him coldly, "I needed to protect my people."

"That's a sentiment I understand." He smiled, "I must say, I know many things, like that Lady Love is a prototype two person Knight, but I'm afraid I don't know who your copilot is."

"I don't have one." She quickly snapped back, "I've configured Lady Love to have all controls on one seat."

"Oh!" A hint of shock could be heard, "Impressive, very impressive … unheard of even."

"I don't know who you are or what you've been up to," she hissed, "but we've been down here training, fighting, dying, for this rebellion. What have you been doing?" She accused him.

"No, no that's fair." He chuckled, "Preparing. If I may draw your attention to your computer…"

Stephanie's eyes went wide as her computer started opening multiple screens. Tons of information poured into it. Current Angel frame numbers, placements, movements. Encampments, supply depots, checkpoints. Reports of rebel activity, pictures, suspects. Everything and anything she could want to turn her small cell into a full rebellion, "How…?" She softly asked him.

"I have my ways." He responded with a laugh, "No one wants the God-Emperor dead more than I. I know more about their inner workings than they do. I've done nothing but study them and prepare for years. I've got contact with multiple traitors within their own ranks. I've got contact with the Southlands and Eastern Dynasty. I've got a whole web that I've been spinning to catch him."

"And where do I fit into your plans, hm?" She asked, "Just another pawn to achieve your goal? I'm a born leader, not a subordinate."

She could feel the smile on the other side of the line, "Good. I only deal with leaders."

"So, what the hell do you want from me then?" She carefully asked him.

"Thrive." He told her, "Succeed. Grow. I want you to make the Eternal Empire sweat, but first you should probably shore up some of what you're missing. A week from now there's a shipment of Knight Mk.2's heading to an incinerator. Most of the workers there would love to join on as dedicated mechanics."

Her computer screen flashed to a map of the area where the incinerator was. "And I'm supposed to believe you aren't asking for anything in return?"

"Oh, but I am." He quickly replied with a smile, "I'm asking for you to succeed. Our goals align. A victory for you is a victory for me." He paused for a moment and sighed, "I understand your hesitation to believe me, but you are already in far too deep to back out now, no? The only way out for both of us, is to keep going deeper."

"Victory or death then, hm?" She asked him, "When do I finally get to meet you in person?"

"You really want the answer to that? Because I have one."

"Yes." She replied instantly.

"When you finally retake the Reach Military Base." He quickly responded.

"Are you insane?" She shouted over the phone.

He laughed, "Possibly, but believe it or not, I do find it to be quite the obtainable goal for you in the future."

"And how the hell am I supposed to do that?" She snapped.

"Let's start one step at a time, hm?" He smirked, "I must go soon, but one last question for you, Stephanie."

She paused for a moment, "What…?"

"I've seen the raw footage of what happened outside of your house last night." He told her, "I know exactly what caused those Angels to explode. I've seen it before."

She went pale as he spoke.

"I'm curious. Where did you find the Archangel of Death? When? And how have you managed to control him?"

Stephanie quickly had to calm herself down. Whoever this was … he had immense power to already have seen that footage. Not even the news had gotten hold of it yet. "I'll tell you, but only when we meet face to face." She hissed.

"Oh!" He exclaimed, "A deal? I like it! Sounds fair to me."

"Good." She snapped, "Because it's the best you're getting."

He laughed, "Don't worry. I don't care nor hold any reservations about you working with him, as I'm sure all your comrades have. If anything, the potential is … nothing I ever could have considered on my own." He paused for a moment, "Anyways, I must be off. May this bunker your parents' and I built serve you well." Click.

The phone hung up before she could respond. Stephanie set it down and slunked down into her chair. "W-who was that?" A-D asked looking up at her.

"I've no idea…" She admitted to him, "But he wants to help. And honestly, we don't have the luxury not to trust him."

Chapter 25: Another Friend

Stephanie spent the next hour trying to sort through all the information her anonymous benefactor sent her. There was too much for her to even hope to sort out even if she took a whole day. Most of the information detailed what was within the Maynor Estate, but there were even generic numbers and locations across the entire Kingdom. Whoever this man was, he had in depth access to the Empire's intel, but one thing was for certain as she glanced over the notes attached to almost everything, he had been planning. He was preparing for a full-on revolution.

A-D even came over and pulled up a chair next to her. He didn't understand any of what she was looking at, but it was nice having someone to talk to. To bounce all her ideas and thoughts off of, even if he was clueless.

Her phone vibrated and she checked it.

Jeremiah: Headed up.

Steph: Sounds good.

She pushed back from the desk and turned to face, A-D, "Well. You ready?"

"F-for?" He asked her.

She smiled at him, "Said a friend was coming up to meet you. Remember?"

"O-o-oh!" He dropped his head down for a second letting his hair cover his eyes and rose his right hand over his mouth again, "Y-yeah." He said softly while standing up.

She ruffled his hair and led him out into their living room. A-D took a seat on one of the stools facing into the kitchen as she poured three more glasses of the coffee and put another up to brew. "You got this, A-D. I believe in you."

"I … I'll b-be okay a-as long as I-I'm with y-you." He responded, taking a sip.

"I don't plan on leaving you alone with him, don't worry." She smiled, "But after he meets you, I have to go have another meeting with some of my people. Will you be okay then?"

He nodded at her, "Y-y-y-yeah … I … it w-wont be like l-last time." He whimpered as he thought about it for a moment, "I-I-I'm sorry."

"You're all good." She told him and sighed, "I think I needed a wakeup call like that…" She said softly … more to herself.

Knock, knock. Jeremiah knocked on her door before A-D could respond. A-D flinched slightly, but stayed put. She quickly got up and let Jeremiah inside, "*Damn.*" He admired as he looked around her suite, "You got one nice set up here, Steph! Full kitchen, full living area … personal dock for Lady Love?" He froze as his eyes fell on the massive, dried puddle of blood staining the floor and wall.

"Large bedroom," She quickly added on, "Full bath, and a washer-dryer combo."

He nodded at her, remembering her warning about it and walked around a bit more, "Wow, amazing. Most of the rooms on the bottom floor are like studio apartments. Theres a few nicer ones on the middle floor, but this is by far the nicest one."

"Well," She shrugged, "I am the leader here."

"Fair enough." He laughed, "So," He looked over at A-D, "This the man we owe all our lives to?"

"Sure is." She walked over next to A-D as he slowly turned around, "Say hello."

"H-h-hi…" He whispered as he used the mug of coffee to hide his face.

"*Ooo* is that third one for me?" Jeremiah asked as he took a seat on the other side of A-D.

"Mhm." Stephanie moved behind and rested a hand on one of A-D's shoulders while taking a sip as well.

Jeremiah grabbed the mug and took a long drink, "Ahh, nothing like bottom of the barrel cheap freeze dried coffee." He laughed, "We owe you one." He looked back at A-D, "Did us a real solid saving Steph's life like that. Thank you."

A-D nodded proudly, "I-I…" He took a deep breath, "I just w-wanted t-to protect h-her."

"Well," He glanced up at Stephanie, "Considering she's right here. I'd say you did a fine job."

"T-t-t-thanks…" A-D muttered softly.

"Think he likes you more than Teresa." Stephanie chuckled.

"Well, I'm not as … energetic as she is." Jeremiah smirked, "Getting the feeling you like things calm."

"Mhm…" A-D mused softly. Stephanie could feel him shaking slightly and she softly rubbed his shoulder calming him down. "B-bad things h-h-happen when I g-get st-st-stressed."

"I feel that one." Jeremiah leaned back, "I've done some pretty dumb things while stressed out."

"You can say that again." Stephanie teased him.

"Ouch." He rolled his eyes, "But fair enough. Oh!" He quickly set down his mug and sat up straight, "My apologies. Never introduced myself." He held out his hand towards A-D, "Jeremiah."

Stephanie kept rubbing A-D's shoulder as he slowly, carefully, reached out his hand and weakly shook it, "A … D…"

"Pleasure to meet you, A-D." Jeremiah said letting go of him and sitting back.

A-D quickly pulled his hand back to his mug and nodded, "Wow," Stephanie shook her head, "I should have had you meet him before Teresa."

"Nonsense." Jeremiah replied, "You and her go back even farther than we do. Plus, she's like your best friend? Nah, she needed to meet him first, for sure."

Bing! The sound came over from her computers for Lady Love signaling the diagnostic was done. Stephanie quickly set down her coffee, and she placed her other hand on A-D's other shoulder. "Oh! That was quicker than expected. I'm gonna go quickly check that, alright?"

"Go for it." Jeremiah nodded at her.

She rubbed both of A-D's shoulders lightly, "I'll just be on the other side of the room. Can keep your eyes on me the whole time if it makes you feel safer."

"O-o-okay…" He finally whispered.

She quickly ruffled his hair and took off sitting down at the computer going over everything they showed her about Lady Love.

"So," Jeremiah leaned in a bit closer to A-D and spoke softly enough so Stephanie couldn't hear, "What do you think of her?"

"Sh-she's," A-D kept his eyes on her as she worked, "P-p-perfect. K-kind. C-caring…" He slowly lowered his mug from his mouth, "Sweet … nice … perfect…" He repeated.

Jeremiah smiled. He knew that look all too well, "Pretty?"

"The most!" A-D said excitedly, thankfully still quietly enough, "So pretty…"

"Anything else about her you like?" Jeremiah was having fun.

"She…" A-D thought for a moment, "S-smells so good. Her-her hands s-so-soft and c-comforting. Her … her voice…" He sighed happily, "Peace."

"You like her, don't you?" Jeremiah asked him.

"O-of course!" A-D responded instantly, "She … she…" He started to breath heavily, "Every … everything t-to me."

"I'll give you this," Jeremiah chuckled to himself, "You got good taste."

"Huh?" A-D looked over at him confused.

Jeremiah laughed and shook his head, "Don't worry about it, man."

"The hell are you laughing about?" Stephanie called out as she walked back over.

"Boy talk." Jeremiah told her and gave A-D a wink placing a finger over his lips. "Don't worry about it."

"Boy talk?" She asked him as she grabbed her drink, "Now I am *very* worried about it."

"She's lying." Jeremiah told A-D, "Don't listen to her."

"Hey!" Stephanie snapped at him and he broke out in laughter.

"Anyways," Jeremiah quickly changed the subject, "How bad's Lady Love looking?"

Stephanie let out a massive sigh of relief, "We are so lucky." She said and leaned her elbows on A-D's shoulders, resting her head on top of his, "When it comes to her looks? Well, that's a whole different story, but functionality wise? Doesn't look like any modules got too damaged. Mostly just cables and connections. Shouldn't take more than two days to fix her up with A-D's help."

Jeremiah also let out a sigh of relief, "She looks a lot rougher than that. We really did luck out." He looked down at A-D, "You help her?"

"Y-yeah!" He said proudly, "I-I h-hand her tools and o-other things."

"Honestly?" She chuckled, "One of the best helpers I've ever had. Doesn't even try to question what I'm doing."

"Hey!" Jeremiah called out, "I was just trying to help back then."

"I know Lady Love." She told him, "I know exactly what I'm doing on her."

"Yeah, yeah, yeah…" He grumbled to himself, "I know that now."

"Anyways," Stephanie finished her coffee, "Might as well get this meeting done sooner rather than later, no?"

"Fair enough." Jeremiah finished his as well and stood up, "Pleasure meetin' ya, A-D."

A-D nodded at him, "T-t-t-thank you."

"I'll meet you outside." Jeremiah waved at them and left.

"You okay?" Stephanie quickly asked A-D.

"Mhm!" He smiled at her.

"I should be back in time for lunch." She told him.

"O-okay." He nodded her, "I'll-I'll be okay this time! I-I-I pr-promise!"

"I know you will." She smiled at him, "Thank you." She left her suite and stopped as Jeremiah was standing right next to the door.

"One thing before we go." He told her.

She looked over at him confused, "What's up?"

"As one man talking about another man…" Jeremiah took a step up next to her and leaned in close to whisper, "He is completely in love with you."

Stephanie froze. "I … I…"

"I don't know what you're planning or doing with him," Jeremiah said, "But I'm behind you every step of the way."

"Thank you…" She said softly.

"Come on," He nodded his head down the hallway, "Let's see what you've got cooked up."

Chapter 26: No Choice

"That kid ain't nowhere near as bad as you made him out to be." Jeremiah told Teresa as he and Stephnie walked into the small conference room.

"In her defense," Stephanie added on as she took a seat, "He's gotten better."

"Before you start asking questions," Jeremiah looked over at Collin, "It's him. I can confirm it. And what she said about him having amnesia seems to be accurate as well. As far as I can tell…" He shrugged, "He's trustworthy like this."

"You've got to be kidding me." Collin grumbled.

"Not in the slightest." Jeremiah continued, "I'd bet my life that he'd do anything Steph asked of him right now. She wasn't lying when she said she has him wrapped around her fingers. As for what happens if he ever gets his memory back…?" He shook his head, "I don't think we'll ever be able to tell what'll happen then."

"Well, what did you think of him though?" Teresa asked, "Like of A-D personally?"

Jeremiah shrugged again, "He seemed alright. Pretty honest, straightforward. I could tell he was trying his best to stay calm though. He's even more shy than I was around Steph back in middle school." All but Collin laughed, but even he was forced to smirk slightly, "If he wasn't the Archangel of Death?" He sighed, "I think I'd actually like the kid."

"*Seriously?*" Collin shouted at them, "Are we just going to pretend he's not the bane of our Kingdom?"

"And what would you have us do?" Stephanie asked him, "Seriously. *What. Would. You. Do?*"

Collin grumbled to himself and slammed his fist on the table, "Shit!"

"Yup…" Stephanie shook her head, "Now you're starting to get how I've felt for the past month."

"How?" Collin asked her, "How do you maintain calm? How do you not lose it?"

"I don't have a choice." She told him coldly, "Either I keep it together, or everything falls apart."

"That's not…" Jeremiah looked over at her worriedly, "That's not good for you."

She shrugged at him, "What else am I supposed to do?"

"That's what we're here for." Teresa looked at the two men, "But enough of this serious dark talk. I wanna know. What was it like when he used his powers?"

"Oh yeah!" Jeremiah piped up and leaned forward, "How … how did it work?"

Collin sighed, "Hate to admit it, but I'm curious too."

Stephanie took a deep breath and sat back closing her eyes, "You really want to know? The truth about those moments?"

"Yes!" They all said at once.

She placed a hand on her temples as she could still vividly see, hear, and feel every moment of those memories, "The first time he used his powers, to kill the men in my house. I had just watched them pepper him with dozens of bullets. He screamed so loudly the rest of us had to cling to our ears trying to block it out as best as we could. It pierced into my mind…"

"And then they just…?" Collin asked her.

"No." She said softly, "A-D started crying louder and the leader managed to get his composure back together and went to shoot me. A-D screamed only one word… 'No.' In that moment where once three men with armor and guns stood, there was now just a red mist."

"He really just … screamed at them?" Jeremiah asked.

"It was … terrifying." She admitted. She still refused to look at them. Better to look exhausted than to let them see the tears trying to form.

"Well, that explains the men, but what about the Angels?" Collin asked her. "I mean that one's even more impressive. You just ask him to?"

She smirked, "I tried to."

"Tried to…?" Teresa asked.

"He was too panicked, too afraid," She told them, "Dropped to the ground crying about how it hurt. How it hurt so much. It hurts … it hurts … it hurts…" She softly said the words as they replayed in her mind. Everyone waited for her to continue in silence, "I heard the lead pilot start the countdown to blow up my house. I begged and begged and begged, but he couldn't do it."

"H … how then…?" Teresa asked her softly.

"Five … four … three…" Stephanie sighed heavily and stopped.

"What happened?" Collin nearly shouted at her. "How did you-"

"I kissed him." She interrupted him. She suddenly opened her eyes and leaned forward in her chair onto the table, "I. Kissed. Him." Everyone stared at her, mouths open, frozen in place, "And the Angel frames … exploded."

They all stared at her in utter shock for what felt like minutes on end. Collin suddenly pushed away from the table and stood up, "No." He said shaking his head, "No. We're not doing this. I'm going to go show him what's what." He turned around and started to head to the door.

"*Woah! Woah! Woah! Stephanie no!*" Teresa and Jeremiah both screamed and jumped to their feet as Stephanie pulled her gun out and pointed it at Collin, her gaze still just as calm as it was.

"Don't even think about it." She warned him.

Collin turned around and froze, "You … you can't be serious."

"Oh, I'm serious." She said calmly, "He's the only hope we really have." She told him, "What, you really think that the small handful of us can actually make a difference? Can actually stand against the Eternal Empire and be more than a minor nuisance? This path we're on leads only to one end. Death and failure. A-D is the only one who can take this pathetic group and turn it into something the Empire might actually fear."

Again, silence filled the room. They all knew … she was right. Collin shook his head, "You'd really kill me over him?"

"Kill you?" She scoffed, "Nonsense. Just take you out for a while. Take out your knee."

"My god…" Teresa whispered.

"And what if I don't like this idea?" Collin asked her.

"Then leave us." She said coldly, "Go start your own cell. Or go die some pointless death charging the Reach Military Base. Sounds like something you'd do."

"Maybe I will." Collin narrowed his eyes.

"Fine." She hissed at him.

"Hey, hey, hey." Jeremiah stepped in between the two of them, "Let me talk to him, Steph." He looked at her, "Man to man. Alright?"

"Really think I care what you have to say?" Collin snapped.

"Will you let me at least try?" Jeremiah asked him, "We're practically brothers, man."

Collin sighed, "Fine."

"How do I know he won't try go to A-D right now?" She asked them all.

"I'll make sure of it." Jeremiah told her. "We'll go just outside this room. You hear me yell for help you know he's running. Plus. Isn't your room locked?" He winked at her. He had a plan.

She smiled and nodded getting the message, "Fine." Jeremiah quickly led Collin out of the room and closed the door behind them.

Teresa slowly looked back to Stephanie, "Would you really have…?"

"Yes." Stephanie responded, "I don't have a choice."

"I…" Teresa sighed, "How are you … really?"

Stephanie laughed quietly, "Honestly? Right now, I wish I was A-D and could just…" She slowly brought the gun to her own head and jerked it to the side, "Boom."

"*Steph!*" Teresa shouted at her, "What's going on?!"

Stephanie set down the gun, leaned back, and stared blankly at the ceiling, "The line between reality and fiction has blurred itself completely."

\ \

"Come on." Jeremiah nodded down the hallway and took a step down it.

"Why?" Collin hissed.

"So they can't hear us, duh." Jeremiah rolled his eyes and led Collin down it. Collin followed him reluctantly. About a third of the way down Jeremiah suddenly spun on his heel and punched Collin as hard as he could knocking him down on the floor as blood started to pour out of his nose.

"What. The. *Fuck?!*" Collin shouted as he put both his hands over his nose applying pressure.

Jeremiah shook his hand grunting slightly in pain, "God I've been wanting to do that for three whole years…"

"So that's what this is about?" Collin slowly got up off the ground, "You wanna fight over her?"

"No." Jeremiah said and took a step back, "I'm over her. I'm happy just being her friend, but that's exactly what your issue is right now."

"Oh whatever." Collin hissed at him and grunted in pain.

"You still care about her, right?" Jeremiah suddenly asked him.

"Yeah, no shit." He responded leaning against the wall.

"Then what the hell are you doing?" Jeremiah asked him, leaning on the wall across from him.

"She's … she's … *gah!*" Collin shouted.

"She's doing everything she can to protect all of us." Jeremiah finished the sentence for him, "She's doing everything she can to help this rebellion. She's taking on all the stress associated with that, alongside cozying up next to the Archangel of Death. We can't even begin to imagine how hard that must be on her. And you know she's made the right choice on what to do about him."

Collin stood in silence for a moment, "So what point are you trying to make here, hm?"

"That if you really cared, you'd be trying to help her in whatever way you can." Jeremiah told him, "Not trying to solve things your way. Not making her life more difficult than it already is. Not threatening to leave. You'd be telling her, 'I hate this, but I'm on board.' Just like Teresa and I have."

"And just let her…"

"Let her what?" Jeremiah asked him, "I was so angry at both of you when you swooped in and stole her from right under my nose, but
I stuck around. I didn't throw hissy fits. I didn't make a scene. I stuck around, because she still needed me, because we were still good *friends*."

"That is a completely different circumstance." Collin rolled his eyes.

"You're right." Jeremiah admitted, "This one is even more serious, because all of our lives are at stake here now. And instead of helping her, you want to throw it all away."

Collin sighed heavily, "So what? I should just … play along with something I hate?"

"Even better," Jeremiah smirked, "Do what I did. Grow up. Get over yourself."

Collin grumbled at him, "Man to man talk, eh?"

Jeremiah chuckled, "Man to man talk." He nodded and took a step forward, offering Collin a hand.

Collin shook his head at him, grunted one last time and shook it, "You're a real asshole you know that?"

"You with us?" Jeremiah asked him.

"Reluctantly." Collin sighed, "Don't really have much of a choice, do I?"

"Now you're starting to get it." Jeremiah laughed and nodded back to the door, "Come on, let's make sure the girls haven't destroyed all the testosterone in that room already." That got Collin to smirk as they headed back.

"*What the hell?!*" Teresa shouted as the two of them walked back into the room.

Collin and Jeremiah shared a quick look and nodded once, "Man to man talk." They said together, and both sat back down.

Collin sighed heavily, still applying pressure to his nose, "I hate everything about this. But I'm in. Got nowhere else to go."

"Thank you…" Stephanie said as she still laid back in her chair. A hint of desperation was in her voice.

"Well, now that we're all on board," Jeremiah continued as Teresa quickly passed Collin some paper towels, "You got a plan cooking yet?"

Stephanie took a deep breath and leaned forward with a smile on her face, "Actually I do. Teresa, you're in charge of the inventory. Jeremiah, there's a cargo hauler down in the hanger. I need you to find someone who can pilot that. Also get a full roster of who's staying in what rooms. Collin," She paused and turned to him. "I'm pretty sure I saw four more Knights down in the hanger as well, no?"

"Six." Collin told her, "Mk.2's even."

"Perfect. Get our best current pilots into those, and our backup's training on the Mk.1's." She told him.

"Why… We planning something?" He asked her.

She nodded at him, "In a weeks' time there's going to be a shipment of Mk.2s arriving at an incinerator. Just so happens most of the people working there are Maynor citizens who aren't so happy with the Empire's rule. We're going to take those Knights off their hands, get ourselves some dedicated mechanics, and take whatever spare parts we can."

"Holy shit." Teresa said, "You aren't messing around."

"No." She told her, "After that our next step will be increasing out pilot numbers. Getting other rebel cells to join us. Hopefully with my destroying the Spoke Embassy, alone I might add, might get some other leaders willing to step down and join the fold."

"You got a long-term plan?" Jeremiah asked her.

"Oh yeah…" She smirked, "But trust me when I say you aren't ready for it." She paused for a moment, "In the meantime I'm going to repair Lady Love, should take no more than two days as most of the damage is just cosmetic. I want a meeting set up with everyone in three days so I can tell them what the plan is. We leave in six days for that incinerator. Sound good to you?"

They all nodded at her, "Now this sounds like the Steph I choose to follow." Collin said with a smile, "I'm sorry for earlier."

"You're fine. The stress is getting to us all." She admitted, "And I'm sorry as well. Let's get to work."

"We'll make sure everyone is on board with the A-D circumstance." Teresa told her, "With Collin on board finally I know that will sway a lot of people who are on the fence about it."

"I can't thank you all enough." Stephanie told them, "I don't know what I'd do without you."

"You let us worry about the cell." Jeremiah told her, "I'm sure A-D is more than enough for you."

"I'll get you six pilots that you can't even tell are rookies." Collin nodded at her, "On my word."

"Now I don't know about you guys, but I'm getting hungry." Stephanie stood up, "Shoot me a text if you need anything."

"You never respond while working on Lady Love." Teresa commented.

"Eh," She shrugged, "I'll give the phone to A-D. He'll let me know if it goes off." She stretched and walked around them, "Home sweet home now." She said before leaving the room.

Chapter 27: No Good Deed…

The former Police Chief Hollander sat in his cell. At least his men had given as many amenities as they could without getting in trouble themselves. Every single one had personally come to voice their support to him, and every single one he had warned them to keep it to themselves. He was just a cop, not even part of the army, leaving alone it was an Angel captain who arrested him. Frankly, he was lucky he was alive.

Two days had passed since that night. There was no word, sight, or sound of any sentencing. He was just being … held. With some luck he had been forgotten about. One more day and he would be released if no one came to press charges. He knew if that was the case he would have to leave town immediately. Head to a different Estate and try to find passage back to the homeland.

His assistant chief, now chief, walked up the door to his cell, "Well, Sir. Looks like you weren't that lucky…"

"Praetor finally wants to see me, eh?"

"Praetor?" The new chief asked him, "No one told you?"

"Told me what?" Hollander asked back.

"He's dead." The chief told him plainly, "Angel frames left in such a hurry because someone hit the embassy with an entire missile barrage."

"My God-Emperor…" He whispered, "Please don't tell me I have to deal with that pilot now."

"No, Sir."

"Then who?" He asked.

"No idea," His friend responded, "All I know is they got the proper clearance to take over this investigation."

"Well shit." He shook his head, "Guess that means I'm as good as dead. Tell my family I love 'em will ya?"

The door opened and the new chief led him down the hallways, "You and I both know I don't have to tell them that." He sighed, "But I will for you."

"You're a good man." Hollander told him, "Don't make the same mistake I did."

"What? Saving people?" He asked as he led them down into the interrogation chambers.

Hollander shrugged, "No good deed goes unpunished it seems." He said as they stopped before his door, "Stay safe, Sonny."

"I will." He nodded at Hollander and opened the door.

Hollander walked into the dark room and sat down in his chair. As the door closed behind him, he was entered into pitch blackness, not even able to see his own hands. "I've been a cop my whole life, you can cut it with the intimidation tactics. I'll speak my piece and let fate guide me."

"It's not for intimidation." A voice being put through a changer echoed around the room, "It's to protect my identity."

"Well, I'll admit." Hollander smirked, "This one is new."

"So, tell me." The voice asked him, "What is your piece?"

"I saved this town." Hollander quickly told him, "I was put to the test. Let this town and everyone in it get destroyed to buy time for our Angel reinforcements to arrive or let a small group of rebels leave. Now maybe I thought I lived in a different Eternal Empire than I do, but I'm pretty sure the tens of thousands of lives I just saved outweigh the small group of rebels I let escape."

"You're from the homeland, correct?" The voice asked him.

"Born and raised." Hollander responded, "Hand-picked by my superiors to come out to the Kingdom of Estates thanks to my exemplary service as a chief back home."

"Then yes," The voice told him, "You did think you lived in a different Eternal Empire. The Empire at home and the Empire across the seas are two very different beasts. Out here only one thing is favored … war."

"Why?' Hollander asked him, "I thought we conquered other lands to help bring them into our utopian fold. To better them in the long run!"

"Wrong again." The voice smirked, "A wonderfully mastered propaganda technique we use." He paused, "We do it for the thrill of it. For the joy in crushing others under foot. For the love of war."

Hollander spat out in front of him, "Then I'd rather die than serve such monsters such as you!"

"That can be arranged." The voice laughed, "But that's not why I am here."

"What the hell do you want then?" Hollander snapped at him.

"Tell me, with full honestly please," It felt as if the voice was right next to him, but no one was there, "What do you think destroyed those twelve Angel frames?"

Hollander froze, "You can ask anyone that. I'm sure everyone's seen the footage of what I saw in person."

"No, they haven't." The voice chuckled, "I've scrubbed it from all records. That footage doesn't exist."

"*What?*" Hollander snapped, "How?"

"What did you see, Hollander?" The voice asked again.

"I…" He took a deep breath, "I've never seen anything like that in person before, but there was only one thing it could remind me of."

"And that is…?" The voice asked him impatiently.

"Looked like the work of the Archangel of Death." Hollander finally said, "But he's long since dead. Empire declared it themselves."

"So, you know the truth." The voice said calmly.

"*What!?*" Hollander shouted, "How could that be?"

"Knowing the truth is a dangerous thing," The voice ignored him, "You know I can't let you leave this room spreading information like that."

"Then kill me and get it done with." Hollander said coldly, "Just leave my family alone, dammit!"

"I mean … I could do that." The voice smirked, "Or … I can offer you a deal."

"A deal?" Hollander asked him, "More like an ultimatum. I take it or I die."

"True enough," The voice responded, "But, with this deal I can promise your families extended safety and protection. Oh! And you get to live another day."

"Well, *boy*," Hollander sighed, "Lay it on me."

"Now that you've seen firsthand what the Eternal Empire is really about, do you still trust them?" The voice asked him.

"If this is how it really is?" Hollander responded, "And everything in the homeland is just a façade?" He paused for a moment, "I signed up to protect the people, not antagonize them."

"Then you're either the perfect person, or the worst person for my offer," The voice sighed, "I need myself a traitor."

Chapter 28: Overdrive

Stephanie couldn't believe how smoothly the next two days had gone. She had gotten the full inventory from Teresa; there was a lot in the bunker. More than enough to last them for months on end hopefully, but she still knew they couldn't live on nothing but military rations. Jeremiah had gotten a full list of every room in the bunker and a roster of who was staying were. There were enough beds to house just over five hundred people down here, assuming no one shared. Although only some of the beds were large enough to share.

Two other hangers had been found around the bunker, each facing a different direction. No more Knights were held in those, but that would make getting to whatever their target was significantly quicker as large corridors that circled the whole compound connected the three hangers so the Knights could move between them.

Collin had sent her some promising updates about their backup pilots. They were still rusty at best, but with a nonstop training regimen they were getting up to speed and fast. Lady Love was also up and running again. She looked far worse for wear, but making her look pretty again could wait. All that mattered was she was ready to head out and lead their Knights.

And possibly most importantly, A-D had remained stable. Stephanie was even able to teach him how to read her diagnostics a little bit and explain the very basics of what she was doing while working on Lady Love. He learned how to make a pot of coffee, heat up some of the MRE's, do laundry. He was starting to become more … normal.

He still spoke very softly, stuttering here and there, but even that had gotten better. Teresa had come up once again to visit and he instantly became far more shy and reserved, but when it was just Stephanie he was opening up.

She got his help to finish zipping up her jumpsuit and turned around to face him, "Do you want to come with?" She asked him, "Can stay hidden in Lady Love while I give my little speech?"

A-D's eyes went wide in fear, "I-i-in front of a-all those p-people?"

"It's solid steel." She told him, "They'd never see you. Wouldn't even know you're there."

"I-I-I … uh…" He started shaking lightly at the thought of that many people around him.

"It's okay if you don't want to." She told him, "Just thought I'd offer."

"D-do you want me to?" He softly asked her.

She thought about it for a moment, she hadn't even considered if she actually wanted him there or not. All she had thought about was hopefully getting him used to being around other people while within Lady Love. It was risky if everyone started yelling at her, but it would be good for him as long as she could control the situation. She sighed, "Yeah … I think so. It's nice having you nearby."

"Th-then I'll go!" He quickly responded and nodded at her. "J-just m-make sure th-they don't know I-I'm t-t-there please!"

She chuckled at him and ruffled his hair, "They'll never know. I promise." She gestured to Lady Love, "Shall we?"

"Mhm!" He nodded again and climbed his way up to the top of Lady Love. Stephanie was right behind him and watched him carefully as he climbed down the ladder to his seat. It was just a month ago she had to beg him to climb up a ladder to get into her house; that he was breaking down completely over seeing Lady Love, but he willingly climbed up and into her without hesitation.

She plopped down into her seat and quickly strapped herself in. It was a short flight down to the main hanger they entered in at, but still better to be safe. Plus, five seconds into her flight and an alarm would start blaring if her or A-D weren't properly strapped in. As soon as they were both in, she fired up the mech and slowly lowered them down into the main hanger, where everyone was waiting.

Pilots sat on top of the Knights next to their friends, some chairs had been brought out and scattered around for others to sit on, and still some just leaned against the wall or over a railing. As soon as she landed, she popped open the cockpit and jumped onto one of Lady Love's shoulders to sit down on, "Y'all doing well?"

Nods and small vocal agreements could be heard. Times were rough, they were tired, uncomfortable in their new home, but spirits weren't down at least. She used this moment to lock eyes with Teresa, who sat next to Jeremiah on top of her Knight. As soon as they locked eyes, she quickly flashed hers down to the open cockpit of Lady Love and back up to her.

Teresa nodded at her and leaned over to Jeremiah whispering barely loud enough for him to hear, "A-D's in there." Jeremiah's eyes went wide for a second, but he quickly smiled and waved at Stephanie. They both knew it was meant to be a secret.

"You all ready to kick some ass?" She raised her voice slightly.

"*Damn right!*" Someone shouted back as the whole crowd was slightly more excited about this question.

She pointed to the one who shouted out, "Now *that's* what I want to hear!" She shouted back, "Because as long as you guys are up to the challenge, we're about to take this small rebel cell and kick it into overdrive!"

Cheers erupted from the crowd. She waited for a moment for them to calm down before continuing, "Three mornings from now I want every pilot suited up and ready to launch. Bring some food and drink for a few days. We're gonna get some scouting done first and hopefully find some fresh, real, food to bring on back."

"Bring back some beer!" One of her men shouted and everyone laughed.

"Assuming one of y'all is comfortable flying that cargo ship," Stephanie responded, "I'll make sure we load as many racks as we can into that baby."

"Hell yeah!" The man shouted back and cheers erupted as more laughter filled the crowd.

"With some luck we'll also be bringing home some new Knights and mechanics as well." She told them, "There's a shipment of Mk.2s headed for an incinerator. We're going to hit it right as they arrive. Steal the Knights, try to convince the workers to come move in with us, and leave before the Eternal Empire knows what happened."

"Wait," someone called out, "you really are planning on kicking this thing off?"

Stephanie nodded at them, "Can't slow down right after I destroyed that embassy." She shrugged at them, "Time to show this Empire what we're made of."

"*Give it to 'em, Stpeh!*" Someone shouted.

"Damn right!" Another one chimed in, "This is the Kingdom of Estates!"

"We'll show these bastards what's what!"

"I've been waiting to give them a taste of their own medicine!" One of her new pilots cheered.

"They shouldn't have pissed you off!"

"They've got no idea what's in store for them!"

"Let's give 'em hell!"

Stephanie smiled proudly at them all as the cheering continued. She waited for it to die down before continuing. "Now, I want to make this clear," she told them, "I don't want you all to feel like there's nothing left but war for us. We're still all friends here, and this is now our home. Make it one. Have fun, relax, laugh, party, and play. Pilots," she turned to address them, "unless you want to keep practicing, take tomorrow off. Have some fun. I've been told there's a whole recreation room with some basketball courts, foosball tables, gaming setups. I want you all flying out there excited to come back home."

"Yes, Ma'am." Collin responded, "Make sure you all thank her. I would have ran you ragged tomorrow."

"Casey," Stephanie addressed her, "I know we've got some children here with us. Think you can come up with some sort of system, whether it be schooling or just daycare? There's a lot of information on the systems down here."

"Way ahead of you," Casey responded, "I've already made sure our seven children will be taken good care of. Jackson is going to teach them math, Lily's got English, Greg has P.E covered, and Thompson and I are dedicated babysitters if needed."

"I'm more than willing to help anyone get a workout routine if they want one!" A female spoke up, "There's a full-sized gym with more machines than the twenty-four-hour ones back home."

"We found a hydroponics room." One of the men said, "I'm not an expert in those, but there were even some seeds in storage. I'll get us a small constant source of fresh food up and running in no time."

"Oh!" Another girl piped up, "I love growing plants! I'll help!"

Stephanie sat back and watched in awe as everyone slowly spoke up, formulating a plan to make this not just a last resort to survive, but a new home. She slowly stood up as everyone keep bouncing ideas around and shouted above them all, "*We are…*"

"*The Kingdom of Estates!*" Everyone joined in with her, "*We will never go down without a fight! Long live the Estates!*" Stephanie stood proudly as everyone cheered at her.

"*Lone live the Estates! Long live the Estates!*" They started repeating. Pumping their fists with each chant.

She looked down into Lady Love, where A-D was staring back up to her. She silently mouthed to him, "Good job," before quickly going back to watching her people celebrate.

Chapter 29: So It Begins

They were travelling halfway across the Estate to reach the incinerator. Above ground they would have been able to make this journey in just a handful of hours, but moving through all the twisting and turning tunnels easily doubled the time it took. It didn't help they needed to move a bit slower than usual as the cargo ship couldn't go nearly as fast as the Knights, nor turn corners as tightly. She was just thankful the main tunnels systems were big enough for it to traverse.

"We should reach our exit by nightfall," Stephanie told them as she led them, "We'll stop under cover there for the night and formulate a plan. Tomorrow evening the shipment of Knights is scheduled to arrive. We'll strike right as they arrive."

"Sounds like a plan to me." Jeremiah responded, "You said there was a warehouse we were going to hit as well? How close is it?" He asked her.

"Close enough." She told them, "I'll run over my plan with you when we stop to rest."

"So," One of the other pilots spoke up, "I know we're all wondering this, so I'll be the one stupid enough to ask. You bring A-D?"

"Yes, I did." Stephanie responded, "He's in my passenger seat as we speak."

"Damn..." They responded in awe, "That's gotta be wild. Sitting right next to him. What's he like?"

Stephanie rolled her eyes, "Truth be told, he's nothing but nice to me."

"No way, for real?" Another asked her.

"Mhm." She replied, "He's been handling the snacks and drinks for me. I don't really have room for anything up by my seat."

"That's absolutely insane." The first one responded, "Never thought we'd be flying side by side with the Ar-"

"You do know *A-D* can hear you all, right?" She interrupted him, emphasizing the name as she spoke. "Like, he's literally right below me."

"Oh shit!" They shouted, "Hey uh... What's up, man?" One of them asked him nervously.

Stephanie leaned down and looked at A-D, "Go on. Say hello." She told him softly.

"H-h-h-hi..." He very softly said.

"Woah!" Another pilot chimed him, "He does not sound anything like I expected!"

"Right?" The pilot of the cargo ship came over the radio, "He sounds so small and weak."

Stephanie laughed at them, "You boys don't even know the half of it."

"I'll be honest, Steph," Collin spoke up, "Hard to believe someone who sounds so timid saved you."

"B-but I *did*!" A-D shouted out.

"Hey, now there's some lungs." Collin chuckled, "Trust me. We all know you did, kid. Steph won't let us forget it."

"All things considered," Teresa spoke up, "You all wouldn't believe how cute he actually is either."

"No way!"

"You're messing with us!"

"You've got to be kidding me!"

"What the hell?" The radio channel filled with a commotion as everyone shouted back and forth at Teresa.

"Really?" Stephanie called over quieting them all, "You had to go there?"

"What?" Teresa asked her feigning innocence, "Thought we were airing out the room a bit about him."

"So, you're telling me," The first pilot spoke up again, "The man who saved your life is not only timid and quiet, but also cute?"

Stephanie had no idea what her three best friends had shared with the rest of them, but she was forever grateful they were playing along. "I mean…" She glanced down and looked at A-D again who was blushing and hiding his face. She smirked and smiled at him, "I suppose she might have a point."

Again, chaos broke out over the radio as everyone shouted in shock and disbelief. She muted herself and reached down towards A-D who quickly grabbed her hand, "You doing okay with this?" She asked him.

"I-i-i-it's n-not as bad w-when it's n-n-n-not in p-person." He said softly.

She smiled at him, "You're doing amazing, A-D. Don't let anyone, especially yourself, try to tell you otherwise."

"I-I…" He squeezed her hand harder, "F-for you!" He beamed up at her, "M-m-must for you! W-w-want to!"

Stephanie blushed, "Just between you and me," She told him while pulling her hand back to navigate a few upcoming corners, "You *are* absolutely adorable sometimes."

"Mmm…" He mused happily to himself but didn't actually respond.

Stephanie unmuted herself as the rest of them kept talking back and forth, "Alright, alright that's enough about A-D." She quieted them down, "He's a bit shy when it comes to people and you all are making him nervous."

"*Fine.*" One of them relented, "As you say, Ma'am."

"The rise up to the surface is going to be a bit tight for you, Pat." She told the pilot driving the cargo ship, "So let's make sure we all give him more than enough room."

"Got it." Pat quickly responded, "She's a bit like driving a boat, a really big boat that flies, but I'll make do."

Everyone had settled down for the night. They had arrived far later than she expected and agreed to go over the plan tomorrow morning. Sleeping in a Knight was never comfortable, but they didn't have much of a choice. They didn't have the space to bring camping sets, nor the materials to even do so.

Stephanie had packed a blanket for A-D, to help keep him comfortable, but she had done this many times before, she needed nothing. Sleeping in Lady Love with her flight suit on was almost second nature to her. They had stopped deep inside of a cave that led out to the surface. With all their Knights powered down they wouldn't show up on the radars of any possible passing Angels, and unless they flew halfway into the cave they wouldn't be seen either.

Stephanie looked down as A-D curled up in the blanket and buried his face in it. She smiled, "You going to be okay down there?"

"Mhm…" He responded softly.

"I'll be right up here if you need anything. Okay?"

He merely nodded in response.

"If I wake up first, I'll make sure I wake you up before I get on out."

"O-o-okay." He replied quietly.

"Goodnight, A-D."

"G-g-goodnight." He responded.

She leaned back in her chair, took a deep breath and closed her eyes.

Sleep came far easier than it should have for her. The night before a small-scale fight, out in Lady Love, A-D below her for the first time in here, tensions still running a bit high in her mind, but before she could think about anything, her alarm was going off the next morning. She quickly shut it off and stretched herself awake. She glanced down and saw A-D stir awake from the noise, "Mornin' there." She smiled at him as his eyes opened.

He rubbed them with the back of his hand and yawned, "M-morning…"

She chuckled as he turned over in his seat and closed his eyes again. She climbed down the ladder and reached over him to their food stash, "Want me to heat up a breakfast for you too? Or plan on sleeping more?"

"*Sleep…*" He pulled the blanket over his head and groaned at her.

"Alright, I'm gonna get some fresh air. So, I might not be in here when you get up."

"Mmm okay..." He said as she leaned away from him with an MRE in hand.

She lightly patted his head, and he let out a sigh of satisfaction, "I'll be back in an hour or so to make you wake up."

"Mmm…" He barely responded as sleep was quickly washing over him. She grabbed a water bottle, chuckled to herself at him, and quickly climbed out of Lady Love. Collin waved at her as he was already up and eating while leaning against a rock, three others were also already awake and waved at her. She waved back at them and hopped down as more of her crew started to wake up.

She got down, heated up her meal, and ate while waiting for everyone else to slowly come to as well. After everyone had finally crawled out of their Knights and were halfway awake, she spoke up, "Morning all."

"Mornin'." They all responded, some slower than others, as they still were waking up.

"Collin," She addressed him, "out of the new pilots, who shows the most promise you think?"

"Hmm…" He pondered for a moment, "Think I'd have to choose Will." He finally said, "Sorry to the rest of y'all."

"Perfect. Teresa, Jeremiah," she looked at them while she addressed them, "I want you to take the other five , alongside Knights six through twelve. You guys will be taking

Pat to that warehouse. There shouldn't be any Angels there, but stay on guard."

"You got it, Steph." Teresa nodded at her.

"I'll send the nav data over to your Knights." She told them.

"Perfect." Jeremiah replied.

"Collin," She turned back to him, "You and I will be taking the rest of us to that incinerator."

He nodded at her.

"Now, I should be able to sneak Lady Love in as I was able to get my hands on a scrambler, but I want you to take Will and draw out those Angels. Once they leave to intercept the two of you, I'll swoop in and knock out their long-range communication tower. The moment that goes down the rest of you, who will be waiting in jet form, will shoot out and cover Collin. Understood?"

They all nodded at her.

"Good." She smiled. "A quick attack like that should make almost instant work of the Angels, leaving just the military encampment around the incinerator itself. Should be pretty straightforward. Just keep your eyes out for missiles and it should go fairly smooth."

"Any backup we should be worried about?" Collin asked her.

"There's a very slim chance a patrol could be within short range communication distance," She told him, "so be wary of that, but otherwise as long as I hit that tower, we should be in the clear for hours."

"Sounds too easy." Will spoke up.

"Believe it or not," Collin responded, "it often is with the Empire. Their hubris is their worst enemy."

"Can say that again." Teresa chuckled, "Do we need to worry about any backup headed our way?"

Stephanie shook her head, "Always exercise caution, but I'd be surprised if you saw any combat."

"If that's the case, why not take some more Knights with you then?" Jeremiah asked her.

"Just in case you *do* end up engaging anything." She told him, "We'll also be fine with what we have, right Collin?"

"Damn right." Collin smiled at her, "Got Lady Love, two Knight Mk.2's, with me piloting one of those, and six Mk.1's? Even without Steph's more technical plan we could easily win against four Angels."

"Should also make loading up the cargo ship a lot faster." Teresa added.

"Exactly." Stephanie nodded her head, "Have just over half of you hop out and start loading her up while the others maintain a perimeter and keep an eye on the employees."

"You know if they're our men or the Empires?" Someone asked her.

"No idea." Stephanie responded, "All I do know is you put a Knight's sword in anyone's face and they'll quickly back down no matter the loyalty."

"Worked pretty well on Hollander." Jeremiah smirked, "So, I imagine it'll work quite well on these folk."

"I want everyone to run an on-board diagnostic before we take off tonight," Stephanie told them, "If anything, even the slightest thing is wrong let your respective leaders know so we can work around it. Understood?"

"Yes, Ma'am." They replied as one.

"Supply team," She looked over at Teresa and Jeremiah, "You all head out at sunset. You've got a bit farther to go than we do. Once the sun is under the horizon we';; head out."

"Sounds like a plan." Collin nodded at her.

Chapter 30: Hit and Run

"How long until you enter sensor range?" Stephanie called over the radio.

"Two minutes." Collin responded.

"Good, the moment you see those Angel's move out towards you let me know and I'll start my run in."

"You got it."

She muted herself and looked behind her at A-D since she was in jet form, "You ready, A-D?"

"I-uh-yes!" He finally decided.

"It's gonna be a bit rough. "She warned him, "So, you just hold on tight, alright?"

"Y-yes!" He quickly responded, gripping the straps tightly.

She unmuted herself, "Rest of you ready?"

"More than ready." One of her pilots responded.

"It's gonna be a tight timing window for you to get to Collin," she reminded them, "So you all better be pushing those engines to full speed!"

"Wouldn't have it any other way." Another one smirked in response.

All their knights hovered in the cave where they made camp while they waited for the signal. The low hum of the engines, the slight movements as their thrusters kept them stable, the tension in the air about them. There was nothing quite like it. The excitement before a mission. Stephanie smiled as she readied to shoot out of the cave.

"That was quick," Collin finally came in over the radio, "Didn't even wait five seconds to start coming-"

Stephanie didn't wait for him to finish as she threw her engines into full power and flew out of the cave,

"-for us. Looks like all four of them took the bait." Collin continued, "Take it away, Steph."

"Way ahead of you." She responded as she flew as low to the ground as she could. The trees below her were nearly uprooted as she pierced the sky just feet above their tips. "Stick to the plan and slowly pull back. No heroics, Collin."

"Yeah, yeah, yeah." He said annoyed, "That's why you gave me Will, eh?"

Stephanie laughed, "Actually no, but now that I think about it maybe I'll pair you with rookies more often."

The man looking at the sensors grumbled as another dot started glitching in and out of his radar. They had just spotted two Knights at the edge of their radar, thankfully the shipment with a detail of Angel frames guarding it had just arrived. "Damn machines." He said kicking it a few times. After the third kick the dot stopped showing up and he grumbled to himself.

"What is it?" His superior walked up.

"Oh nothing. Just a damn glitch in the system."

"Keep your eyes on that screen." His superior reminded him, "Last thing I need is an incident with Angels around."

"Of course, Sir."

Stephanie smiled to herself. The scrambler was working. She was nearly on top of their base and they still hadn't sent anything out to intercept her. She wondered if it would also keep their missiles from locking onto her, forcing them to switch to heat locks, which were far easier to evade. She steeled herself as the incinerator came into sight. Thick black smoke poured out of a pair of massive concrete chimneys. She would find out shortly.

She set her missiles to lock onto the long-range communications tower as soon as she entered into range. The trees ended abruptly and she blew past the tall, barbed wire fence surrounding the scrapyard. She pulled up and smirked as she passed the first missile turret. This was going to be even easier than expected.

Bing!

Target locked.

She launched two of her missiles and quickly pulled to the side heading around one of the chimneys.

\ \

BOOM!

The whole room shook as the communications towers exploded. "What the *hell* was that?" The commander screamed, "*Report*!"

"No idea, Sir!" The man watching the radar quickly responded, "Still nothing on radar!"

"Shit!" He grumbled and quickly grabbed the emergency radio. "*Battle stations!*" He screamed over the intercom, "Switch to manual heat lock! They have a scrambler!"

\ \

As Stephanie came around the other side of the chimney, she unleashed a short burst of bullets blasting the nearest missile turret to pieces right as it started to turn towards her. As the rest of the turrets turned towards her she quickly locked on to the two nearest ones she was about to blow past and launched a missile at each one.

She quickly flew past the small command tower and made a sharp turn around it. She still had seven missile turrets to deal with. Alarms went off as her Knight informed her she had been locked on to and fired at. She quickly fired a burst of bullets at the turret in front of her and spun over the missile as it neared.

She shot back towards the chimneys with five missiles right on her tail. As she thought, the missiles, locking onto heat, turned into the chimney as she skirted right next to it. As the rubble exploded she came around again and quickly locked onto two more turrets, destroying them with the push of a button.

She was out of missiles now though, unless she switched to fighter form, but there wasn't time for that as a whole barrage of missiles came flying at her from the remaining four turrets. She smiled to herself. If the plan worked on one chimney, may as well use it on the other. Right as she whipped Lady Love around to head back, she gasped.

"No." A-D whispered softly and all the missiles in the air suddenly exploded.

Wasting no time, she turned her 180 into a full 360 and quickly fired a barrage of bullets at the four turrets that guarded the entrance of the base. As they exploded, she quickly shifted Lady Love into its fighter form as she had a few seconds to spare and looked down at A-D in awe, "Thanks."

She didn't have time to be excited about him using his power to protect her. There was going to be guards running out with rocket launchers in moments. He looked up at her and smiled, "N-n-no v-v-voices."

"Two Angels headed your way, Steph!" Collin shouted over the radio, "They just turned back!"

"Understood." She responded.

"On route to intercept." The pilot of their other Knight Mk.2 responded, "Knight's 3 and 4 with me."

"Timeframe?" Stephanie asked.

"Should be arriving right when they do."

"Remember your training!" Collin shouted at Will, "Dodge and weave, boy! Dodge and weave!" He unleashed a wide barrage of gunfire at the incoming missiles, destroying all of them, while simultaneously launching off six of his own. The rookie barely moved out of the way in time to avoid a missile headed towards him, but quickly spun and shot it before it could come back around, "Good shot!"

"Phew!" Will came in over the radio, "This is terrifying!"

Collin laughed as he charged towards the Angel targeting Will, "Nah, kid. This is fun." He swung his sword and the Angel pilot barely rose theirs to block him in time. He slammed the barrel of his gun against the chest of the Angel and they quickly spun out to the side before he could pull the trigger. "Bad move." Collin smirked to himself as he launched a missile at point blank range while over charging his thrusters to push him back far enough from the ensuing explosion.

"Oh, you wanna play?" He said as his screen went red, warning him of more incoming missiles from the other Angel. He spun around and smiled as Will quickly shot the missiles out of the sky.

Before Collin could take the shot the Angel exploded and their back-up flew past them, "Target cleared." One of their pilots came in over the radio.

"Kill steal!" Collin shouted at them, "Come on, let's get to Steph!" He shouted at his rookie and took off as quickly as he could towards the incinerator.

\ \

The problem with rocket launchers being fired from soldiers, was that they didn't show up on Stephanie's radar. She had to wait for a rocket to get launched at her and quickly retaliate. She dove in and around the scrap. She was far from worried about getting hit, but this was annoying and tedious.

She flew around a corner and quickly turned a group of soldiers into dust.

"One Angel stopping to intercept us." Her Knight Mk.2 pilot said, "Knight 3. Continue to Stephanie, we'll handle this one."

"Understood." He responded.

"Knight 3, circle around to the other side of the compound." She told him, "Then come in and swing around the backside of the chimney. I'll lead him there."

"Yes, Ma'am." He quickly replied.

Stephanie quickly boosted up into the sky and made her way to the chimney; she had thirty seconds until they would arrive. As long as she was right next to it the Angel pilot wouldn't even be able to rely on heat targeting. Unless he decided to destroy the whole thing, but then that'd leave him open for a counterattack.

She quickly spun around and fired a missile at the command tower while pulling back to the chimney. After this Angel, the battle was all but won. She flew around to the right side of the chimney and waited for the Angel to arrive. The moment it entered her line of sight she fired a barrage of gunfire at it. Her screen flashed red repeatedly as the Angel pilot kept trying to lock onto her, but couldn't. The fires from the chimney were just as potent as the heat from her engines.

The Angel swiftly dodged her incoming fire and shot a few bursts of bullets back at her. She pulled back around the chimney, using it to block the incoming fire and sat back in her chair. "All yours." She said as the Angel closed in. Right as it came around the corner Knight 3 came in from behind her and shot it out of the sky. "Well done." She smiled, leaning forward and putting a few more bullets into the Angel frame ensuring the pilot was dead.

"All clear?" She asked over the radio.

"All clear." Collin responded, "We'll be there in moments."

"Perfect. We'll work on cleaning up the stragglers and finding our sympathizers." She replied and quickly got back to work clearing out the last few small groups of soldiers who hadn't started to run away yet.

Chapter 31: New Recruits

Out of the corner of her eye Stephanie saw someone waving her down with a flare in the scrap around the incinerator. She quickly landed Lady Love by them, "You one the of the workers here?"

"Sure thing, missy." The man responded in a low gravelly voice. He stopped as his eyes went wide for a moment, "Well I'll be damned, that right there is Lady Love ain't she?"

"You've heard of her?" Stephanie asked, a hint of excitement in her voice.

"Who the hell hasn't?" He laughed, "Single handedly took out the Spoke Embassy. You were all over the news for a day before the Empire started pushing it all under the rug. Goddamned hero amongst us rebels though."

She gasped. Word had already spread. This was amazing, better than she ever could have hoped, "You know, I could use some mechanics on my team. We're a bit lacking in that department."

"Holy shit-wait what?" He took a step back flabbergasted, "You got somewhere safe for us to stay?"

"Yes, I do. Rooms, food, drink, space to work." She smirked, "In fact we came here to pick up that shipment of six Knight Mk.2s that just arrived. Was hoping you had a cargo ship or two we could load them up on and bring them home."

"Say no more, missy." He quickly grabbed the radio on his collar, "Everyone!" He shouted, "Time to pack up and head out! Fill those loaders with any useful scrap you can and get them in the air!" He stopped and looked at her, "You got any idea how long we have before we need to move?"

"Two hours max. I want to get part of the way-" She stopped as five frames showed up on the edge of her radar making their way in. They had Knight transponders. She quickly switched to the open radio channel, "Unidentified Knights, identify yourselves immediately or we will be forced to intercept!"

Silence.

"I repeat. Identify yourselves!"

The mechanic chuckled, "Ah, their radios are probably shot again. Can never seem to keep those things working."

"You know these people?"

"Truth be told, I was expecting them." He said, "Not until later though. They probably saw the stunt you just pulled and decided to come in."

"Knights 1, 2, and 3." She called over her radio, "Intercept, lock missiles, but hold your fire. They may yet be friendlies. Bring them on in."

"Yes, Ma'am." They responded and quickly took off to intercept the incoming Knights.

"Oh, they're friendlies alright." The mechanic smiled at her and got back onto his radio. "I'll stick around for their arrival. They know me."

"Sounds good." She turned to face the direction the unknown Knights were coming in from.

"Oh, by the way." He told her as he walked next to Lady Love and leaned against its leg, "Name's Gerald."

"Stephanie." She responded.

Gerald quickly grabbed his radio, "I need you guys to get those new Knights that just came in loaded up. Should take up two of our loaders. Use the rest for parts." He shouted over it, "And if I learn that any *one* of you touched my baby, I'll have your damn hides! Not one bolt better be out of place!"

"Your … baby?" Stephanie asked him.

"Ah, just something I work on to keep myself sane. A passion project if you will." He held up his hand as the five Knights came over the fence and slowly landed in front of

Stephanie. Her Knights hovered above them keeping their missiles locked on.

"Sorry about the no response." The lead Knight spoke up through his speakers, "Outgoing communication is down … again."

Stephanie had never seen Knights like these ever before. They looked like their base was the Mk.1, but they had been heavily modified, and were barely holding together as well.

"Sorry about that." Gerald said, "Only so much I can do with scrap, my boy."

"That's why we keep the hand radios." He responded, "I didn't think anyone else knew abou-" The pilot froze as he spoke, "Holy shit is that … are you … *Lady Love*?" He shouted.

"Name's Stephanie." She told him, "And Lady Love is my Knight."

"It's an honor to meet you!" The Knight quickly replied and lowered its head in respect, "A Knight that can change form while in motion! *How?*"

Stephanie chuckled, "It's an old, abandoned prototype I finished putting together."

"Was meant to be the Knight Mk.2.5." Gerald spoke up, "But was deemed too difficult to get two pilots thinking on the same wavelength twenty-four-seven."

"You know your stuff." Stephanie responded.

"Know it?" He laughed, "I helped design it! Can't believe you found a copilot to fly that with successfully."

"I didn't." She responded, "Rewired everything to the main seat."

"There ain't no shot…" Gerald laughed and shook his head, "They told me expecting one pilot to do everything this baby was supposed to do was impossible."

"It took a lot of practice." She chuckled.

"Ah shit." Gerald took a step back, "I ought to get packing up as well."

"You guys headed out?" The unidentified Knight asked him.

"Yup, Lady Love here needs herself some mechanics." He responded, "Said there's somewhere safe we can stay."

"Can we come with?" The Knight instantly asked her, "This is all that's left of us. We ain't much, but-"

"Can your Knights make a day and a half flight?" She didn't even wait for the pilot to finish.

"They might not make it off of the ground after that, but we should be able to make it."

"Welcome aboard then." She said with a smile.

"Name's Kyle. You won't regret it."

"You're one of us, Kyle." She told him, "I know I won't." She glanced back at Gerald who was walking off, "Anything we can do to help?"

"Nope. We've been waiting years for this day. We'll be ready to head out in under two hours."

"We'll keep an eye on the perimeter just to be safe." She signaled at her Knights, and they quickly took off to patrol the border of the incinerator.

"Where's your safehouse that you can afford to hide so many people and Knights?" Kyle asked her.

"Deep underground." She told him, "I've got about another fifty some odd people there already. All from my original cell."

"No way…" He said in disbelief, "You're looking at starting a real rebellion…"

"Yes I am." She smiled, "You guys look like you've been through hell and back. What happened?"

"I wouldn't know where to start." Kyle forced a laugh, "Most of this damage came from when we got caught out by a double patrol of Angel frames. Doesn't help we've only been able to get super short repairs for months by sneaking in here."

"Well, we'll make sure you get those Knights back up to full speed once we get home." She told him.

"We owe you big time." He replied.

"Nonsense. If we want to stand a chance against the Empire we need to stick together. Do what you can to keep your Knight's in the air, I'm going to try and contact my other team."

"You have another team?" Kyle quickly asked her.

"Mhm, getting us supplies from the warehouse a few hours east of here." She turned off her speakers and called Teresa.

"What's up?" Teresa picked up the call almost instantly.

"Status report. What do you think?" Stephanie rolled her eyes.

"We're about to head back to the cave." She told her, "Went smooth as butter. You?"

"They said it should take about an hour and a half to get everything loaded up and in the air," Stephanie responded, "But better than expected. Even picked up another small cell."

"Wait, like more pilots?!" Teresa said excitedly.

"Mhm." She replied, "Five to be precise. They were headed here to try and get some quick repairs from our new mechanics. Asked to join on."

"That's huge!" Teresa shouted, "Can't wait to meet them. We'll see you back at the cave."

"Don't shut down your Knights." Stephanie told them, "I want to start the journey home, get maybe a third of the way there before we stop for the night. Make it impossible for the Empire to figure out where we went by the time they come searching."

"Understood, we'll be ready and waiting. Teresa out."

Stephanie hung up and turned her attention back to Kyle, "So, what's with all the mods?"

Kyle laughed, "Gerald's idea. They might only work half of the time as they were very hastily installed, but they keep our Mk.1s on par with the modern Angels."

"So, like a fake Mk.2?"

"Well, if everything worked as it should all the time." Kyle chuckled, "I'd argue even better. Might finally have something with these babies if Gerald can spend some solid time patching them up."

"Better, eh?" Collin said as he landed next to Stephanie in his Mk.2, "Find that hard to believe."

"Kyle, meet Collin, he's one of my captains." Stephanie quickly introduced them, "Collin, meet Kyle. He's just asked to join us."

"I'm also the best fighter you got, Steph." Collin added on, "Welcome aboard."

"Thank you." Kyle responded, "Can't believe someone is actually starting to pull together the different cells."

"Well, I just started doing that." Stephanie told him, "But that's the plan. If we all work together, we can take the Maynor Estate back."

"How many people can you hold underground?" Kyle asked her.

"What'd Jeremiah say?" Stephanie asked, "Like five-hundred or something?"

"Five hundred in total." Collin corrected her, "That includes non-pilots. And that's just comfortably. We could easily make some basic bunks instead of beds, transform some of the rooms into dedicated compacted sleeping quarters."

"We'll worry about that if we ever get to five hundred." Stephanie told him, "We've still got a long way to go."

"Fifty-four of us, about what ten mechanics, and these five new pilots?" Collin asked her, "I suppose you might be right."

"She single handedly destroyed the Spoke Embassy," Kyle spoke up, "If you go out looking for recruits, you'll quickly find them. You've given us a hope we never thought possible."

"One step at a time, kid." Stephanie responded, "One step at a time."

Traversal home was even slower with a total of seven cargo ships/loaders following them. The mechanics were much more skilled at flying them than Pat was, but it still was very time-consuming. They went late into the night, even into the earliest hours of the morning before stopping to rest for a few hours. Stephanie felt comfortable enough that they were hidden.

She ensured their new mechanics and pilots got food for the night and told them that they were only stopping for six hours before returning to Lady Love for the night. She climbed down and leaned on the ladder while looking at A-D. She hadn't been able to properly talk to him, and she needed to. "You … you used your powers." She said softly, "Are you feeling okay? No voices? No…?"

He shook his head at her, hiding his face behind his hair and hands, "N-n-no…" He barely responded, "T-t-they s-start to c-c-c-come back when y-you l-l-leave," he told her, "b-b-b-but they g-go aw-awa-away when you-you're near."

She smiled and gave him a hug, "I'll have you know, I had that situation completely under control … but you made my life so easy up there. Thank you, A-D. Truly." She couldn't believe it. Her plan, it was actually coming together.

"I-I…" He hugged her softly back, "I j-just wanted to-wanted to he-help."

She squeezed him lightly, "You did help! You did! It was … amazing!" The excitement in her voice was easily noticeable, and it wasn't fake. "And it didn't hurt you?"

"N-n-no…" He whispered.

"You promise?" She asked him, "You don't sound very convinced."

"I-it didn't!" He rose his voice slightly, "It just … it just…" He shook as tears started to fall, "It's, it's, it's w-why every-everyone h-h-h-hates me! I-I-I-I'm a m-monster!"

"No, no, no, no, no…" She assured him, "That was amazing, A-D! I couldn't believe my eyes!" She sounded giddy, "I loved it!"

"Y-y-you…" His crying slowly stopped, "You d-did?"

"Yes!" She shouted and pulled back ruffling his hair, "As long as it doesn't hurt you, okay?" She reassured him.

"I-i-it doesn't." He smiled softly, "As-as-as l-long as I'm w-w-with you."

"I'll always be by your side. I mean this is my Knight," She chuckled, "So you'll never have to worry about me not being right above or in front of you. And unless something goes horribly wrong, I shouldn't be in danger outside of her."

"O-o-okay…" He took a deep breath, "I-I-I…" He took another one, "I can d-d-do this. I c-c-can k-keep you safe."

"I know you can, A-D." She sighed happily, "You already have." She paused for a moment, "Now get some rest. We need to get back home tomorrow." She ruffled his hair one last time and climbed up into her seat.

"G-g-goodnight." A-D said softly as he pulled the blanket around him.

"Goodnight." She said back with a smile on her face. With A-D willing to use his powers while in Lady Love … anything was possible now.

Chapter 32: They Even Had Beer

"Lady Love to bunker, come in." Stephanie called over the radio.

"Reading ya loud and clear, Steph." Casey called back, "Opening doors. Welcome home."

As the massive doors to the cavern opened everyone came in and started to land. "I'll be back down in a moment." Stephanie told them, "Don't wait for me to start celebrating," She quickly left for her private dock. As soon as she landed, she quickly climbed out of Lady Love and jumped to the ground. She turned around and held out her arms for A-D.

"I-I-I can do it." He said wearily as he looked down from her mech.

"You gonna complain?" She asked him and gestured for him to jump.

His eyes went wide and he smiled, "N-no!" He said and quickly jumped down into her arms.

"*Woo!*" She cheered as she spun around twice with him in her arms before setting him down, "I don't know about you, but I'd call that a success and a half!"

He merely smiled, staring at her in awe.

"We got the Mk.2s, we got the mechanics, we got food and drink supplies, and we got five new pilots!" She suddenly pulled him into a tight hug and jumped with joy, "It couldn't have gone better!"

A-D laughed and hugged her back, "Y-y-you're so happy!"

"Yes!" She nearly shouted and pulled back, still holding him by the shoulders, "And you did a wonderful job as well!" She lightly booped his nose with her finger, "I couldn't be happier right now."

He smiled at her, "Y-y-you got to g-go down and c-c-celebrate with them?"

She nodded at him, "Yeah, part of being a leader. Can't just stay up here *all* the time."

"T-that's okay!" He nodded his head at her, "I-I'll wait here!"

She slightly frowned, she felt bad always leaving him behind, "You know you can come if you want?" She asked him.

"*No*!" He shouted, "No, no, no, no. Too … too-too many p-p-people!" He shook his head, "I-I-I'll just stay here!"

She placed her hands on his cheeks and leaned towards him, "I'll think of something for you. You deserve to celebrate a bit too."

He completely froze, nearly melting as well, in her hands as they locked eyes. His mouth fell slightly open as his breathing slowed.

Stephane immediately knew what she had done, what he was expecting. She quickly moved her head to the side and gave his cheek a quick kiss, "I'll be back soon!" She told him as she let go of him and headed for the door.

"Mhm…" He mused softly to himself while placing a hand where she had kissed him smiling from ear to ear and blushing.

Cheers erupted from everyone as Stephanie entered the hanger everyone was currently in.

"Hey, Steph!" She recognized the voice as it called out to her, "They even had beer!" He shouted as he threw a can up to her. It was the same man who had joked about getting some days ago.

She quickly caught it, popped it open with one hand and took a long drink from it. "Never catch me saying no to a free beer!" She called back out and laughed, "Fine job everyone! I want you all to meet our new friends!" She gestured over to Gerald who was ordering his men around unloading everything, "Gerald and his mechanics! No longer do I have to rely on your guys' suspect repair jobs!"

Laughter erupted throughout the room.

"Hey there, missy." Gerald called back out, "Still depends on what tools I have access to."

"Each dock comes equipped with basic repair machines," She told him, "But there's a whole workshop as well with anything and everything you could dream of. Could build a Knight in there if we had the time and parts."

"Plus, there's a whole stock of backup parts." Jeremiah added in, "You're set up for success my friend."

"Well, I'll be damned…" Gerald whistled loudly while cracking his knuckles, "It's been ages since I got my hands on a proper workshop. I'll have every Knight in this bunker running as smooth as a baby's butt in no time."

"I also want to welcome our new pilots," Stephanie called out pointing over to Kyle and his small group, "Kyle and the remnants of his rebel cell!" Shouts of joy came out, "Hey! Give them some beers too! They're all part of us now!"

"Yes, Ma'am!" A handful of her people responded as they all quickly tossed cans over to Kyle and his crew.

"Hope we don't disappoint you!" Kyle called out as he popped open his can.

"I wouldn't worry about that!" She responded, "They happened to be in the right place at the right time." Stephanie told them all, "Asked to join up and I was more than happy to oblige." She paused for a moment, "Make sure all of them are welcomed here like they've always been one of us! Gone are the days of separate rebel cells who might work together here and there. Now are the days of a true rebellion!"

More hoots and hollers echoed throughout the bunker. Even the newcomers joined in as they all celebrated. Stephanie jumped over the railing and immediately got to mingling with everyone. Exchanging hugs, toasts, congratulating all her pilots on a job well done.

She approached Gerald and shook his hand heartily, "Welcome to your new home, Gerald." She said sincerely.

"Appreciate it." He responded with a smile, "Was getting real sick and tired of melting down all that hard work put into Knights."

"Well, now you can help keep them in business." She smiled.

"Damn right." He responded, "Now I gotta know. You fly an old prototype Knight, name's Stephanie … you a Maynard?"

Her eyes went wide in shock, "You know me?"

"Nah." He shook his head, "Gave away a prototype two person Knight to a couple of Maynard's ages ago, back when I still worked for the Kingdom." Her mouth slowly dropped, "Can't believe I'm saying this, but you've done that baby of mine proper justice."

"You actually *made* Lady Love?" She nearly shouted.

"Oh no," He smirked, "You made her into Lady Love. What I gave away was just the basic framework of a Knight. You must be the best damn pilot left in the Kingdom though if you can pilot her solo."

She blushed slightly, "I take pride in my work, just like you do it seems."

"She's an old baby of mine," he replied, "But she's all your now. Tell me though. What's your best transformation time?"

"Just under three seconds while stationary and just under nine while moving." She told him proudly.

He whistled again, "*Damn.*" He shook his head in disbelief, "You managed to transform while moving faster than a normal Knight can while stationary? We were hoping for a similar time, never even considered one could be faster."

"I'm a very good pilot." She beamed with pride.

"That you are," He nodded at her. "You need any help doing anything with her and I'll make it a top priority."

"Thank you," She nodded at him, "But all she really needs right now is a fresh paint job." She laughed.

Gerald laughed with her, "'Fraid I can't help you with that one. Not unless you find me some paint."

"You can bet I'm keeping an eye out for it. She just ain't the same all scratched up." She chuckled and waved goodbye to him continuing to mingle about.

She made her way over to Kyle, who Teresa and Jeremiah were already talking to. "Mind if I butt in?"

"Steph!" Jeremiah cheered as he gave her a tight side hug, "I like this guy already!" He pointed over at Kyle, "He's got some jokes."

Kyle blushed slightly and waved his hand dismissively, "Sarcasm has carried me this far in life, why stop now?"

Jeremiah laughed as he let go of her. "Six Mk.2s," Teresa spoke up, "Five new pilots with heavily modified Knights, a whole set of mechanics, and some fresh supplies to boot?" She whistled, "You weren't joking when you said it was time to kick it into overdrive, Steph. I'm impressed."

"Thanks, Teresa." Stephanie smiled at her before turning to Kyle, "Whatcha think of our home?"

"Phew…" He shook his head, "This sure is something else. Whole underground compound? Never would have believed it if I didn't see it with my own eyes."

"Same." Stephanie agreed with him.

"I'll kept it real, Stephanie," He looked over at her, "No offence meant, but I never would have guessed it was going to be a female commanding the most successful rebel cell in the area. Most are hardheaded men, not pretty girls."

"None taken." She responded with a smirk, "Even more surprised I'm the one who destroyed the embassy?"

"No!" He quickly responded, "I saw that footage. Us guys are too stubborn to pull off whatever the hell you did there. That was like watching a gymnastic maneuver. Insane." Everyone around him laughed. "What? Tell me I'm wrong!" All the men quickly shook their heads and agreed with him.

"Hey Steph," Teresa addressed her, "How's the boy doing?"

"Boy?" Kyle asked up.

Stephanie rolled her eyes at Teresa, "He's doing good. Offered for him to join us down here, but…" she shrugged

"Yeah, that was a pointless ask." Teresa laughed, "Would be nice to see him actually mingle though one day."

"I highly doubt that's ever going to happen." Stephanie shook her head and then turned to face Kyle, "I'll explain more about A-D to you after you've gotten settled in, but let's just say this. He's our ace in the sleeve."

"Not you?" Kyle asked her confused, "I thought you would have been that!"

"I'm the ace on the table." She smiled at him, "A-D? Well, he's our five of a kind."

"Aren't you just full of surprises, Stephanie?" He said with a smile.

"I try to be." She smirked, "Hey Jeremiah, make sure all our new people get proper lodging."

"You got it." He responded. "It's late, so I'll let them crash in whatever empty room they choose and help sort out proper assignments tomorrow."

"Sounds like a plan." She smiled at them, "Anyways, I best get to mingling some more before I call it a night. Have fun you all." She waved at them as she stepped away. They all waved back and went back to their conversation.

Stephanie spent another bit down there mingling and celebrating with everyone before she started to make her way back to her room, she made one quick pit stop though. She had figured out what to get A-D, she just needed to use a printer.

"Hey A-D!" She called out as she entered their room, "I brought something for you. A gift."

She heard some splashing from the bathroom for a moment as A-D got out of the tub and walked out to see her, "O-oh?" He asked her, still dripping wet.

"Oh!" She exclaimed, "Sorry, I didn't know you were taking a bath. It can wait until you're done."

He shook his head, "N-no. I-I want to see it!" He smiled at her and walked up. She held up her hand and he stopped.

"Grab a towel and dry off first." She told him, "Requires us to hop in Lady Love. Last thing I need is water pooling in the bottom."

"Okay!" He quickly turned around and got a towel to dry himself.

"Might as well hop in that bath myself when we're done." She told him, "I'm disgusting."

"N-n-no!" He told her, "Y-y-you're wonderful!"

She chuckled, "I meant I'm gross. Haven't showered in days and have been wearing nothing but this flight suit." She paused for a moment, "Speaking of…" She turned around. A-D quickly came up and undid the zipper for her, "*Thank you…*" She said while peeling it off her skin, "Oh my god it feels so nice to get out of that finally."

She looked back at him as he finished drying, "Aight come on. Let's go." She grabbed his gift and led him back into Lady Love. Making sure he couldn't see what she held in her hands. She let him get into his seat and climbed in next to him.

"Close your eyes." She told him. He quickly obeyed. She leaned over him and fidgeted about as she fixed something to the bottom of her seat. "Alright, you can open them." She said as she leaned back onto the ladder.

He opened his eyes and smiled as she had pinned two pictures where he could see them. The first one was the picture she had taken of them in her house. She had written on it with sharpie in the white outline, "My first friend!" He looked at the other one and squeed with joy. It was the picture Casey had taken of her. In the white outline she had written, "*My first friend!*"

He gasped and gave her a hug, "Thank you, thank you, *thank you*!" He shouted.

She laughed and gave him a light hug back, "You earned it, A-D." She told him. "Got them printed just for you."

He squeezed her even tighter, "I-I love them!"

"Good," she smiled, "Now let's go get me cleaned up. I feel utterly disgusting."

My first friend! ♡

www.ingramcontent.com/pod-product-compliance
Lightning Source LLC
LaVergne TN
LVHW020706110826
845149LV00012B/2135
9798996310401